go blue

go blue

JACK BEAM

F|7

Face to Face Books

Shorewood, Wisconsin

Face to Face Books is an imprint of Midwest Traditions, Inc.,
a nonprofit press working to help preserve a sense of place and
tradition in American life.

For a catalog of books, write:

Midwest Traditions
3710 N. Morris Blvd.
Shorewood, Wisconsin 53211
U.S.A.
or call 1-800-736-9189

Go Blue
© 1999, Jack Beam

This is a work drawn from the imagination, and nothing herein is
intended to be taken as anything other than fiction.

Cover design by Heather Fukumoto.

ISBN 1-883953-29-4

Original Paperback Edition
10 9 8 7 6 5 4 3 2 1

ACKNOWLEDGEMENTS

"Lyin' Eyes"
by Glenn Frey and Don Henley
©1975 Red Cloud Music/Cass County Music
All Rights Reserved.

"Ramblin' Rose"
by Mari John Wilkin & Fred Burch
© 1961 Cedarwood Publishing
All Rights Reserved.

"Money Changes Everything"
by Tom Gray
© 1978 Gray Matter Publishing Co.
All Rights Reserved.

"You Must Go"
by John Hiatt
© 1995 Careers-BMG Music Publishing, Inc. (BMI) /
Whistling Moon Traveler Music (BMI)
All Rights Reserved.

"Blue Angel"
by Paul Gurian
© 1997 Bow Tie Publishing
All Rights Reserved.

"Blatz Beer Commercial"
Lyrics © The Stroh Brewery Co.
All Rights reserved. Used by Permission.

"Be Kind To Your Web-Footed Friends"
Words and Music by Lennie Carroll
© 1959 (Renewed 1997) EMI BLACKWOOD MUSIC, INC.
All Rights Reserved. International Copyright Secured. Used by
Permission.

And on keyboards, Mr. Doug Banker — thank you for the inspiration
and encouragement.

for
Bjorn,
Bianca,
and
Renee

❖ ❖ ❖

The fifty-something woman sat at a table in a cloistered, dimly-lit room. She punched "total" on her ten-key calculator. It made a scratchy cluttered sound, like a rattle being shaken by a high priest over a dying body. She took off her reading glasses and snapped a rubber band around another stack of wrinkled green bills. "Not bad for a Monday this time of year." She tore off the long coil of white paper from the adding machine, and handed it to Jonah Wasaquom.

Jonah looked at the bottom line. His black eyes frowned, a sour look. The same look would have passed over the face of one of his ancestors, a few hundred years ago, inspecting a scrawny half-starved doe being brought into camp for the supper entreé. Wasaquom's head darted up to catch movement through the one-way mirror looking out onto the main floor — such as it was — of the dingy Beaver Sands Casino. There was some commotion over by one of the blackjack tables. He handed the tape back to his bookkeeper.

"It's enough money to send my son to college," said the woman. She meant to be encouraging. It was obvious to her that Jonah had been preoccupied with something, ever since the evangelizing white man from Nevada had come, telling his grand tale of fantastic growth that would increase Ottawa gambling revenues by unbelievable multiples. "How?" the Ottawa elders had asked. And they had listened in rapt attention to the silver-tongued, white-haired man and his answer.

"When the buffalo returns to this land again, your son won't need to go to college," Jonah said sternly. He put on his jacket and unlocked the door. "I'll take care of this," he nodded at the commotion out on the floor. "Then I'll be gone for the rest of the night."

Two good old boys were arguing with a dealer and the pit boss. One of the gamblers was distinguished by a lime-green nylon jacket that read "Ralph's Asphalt" in big yellow letters on the back. The other one sported a cap that read "Eat Pork Rinds." They were drunk as skunks.

Jonah sized up the situation in seconds. He nodded to uniformed security, who promptly "eighty-sixed" the boys out a side door, over their profane protests about "this cheap ass nickel-dime dive" and "rot-gut Indian firewater."

Jonah Wasaquom looked at his watch.

Make no mistake about it. When a branch breaks in the woods, it is always heard by someone or something. After an unseasonably dry Michigan summer, the hard, sharp crack reverberated like a shot, echoing back into the swamp and up towards the cottage set high on the bluff. The sound raced out over the lake and was gone.

"What was that?" asked Hazel.

"Nothing dear. She's probably starting to kick up tonight. It is October," said Albert, digging into a fresh pouch of fragrant pipe tobacco. He wasn't suppose to actually smoke the stuff anymore. The cardiologist at Mercy Hospital down in Grand Rapids had delivered a lecture on that as soon as he got Albert into one of those hospital gowns they always put you in so they can get the upper hand.

Hazel was up in her stocking feet. She tip-toed to a low,

cluttered bookshelf and leaned over it. Pressing her face to the glass pane, she peered out one of the two latticed windows on either side of the fieldstone fireplace that anchored the living room of the little clapboard cottage. On a cloudless full-moon night, from this precarious perch, she could catch a glimpse of whitecaps, far away out on the darkening water beyond the bluff upon which their nest was nestled.

Albert looked over his bifocals at the posterior view he was now being presented by his bride of fifty-one years. Still lovely, he thought, as he resumed reading the *Manistee New Advocate*. He started sucking on his corncob pipe. The pipe always reminded Albert of the returning General MacArthur, who he, Albert, had witnessed — along with hundreds of other sailors hanging from the upper decks of the *U.S.S. Missouri* — the day the Japanese had surrendered.

"She is smooth as glass," Hazel observed, stepping down with a fair amount of grace for a woman her age. She straightened up her copy of Norman Vincent Peale's *The Power of Positive Thinking*, which she had knocked over when leaning on the bookshelf.

"Then it's that crazy wolf that escaped from Isle Royale and stowed away on a freighter out of Duluth. Came right through the Soo Locks, they say. Easy as a zebra mussel up the St. Lawrence." Albert was deadpan serious, but his eyes managed a twinkle, thanks to successful cataract surgery, which he had undergone the year after the triple bypass. If he was going to live awhile longer with his old ticker, he reckoned, he might as well get a last good look at things.

Hazel pouched her weathered cheeks to give her old hubby a look of incredulity. She knew Albert was working up to one of his increasingly frequent diatribes about how the zebra mussel had been carelessly introduced to their lake. And how they never should have opened up the St. Lawrence Seaway to ocean-going freighters in the first place. And what did the goddamn Army Corps of Engineers think they were doing anyhow! She hoped God wasn't too sensitive about all the cussing. And besides, she figured, He probably wasn't too keen on the zebra mussels bothering his beautiful Great Lakes either.

"It's true," he continued. "A bus load of Leaf-Peepers said they saw the wolf up on deck howling as the freighter passed under the Mackinaw Bridge. Front-page news, if you don't believe me." And he added, "Heard those zebra mussels are in Green Lake now. They attach on boats out in the Big Lake and next thing you know ... goddamn Army Corps of Engineers and their goddamn ..."

"Albert Hanker," she said, with the same no-nonsense tone she used to use on four decades of second-graders.

Albert knew the tone. "Sweetheart, why did they name a blue-eyed beauty like you 'Hazel'?" It was Albert's favorite line, always good for changing the subject. It was a line he would use successfully until the day he died.

"Because they just didn't appreciate what they had. Go see if the raccoons or that wolf are getting into the garbage."

"Put another log on the fire," said Albert, trying to have the last word as he got up out of his favorite chair.

"Put on your coat." Hazel always got the last word.

Only Fudgies, of which Leaf-Peepers are a subset, forget to firmly secure garbage cans in Michigan's north woods. Albert was the son of a copper miner from the Keweenaw — that long, narrow appendage of Michigan's Upper Peninsula which juts out madly into Lake Superior like the ragged ear of a wolf. Still, just to make sure, Albert tugged at the bungee cords that secured the metal lids to the cans lined up in back of the garage. He could honestly tell Hazel that he had checked them. The night air was crisp, but far from bitter. Albert walked back around the garage up to the cottage. Like a peeping Tom, he looked in a side window.

Hazel was seated in a Biedermeier chair stuffed with musty pillows, next to a Biedermeier table. Her knitting, which she had just resumed, was lit by the fire's yellow glow and a Tiffany lamp. The gracious interior, in the style of the Arts and Craft Movement, was rudely disrupted by Albert's mustard-colored reclining chair. Of course, Albert did not see it that way. He saw only cozy comfort — and his bride, whom he was beginning to worry about.

Just a few day ago, after walking down their long winding drive to the mailbox, she had reported a car with out-of-state plates speeding off. "Illinois, Indiana, Ohio. People come a long way to see what we have in our own backyard," Albert reassured her, as he pointed to one of the maples that had turned early, an electric-orange color that a hunter would feel safe wearing.

"No," she insisted. "I think it was New Hampshire. The bumper sticker said 'Live Free and Gamble,' or something like that." Hazel had been a little confused about the exact wording, or any details of who had been driving the car.

Albert rustled through the leaves around the corner of the cottage, to where his lawn opened up and then abruptly ended at the edge of the bluff. He walked right up to the border of the escarpment and looked out. The heights were not at all wuthering. A hundred feet down, there were no jagged rocks upon which a fall would bring instant death. Instead, below lay the soft, golden, sandy shore of Lake Michigan.

He looked out onto the lake like a father, hidden and unseen and loving, watching his daughter brushing her hair in a mirror. For Albert and Hazel, the lake held all their youthful passion, all their dreams, all their past and future. Their many years of hard work — she at the elementary school and he at the wooden-floored hardware store — were invested in this lakefront property. Some childless couples, late in life, put all their caring into a scrunch-faced lap dog or an aloof cat. The Hankers had a lake and they loved it like a child.

Albert spoke softly to her. "Honey, Mother is getting on in years. She's starting to hear and see things." Albert paused. "I guess I am, too. The point is, we won't always be here. If something happens to us — remember what I've told you about strangers. Some men will take advantage of a nice-looking girl like you." Albert paused again.

These were awkward things for a father to say. "You're our one and only. Mother prays every night that neighbors and friends will step up when we're gone and you really need something." He whispered to himself nervously, "Sure as hell hope she's right."

Albert was relieved he got all that off his chest. He stood there quietly for a moment. "You're so still tonight. I guess that means you'll let me have a quick smoke, hey?" Albert looked back at the cottage to make sure Hazel wasn't peeping out at him. In the windless night, he lit his pipe with one match. He savored a puff and smiled at his world.

Only a few yards away from Albert, sugar maples stood shoulder to shoulder in the high dry soil. They grew thin, not thick, as each stretched for the sun. Jonah Wasaquom tried to make himself as thin as the maple he was hiding behind, but too much rich living had paunched him out. He could barely see his expensive footwear. Would the iridescent swoosh reveal him in the glow of the rising moon? If he had worn the cross-training deerskin moccasins of the ancestors, he would have felt the tension of that branch in the soles before it snapped.

❖ ❖ ❖

"Can I give you a hand with that?"

Mitch was staggering up the stairs towards her, carrying a blue plastic milk-crate stuffed with old record albums, on top of which were stacked a few too many of his law books. His chin was trying to keep the whole thing in balance but, while not wholly devoid of character, his chin was not really prominent enough for this particular task.

She caught two of the books as they slid off. He watched in slow motion as a third book slapped to the floor. She scooped it up as if it had bounced. She faced him, cradling all three books in her arms like a schoolgirl.

"Thanks." He looked at the titles in embarrassment. *Extra-Judicial Adjudication: A Guide to Self-Help Dispute Resolution* by Professor Robbie Joe Cryer was closest to her chest. Towering above his students in all his six feet and four inches, Robbie Joe had looked like the tight end from Ole Miss that he once had been. With a voice deeper than God, the Rhodes Scholar had shaken the South out of his speech at Oxford. At Northwestern Law School, Robbie Joe had killed more brain cells with his liquid lunches than most people were born with. Half in the bag, he could still out-think forty sober law students without even trying. He held some non-practical notions about what he called preventative law — for example, that litigation was not only expensive, but wasteful. Fortunately for all the hourly lawyers of LaSalle and Wall Streets, who thrive on obstructions in various forms, Robbie Joe was devoured by cancer before anyone nominated him to the bench.

But Robbie Joe had risen again. Let the trumpets proclaim. It was her nipple. The woman's right nipple was pressed firmly against that hardbound copy of *Extra-Judicial Adjudication.*

Everyone has felt envy for inanimate objects. At the moment, Mitch was jealous of that book. But he was happy for his old proctor Robbie Joe, whose legal theories were being embraced by a heavenly body.

Still in slow motion, Mitch looked up into bright confident eyes. He saw they were blue, and that she had beautifully soft, luminous skin that went well with the eyes and with everything else, including the nipple.

"Are you alright?" she asked.

"Yeah." He shuffled towards the door and lowered the crate of albums carefully on the landing. He vacantly searched his pants pocket for his new apartment key.

Laura reached down and pulled out an album, *Magical Mystery Tour*. She looked at it closely. "Vinyl LPs. Wow. That is totally Smithsonian," she said. "I would say by the looks of these artifacts you're either an archaeologist or a lawyer."

"I'm Mitch Miller," said Mitch, not as quick as he used to be to admit to the lawyer part these days.

"I'm Laura Knight. I come with the property." She smiled as she reciprocated his firm handshake. "You need to pull the door towards you. Like this." She took the key from his left hand, stepped in front of him, and opened the door. She walked in first. "We just installed new weather-stripping. Everyone is complaining, but it will save a couple of bucks on your heating bill this winter."

"I didn't think you had rough winters in this part of Michigan anymore," he said as he followed her into his own apartment. He hadn't thought there was a Santa Claus, either, but that might all be changing before his eyes.

"How much winter do you need?" she asked, opening the living-room curtains.

"I can never get enough winter," he said, taking his eyes off her for the first time in his life. Out through the window, he glimpsed a large pond with a backdrop of dense woods, mostly oak and pine.

"Last year the pond froze, and we had snow on Christmas Eve." She also was taking in the view as if for the first time, still cradling Robbie Joe.

Oakwood Village was an attempt to create a slice of Marina del Rey in the blue-collar town in Michigan called Wyoming. But there was nothing contrived about the woods and water that surrounded the outskirts of the village. Besides, he could have chosen Marina del Rey or even Malibu, if he had wanted to drive a million miles on a freeway twice a day. An appointment with the U.S. Attorney in L.A. had been his for the asking. There were a lot of nipples there, too, and the offer had been tempting. But Michigan was where Mitch had grown up, and he had found himself surprisingly longing for his boyhood home of freshwater lakes and bays.

She turned. "Well, Mr. Miller, this is home." He watched her as she walked over to the only piece of furniture that wasn't covered with a box of his stuff. She laid Robbie Joe down gently. She caught Mitch's eyes as she handed him back his keys, and lingered, and smiled.

"If you don't have plans, would you like to come to dinner tomorrow night?"

Forget Robbie Joe. Mitch gave her a speechless grin.

"I guess that's a yes." She smiled again, notching up the

candle-power in her eyes. "Nothing fancy. Just a little wok," she said as she headed down the hall. "About seven."

"Hey, where do you live?" he called after her.

"Right above you," he heard her exclaim, as she walked out of sight.

❖ ❖ ❖

The next morning, Mitch surveyed the boxes and furniture scattered around the one-bedroom apartment. The movers had managed to put the bed in the bedroom. Everything else was helter-skelter. There really was not a lot to unpack. He had done this drill before, moving from college to law school, from law school to D.C., from D.C. to Philadelphia.

There was a bed, a desk, a sleeper-sofa, and a four-legged monstrosity that passed for a kitchen table. No doubt he would upgrade his home furnishings now that he was ready to start work in nearby Grand Rapids, known as the Furniture City. It had already started at dinner last night, with his mother's promise of an armoire she had seen at Klingman's. "Of course, you could save a lot of money and live with your dad and me."

But Mitch had found himself thinking: what if this new girl I just met is a screamer or a moaner? "No thanks, Mom, I'm kind of used to living alone. You know, being almost thirty." She had protested, "You are only twenty-eight." His dad finally came to his defense, albeit with his characteristic bluntness. "Maybe he's got a hot blond." Blondes to him meant Carroll Baker in *The Carpetbaggers*. But his dad was on the right track with the hot part.

Mitch walked to the cardboard box that had a red string wound around a red button. With reverence, he unwound it and spread the flaps to reveal a coffin-like styrofoam case. He lifted up the styrofoam. "Sansui — the receiver of choice for our boys in uniform," That's what Giovanni used to say. And that was how he said it. "I, personally, opened up trade routes for Sansui. It was a small price to pay for quality sound. Damn glad I could be part of it."

Mitch had never been able to tell if Giovanni was kidding. Mitch would wait for a little smile or even a twinkle in the eye after Giovanni said something like that, but it never came. Giovanni had dropped out the first semester of his sophomore year. Back then, most college curriculums were being inflated by so-called relevant courses. But Giovanni was in Engineering School — electrical engineering. Social relevancy was harder to achieve in "Double-E" School. You couldn't teach Afrocentric logarithms or Native American titration. Physics was physics, without reference to race, creed, color, or previous condition of servitude. And you couldn't BS on a calculus exam like you could on a sociology exam. Giovanni most certainly would have flunked out, if he hadn't dropped out.

Instead, he made the Tan Son Nhut connection. He went right into the jungles of Vietnam and started shooting. He said he never stopped shooting. He didn't know if he ever hit anyone. He just decided to create a wall of outgoing lead around him. Apparently it worked. Giovanni came back without a scratch. Two decades later.

"My buddy and I promised each other when we got out of that place, we would see the rest of the world. I spent twenty years seeing the rest of the world. Kept my promise," Giovanni explained. "Now I'm ready to complete my formal education."

"So what happened to your buddy?" asked Mitch, walking into an obvious ambush as he and Giovanni lifted another keg into the Ford van.

"Son of a bitch went and got his name on The Wall."

That was the first day they met, during their part-time jobs at the campus corner store shuttling kegs to TGIF frat parties. For the rest of the first semester of Mitch's senior year, the two of them spent hours taking a magical mystery tour of politics, religion, and music.

"The coincidence of the decline of rock 'n' roll and global warming — that's going to be my doctoral dissertation," Giovanni claimed, in the midst of finishing off his first six-pack one Friday night at his creaky one-bedroom apartment just off Packard Street.

"Will this be for a Ph.D. in philosophy or sociology?" Mitch tried not to laugh.

"Mathematics. I don't know. Look. I leave this country in '67 with the lads from Liverpool on top. I come back to brown winters and some dweebs called Milli Vanilli. What does that say? Stop, look, and listen, man." Giovanni pointed to his blue milk-crate full of albums.

"I agree about the winters, but I do like Men at Work," Mitch yelled, trying to raise his voice above the Led Zeppelin tune spinning on the turntable.

"One-hit wonders. Where are they now? And where is the snow? It's almost December 7th."

"Hey, Madonna was a U of M drop-out, but she's no one-hit wonder," Mitch said, trying to re-direct Giovanni's mania — or whatever the *DSM IV* psychology textbook diagnosis was that made him such a hyperbolic conversationalist.

That was one of their last times together. Giovanni was killed that Christmas vacation. He was helping an old purple-haired lady change a tire by the side of the road, near his family home outside of Columbus. A passing tractor-trailer blew a tire that hit him in the head. That's what his sister told Mitch when she drove up to Ann Arbor to pick up Giovanni's stuff. Rubber shrapnel, thought Mitch, as he helped her pack the car. They talked for a long time.

Mitch told her how he and Giovanni worked together on Fridays and sometimes studied together at the graduate library on Saturday nights. It was rare that either of them ever had a date — Giovanni because he didn't want one, Mitch because he didn't know how to get one. He didn't tell her Giovanni was the first person he had smoked pot with. He did say Giovanni was a real nice guy, which was actually true. That made her cry. After that, she said she wanted Mitch to have all her brother's relics: speakers, turntable, Sansui receiver, and his old vinyl records.

Mitch had tried to convince her to keep the LPs, as Giovanni had believed vinyl would come back someday. She said, "I doubt that. My brother had a lot of crazy ideas. He was perfectly fine when he finished his tour in Vietnam. It was those Buddhists in Kathmandu who brainwashed him."

Mitch now stood at the sink looking at himself in the mirror. His knuckles formed pods on the Formica vanity, and he leaned forward, trying to define his *pectoralis majors*. He had just completed what he thought was a bloodless shave, but as he surveyed his young face, he saw the blood and Barbasol by his earlobe.

On Giovanni's system in the other room, a well-sung song was finishing, but it was because of the next song that the Eagles LP had been selected from Giovanni's collection to christen his homecoming. Mitch pulled down his underwear to his feet.

City girls just seem to find out early,
How to open doors with just a smile;

A rich old man she won't have to worry,
She'll dress up all in lace and go in style.

He looked at his body. He had always been self-conscious about it.

And it breaks his heart to think her love is only
Given to a man with hands as cold as ice.

In his mind, the song had long since become a forlorn anthem to his long-lost love, Maggie, from his days in D.C. Why, he wasn't sure; it was one of those things songs do to you which make no sense at all. Maggie had never lied to him. She had never loved him. She had never even laid him. God only knows the boy in the mirror deserved points for trying.

There had been some sweaty passion. There was that delicious autumn day when the two of them had driven to Harper's Ferry in search of red in the trees. Then all of a sudden she was gone, faster than the leaves had fallen from those trees. She moved from the Potomac to the Pacific — to Redondo Beach. Surfin' USA. The Eagles may have written her anthem, but the Beach Boys were the demographic force that really mattered.

Thought by now you'd realize
There ain't no way to hide your lying eyes.

With grace, as if he had once kicked bare-footed field goals, he flipped his underwear up over his head, spun, and caught it on the finger tips of his right hand. He stepped into the shower. With any luck, his saccharine memories of dear departed Maggie would soon be a thing of the past.

Finished with the shower, he moved into the living room. Outside his sliding-glass picture window, ducks passing through from Canada were swimming in the pond. It had been a nippy October afternoon. The promise of more color in the leaves made him call an audible, "I love Michigan." Tonight he would stop being a voyeur and start being a player.

Sucking in his stomach, he got down on his knees like a Moslem turning to the East to pray, and started thirty push-ups to pump his pecs, just in case she made him take his clothes off. His towel slipped off at twenty.

❖ ❖ ❖

Si quaeris peninsulam amoenam circumspice. Michigan is and always will be a peninsula — unless someone decides to drain the Great Lakes so that Las Vegas can force up a few more skyscraping arcs of water to evaporate into its zero-percent humidity.

On that peninsula was the town of Wyoming, Michigan. It was a town named backwards. De Tocqueville noted that as manifest destiny drove Americans west, they often named their new towns after cities they had come from back east. Was Wyoming then named by some disgruntled pioneer who, after a few too many years hunkered down on the high and dry plains, hightailed it back home?

Although contiguous with Grand Rapids, Wyoming was not a suburb. It was its own place, a blue-collar town with automotive plants. Most of its houses paid homage to Mr. Levitt's grand idea: sameness. Like Flint, Wyoming was a creature of the auto industry and depended on it totally. It was just brighter and whiter than Flint.

But within that blue-collar town, Oakwood Village was an enclave of higher aspirations. There, wine was even stored in the horizontal position. At least that was what impressed Mitch as he entered the Oakwood Village Wine Shop.

"May I help you, monsieur?" The wine keeper's tone was cold enough to suggest that he was not only French, but probably Parisian.

"I need some wine. Something with a cork." Mitch flashed back to Giovanni, praising Boone's Farm as the drink of choice at Michigan home games in the Sixties. No later than the second quarter, the chant would go up from the student sections: "Boone's Farm, Boone's Farm!" Bottles would pass up from hand to hand — first hundreds, then thousands. A glassy sea rolled up out of the end zone and crested at the rim of the great human bowl. And then, if it was third down and short yardage, another chant began: "Go Blue, Go Blue!" The Michigan battle cry.

Another Wyoming cowboy, thought the little Frenchman. The backwards naming of the city had confused him since the day he arrived. It wasn't until he got slapped by a woman he had approached at Rogers Mall, in only his second week in the new country, that he realized he had the wrong Wyoming. "I vont, how you say, please — your beauty-full big Tetons."

Mitch walked over to a latticed bin and grabbed a bottle of red. He held it up and squinted at the sediment as if he was looking into a jar of formaldehyde at some dissection.

"Do not treat the wine like that you — you cowboy!" The little Frenchman violently grabbed the bottle from him and then ever so very gently laid it back in the bin.

The winekeeper was about to hurl an epithet nastier than "cowboy" and in French, when from across the cellar came a voice to the rescue. "Girard, maybe I can help him. Here's a Puligny-Montrachet."

"Oh monsieur, I did not hear you come in." With much ado, the little Frenchman danced across the floor to his newest customer. "It has been too long." He kissed him on both cheeks. "Where have you been?"

"Tour de gran, Girard." The lone stranger smiled.

"While you were gone, Monsieur Magliola returned from

Tuscany. He bring ten cases of this very pretentious Italian white, I told him we need to save one for my best customer. I go get it for you, ouí?"

"Mercí."

Girard disappeared in the back as the man walked up to Mitch. "Don't mind Girard. He is harmless."

"And a nice guy once you get to know him, right?"

"Exactly." The lone stranger quickly continued, "If you are looking for white, this is more than decent. What are you having for supper?"

"Nipples." Had he said that out loud? No. He wasn't sure. "I mean, wok." From the looks of this guy, Mitch thought, he must know what wine to serve with wok.

"Here try this," the lone stranger handed him the bottle he had been holding. "And for a red, how about ..." He walked over to a wooden case. "Here, try this Bandol. It will go with anything born on two or four legs. Now you are covered."

They both walked to the counter, where an effervescent Girard stood patting the sides of a case.

"Monsieur, let me have this delivered for you?"

"I can handle it. Put it on my tab." With that he picked up the case. "Thanks Girard. Good luck," he said to Mitch and walked out the door.

The little Frenchman said, more politely now, "That will be ninety-seven dollars and twenty-four cents."

"Ninety-seven dollars!" There was no question he said that out loud. He rummaged through his brown leather bill-fold, looking for his secret fifty. In one of the outside flaps was an embossed circle about the size of a fifty-cent piece, a condom's foiled wrapper, the grown-up Boy Scout's "Be Pre-pared." It had been restocked much less often that the secret fifty.

❖ ❖ ❖

Mitch had been taught that being on time was the polite thing to do. Promptly at seven, he walked up the stairs to the apartment above him; red wine in one hand, white in the other. He stood in front of her door, the only door on the third floor. His heart was pounding so hard he questioned whether he even needed to knock, but he did.

"Will you get that?" came a female voice muffled by the door.

In the seconds before the door opened, his mind raced through the possibilities for "you." The "you" could be her cat, highly trained and able to open doors. They didn't allow pets at Oakwood Village. Well then, and this was promising, she was desperately lonely for a man and had recently taken to talking to herself. But, she wasn't lonely. She seemed happy. So, the "you" was her female roommate, waiting for her boy-friend to pick her up. Maybe. In the remaining seconds before that door opened, he tried to conjure up an exciting triangular configuration with him and two women. But he couldn't sup-press a sinking feeling.

He was right on the geometry, wrong on the sex part. It was the man from the wine shop.

Stunned and frozen, Mitch could only swivel his hands up to eye level, holding his two bottles of wine.

"Excellent choice," said Rick with a smile.

That night, they all ate their vegetables. Rick ate his because he was a vegetarian. Laura ate hers because she loved Rick. And Mitch ate his because he had never tasted vegetables before. He had never tasted anything so wondrously fresh and spicy — a plate of color that cheered for a person's longevity.

Of course, he had eaten vegetables before. He had been raised in the Middle American tradition where vegetables, fresh or from a can, were cooked until they were dead like meat. Vegetables had always been obligatory in his life, never desired. Mitch took another sip of wine. Everything in this well-appointed place was desired.

The main floor of their apartment had a vaulted ceiling rising up above a loft. A big wicker chair was dwarfed by large looming ferns and a giant ficus tree. A plush white L-shaped sofa was arranged over by the balcony picture window. There was a funny-looking horizontal wooden bed with springs, which looked like something from the Spanish Inquisition. In fact, it was a "Pilates Reformer" — not connected to the local Christian Reformers, as best Mitch could tell when Laura tried to explain the contraption to him. The center attraction was a baby grand piano.

Rick went into the kitchen to open yet another bottle of wine. Laura seized the opportunity to lift her glass to Mitch as if to toast him. Instead she closed one eye like an artist and surveyed him using the glass as some sweet prism. "So you call yourself a lawyer. Does law have anything to do with the search for truth? Or is it a type of philosophy? I get those two mixed up." She mocked him.

Mitch emptied his glass and sat silently, not sure what to say. The floor was hers.

"I'm sure you would even consider defending a wife-murdering, bonehead football player," Laura declared. "That's our American system of justice." She grimaced. "But how far would you go to achieve some ultimate Platonic good?"

Mitch considered his defense, a valiant version of himself, easily done from the safety of this wine-soaked dinner party. But Rick walked in with an uncorked bottle and three fresh glasses.

Having emptied her glass and rested her case, Laura got up. She walked past the baby grand to an electronic Yamaha. As she flipped a couple of switches, Rick explained, "She went to Interlochen with Jewell." Mitch knew Interlochen; the music academy south of Traverse City, Michigan, was the Juilliard of the Midwest. And Jewell? Her star was rising, even as Laura covered an old Cyndi Lauper tune.

> *... money*
> *money changes everything.*
> *money, money changes everything*
> *we think we know what we're doin'*
> *that don't mean a thing*
> *it's all in the past now*
> *money changes everything ....*

BMI and ASCAP should have collected performance royalties that night from everyone except Mitch, who was so tone deaf he would lip-sync Happy Birthday at his own mother's birthday. Rick played the piano — while laying on his back on the bench like a weight-lifter doing a dental press. But the show stopper was a duet by Laura and Rick, a medley of classic rock 'n' roll which Mitch knew was surely bringing tears to Giovanni in heaven.

Sunday mornings came early in many neighborhoods of Grand Rapids. A decent percentage of the populace were members of the Christian Reformed denomination, or "CRs," as they were affectionately referred to. CRs went to church twice on Sunday, so they started real early. Rick, however, saw no need to get hung up on the religious implications of Sunday, in Grand Rapids or anywhere else in the free world. He figured the chances of Sunday being the holiest day of the week were one out of seven.

Rick's manual dexterity extended well beyond eighty-eight ebony and ivory keys — to computers and phones. He could punch in the number of his bookie faster than any gambler in America.

As he waited for Jojo to pick up in Las Vegas, Rick turned and looked at his big brass bed and its sleeping occupant. Laura was the best thing he had ever seen. She slept, not curled like a kitten, but with muscle fibers extended like a thoroughbred. And race they had, as soon as their blurry-eyed guest gave thanks for the great vegetables and teetered down the stairs. Last night Rick had been the thoroughbred, or at least tried to be. She had been the jockey, urging him on with an occasional whip at the stretch in case he had some mistaken notion that it was a short track. He was surprised by her aggression.

Her behavior was explained Sunday morning by the

Cosmo article he found lying underneath the bed: "Mad at your Man? Ride him for Awhile: A Female Jockey Shares Six Sexual Tricks to Vent Your Aggression." Well, Laura had a right to be mad. She had given up a promising career for him. And his career as a music promoter was sputtering. If it weren't for concert sales of T-shirts and a decent string of winning bets on football ...

"Jojo. It's Rick. You've got me for the Jets, Dolphins, Raiders, and the Pack for the line. No. That's it. I need sure things," said Rick.

Jojo scribbled the bet in his book. He grunted as he wrote. "Hey, got some young lawyer out by you who dropped a bundle yesterday on college," said Jojo.

"Who's the lawyer?" Rick asked.

"I'll tell you next time you're in town," said Jojo.

"College games are for rookies," Rick said, and he hung up. He wondered if it was his new neighbor. Mitch didn't seem like the type. But Rick knew enough about vices to know that you never know.

❖ ❖ ❖

Ken Calley relished being the top dog at Holland, Dawson & Hager. Overweight, and more or less the spitting image of W.C. Fields, only redder in the face, he knew that pure power trumped all cards.

"Hold all my calls." Calley stared without expression at the associate standing across from him. Fletcher Cratchett was not prematurely gray for his age. He was prematurely gray for an associate. If he had been a partner, his hair wouldn't have been an issue. Jim Bater had been made a partner at twenty-nine. The next year he lost his hair. No one noticed because Bater was a partner.

"Fletcher, it doesn't matter to me, but you might want to get the door." That was a good opener, thought Calley. He saw the associate's knees buckle a little bit as Fletcher returned from closing the solid-oak office door.

Fletcher looked for a place to sit but the two chairs and couch were covered with stacks of brown accordion files.

"Fletcher, let's get to the point." Calley leaned back in his chair with his arms winged in back of his head. "The partners have voted against making you a partner. Your billable hours are down this year almost ten per cent."

"That's because of my son's surgery ...."

"The partners are mindful of that, Fletcher. But you know that it is billable hours that form the foundation of any enduring law firm."

Fletcher's knees were starting to crumble again. He grabbed the chair beside him. The guy was scared.

Calley was pleased to see this. His cronies on the personnel committee had cautioned against too much sadism. Of course, they regaled in Calley's stories of firing selected associates and otherwise swallowing them whole, but even they thought his fun with Fletcher over the years had run its course. "Don't get him pissed off, unless you want to write your own briefs," they had admonished Calley.

Fletcher had talent. He was responsible for most of the firm's hardcore appellate research. The guy was an eloquent writer. The reversal he had won for Kendore Furniture had saved that client millions. He had not argued the case in court; the firm wouldn't let him and he wouldn't want to. But it was the sheer force of his intellectual argument that had captured the Michigan Supreme Court's attention.

More importantly, it was Fletcher's research that formed the legal foundation for the brainstorm which had whirled out of Nevada like a desert cyclone. Fletcher's brilliant memo, "First in Time, First In Right," traced the seminal 1908 Supreme Court case of *Winters v. United States*. The *Winters* decision had established the principle that Indian tribes hold reserved water rights. The holding in *Winters* explained that such crucial water rights were needed to fulfill the purpose of the Indian reservations, "which is to change their nomadic and uncivilized habits and encourage them to become pastoral and civilized people."

Fletcher was an artist. He had crafted a cogent legal argument, stacked with supporting citations, showing that a tribe's water rights date back to time immemorial. Of course, the Ivy League-educated WASPs who packed the highest court at the turn of the last century only intended to be condescending, reinforcing the federal government's role as paternal trustee with fiduciary obligations to the red man.

But in Arizona, the Tohono O'odham Nation had been quite happy to live with such condescension. Relying on the *Winters* decision and its progeny, they sold their water rights to the thirsty city of Tucson. But that lease of 13,300 acre-feet per year, to last for 99 years — called the Salt River Pima-Maricopa Indian Community Water Rights Settlement Act — was a mere drop in the bucket compared to what HD&H's newest and boldest client had in mind.

Calley looked at his prey, acknowledging only contempt for the weak-kneed associate standing before him. What Calley would never admit to himself was that his contempt was rooted in jealousy, because Fletcher was a legal genius trapped in a law clerk's body.

"Fletcher, we have decided to elevate you to an associate *emeritus*."

"Associate *emeritus*?"

"That's just an unofficial title between you and me."

"Thank you, sir. Thank you very much," He felt relief as some strength returned to his legs. He wasn't being fired.

Calley blared into his intercom for his secretary: "Get me O'Leary and Miller." Calley looked up to see Fletcher still standing before him. "You can go now."

"Go?" Fletcher asked.

"Go back to the library."

"Yes sir. Thank you, sir."

Cheer Cheer O'Leary nearly knocked over poor Fletcher as he came rushing in through Calley's door. Cheer Cheer was what folks in South Bend referred to as a "Double Domer," having gone to both Notre Dame undergraduate and law school in the shadow of that great golden dome. Cheer Cheer was possibly even more competitive about Irish football than about the law, but not by much. He stood poised in front of Calley's desk, like one of those players on the Irish sidelines in whose ear the coach is calling a play to send in to the waiting huddle. Cheer Cheer had that invisible spring in his knees, his whole body saying: "Let me in, coach, let me in." He was ready to burst forth onto the field.

In came Mitch, just as Calley was calling the play. Mitch nodded to Cheer Cheer; he was the first associate Mitch had met when interviewing at the firm. Cheer Cheer had been hired by HD&H right out of law school. He was roughly on the same partnership track as Mitch. And they were the only single guys in the firm, so they naturally gravitated towards each other.

"I ..." said Calley, to distinguish himself from the half-dozen other senior partners, "... have been designated by our client, Mr. Malone of MDDC, as lead counsel for the twin ballot referendum."

"The Malone Desert Development Corporation!" Cheer Cheer was ecstatic. "Fantastic. Congratulations, Mr. Calley." Cheer Cheer was not being insincere, though certainly neither he nor any associate bent on making partner would ever miss such an opportunity. His was spontaneous joy. He didn't need his accounting background to estimate the staggering billable hours such a project would generate from beginning to end. If there ever was an end.

Calley was pleased with Cheer Cheer's exuberance and he added, "Actually, I was informed by Mr. Malone's people that this firm will be handling the Desert Development Corporation's interests throughout the Great Lakes states."

"We beat out the Detroit firm?" Cheer Cheer asked.

"And Chicago. And New York. We are going to be a law

firm to reckon with in the 21st century." Calley slammed his hand on the table. It was boastful, but not impossible. After all, Grand Rapids was already the headquarters of the Amway Corporation, which had been founded in a garage by a couple of Christian Reformed Dutchmen. Their mixture of evangelical enthusiasm and laissez-faire capitalism had quickly grown into a billion-dollar global giant. Why not the law firm of Holland, Dawson & Hager?

Mitch had not said a word through all this. He had been staring out the window looking at the orange-red Caulder sculpture. The striking piece had anchored the city's first wave of urban renewal in the sixties, back when there was public money for such cultural improvements.

"Mr. Miller, I hope it does not offend your values that, by transferring an immeasurable amount of our natural resources to our fellow Americans in the Great Southwest Desert, our Native Americans are going to have the opportunity to truly prosper. And that once-arid land will be made green."

Mitch had been hired for his white-collar trial experience. In fact, Calley had objected to his hiring, because Mitch didn't have any experience in transactional law or commercial litigation. Thus, Calley was already considering grooming him for associate emeritus, like Fletcher, instead of partner.

"The truth is ..." Mitch was thinking about what Laura said. "The truth is, I'm a lawyer, not a philosopher. If that's what the people want, then that's what a democracy should give them."

"That's very good, Mr. Miller." Calley was not impressed. "Anyhow, here is a small case involving the family of one of the primary supporters of the coming ballot initiative." Calley tossed a file across his desk. "Don't screw it up. You can go now."

Calley turned to Cheer Cheer. "I need to talk to you about other matters in private."

❖ ❖ ❖

The Medical Examiner ruled that the cause of death was natural. Natural as carbon monoxide. There was no evidence of any trauma. That made sense to everyone in Manistee. Everyone thought it perfect that the well-liked old couple had gone together. Everyone except Ted Moore, a heating and air-conditioning contractor and all-around handyman.

He had been the one who found the Hankers. He had driven out there to see how their furnace was doing — the unit he had inspected and cleaned at the end of the summer. And to give them a bid on repairing their sea-wall, built at the bottom of the sandy bluff to protect it from erosion in the years Lake Michigan's water table was high.

When Ted Moore walked into the cottage, he found them both sitting in their chairs. He knew they were dead. He just didn't think they looked natural. There was something odd about the way the *Field and Stream* was lying so neatly on Albert's lap. And the way their old hi-fi was making a scratching sound like, well, a broken record.

Ted had gone over to the hi-fi even before he called the sheriff. What he heard would haunt him forever. He picked up the arm of the turntable and randomly set the needle back down on the *Mitch Miller Sing-Along Album*:

> *Be kind to your web-footed friends,*
> *For a duck may be somebody's mother.*

Be kind to your friends in the swamp,
Where the weather is very, very damp.
Now you may think that this is the end,
Well it is.

That's when he called the Sheriff.

❖ ❖ ❖

The white steeple with its soaring cross rose above the leafless trees. The hill was so heavily wooded that in the summer you wouldn't know anything was up there, but for the sign on the street: *The Christian Reformed Church for Biblical Justice. Peter V. VanderHook, Sr., Minister.*

Mitch turned off Lake Michigan Drive just past the sign and down-shifted his Honda to first gear with a jerk, as he started to climb. It was a steep incline up the tree-lined drive. Must be a bitch on ice, he thought.

He continued up the drive for a good sixty yards. Then he saw it. There in the clearing was an enormous red-brick church, with a stately white portico supported by six thirty-foot pillars. Ionic? Laconic? He didn't know the difference and didn't care. It was magnificent. It had a presence like Mount Vernon seen from the Potomac.

In the clearing, the driveway split around an enormous but well-proportioned lawn, and circled to meet itself under the portico. The only imperfection was the brown color of the lawn, unavoidable this time of year. A blanket of snow would cure that in another month or two.

He took the counter-clockwise route. He stopped short of parking his Honda under the portico. His tiny foreign car was not worthy.

He got out and walked up the walk, and then up the steps. Stretching his neck, he read the gold letters written above the six doors: "Upon this rock I will build my church."

Then he was pulling on the gold door-handles, and thinking that each gold letter probably cost a good chunk of his annual salary.

"Try the one on the far right," a voice said.

He must have jumped a foot. "Christ, you scared me," Mitch said.

"A little testy, aren't we?"

"Forgive me," he said.

"That's not my job. I'm only the minister's daughter."

She wore a sweatshirt that said Hope College, but she quickly confirmed that she went to Calvin. She did most of the talking, as she lead him down the primrose path to the parsonage around the side of the church. The parsonage, of course, was perfectly in proportion to the church. They went in the side door, which entered the kitchen. Her mother was trimming the dough around the glass rim of a generous fruit pie.

"Mother, this is Mitch Miller. He is the lawyer here to see Peter."

Like her daughter a few minutes before, the mother came forward with an engaging handshake. "Ruth VanderHook." Like her daughter, she was blond and handsome. Even in an apron, she was no matron. There were wisps of gray at her temples, but middle age was still a few years away and in any event would be entered gracefully.

"I'll get Peter," Sarah said, heading for the backstairs that ran to the kitchen.

"Have you been a lawyer for long? You look so young."

Mitch followed the pie with his eyes as it slipped into the oven, concerned that she not spill the delicious creation, even if it was not intended for his lips.

"I was a federal prosecutor in Philadelphia before I came home to Grand Rapids." He wished Sarah was in the room to hear that. He always impressed himself when he said it.

"So you're from Grand Rapids. Miller ..." She tested the sound of his name. "Did you go to Calvin?" It was a circumspect way of asking if he was one of them.

"Michigan and Northwestern."

"My oldest daughter is in medical school in Ann Arbor," said Mrs. VanderHook proudly. "The undergraduate school is such a radical place isn't it?"

"Not like it used to be, according to a student I once knew," said Mitch. Ruth VanderHook was not much older than Giovanni would have been.

There was a contemporary Christian radio station playing softly overhead. Mitch was tempted to test Giovanni's global warming and decline of rock 'n' roll theory on her. Had she heard of Milli Vanilli? He was about to ask her, when young Peter came bounding down the backstairs.

"Mr. Miller," said Peter, oozing politeness in front of his mother and Sarah who had followed him down.

"Why don't you go into your father's study?" Ruth VanderHook suggested.

"Sure, mother," said Peter, as if that would be a treat.

As soon as they walked in and closed the door, Peter said, "So tell me, you wouldn't like to hose my sister?"

"I ..." The defendant's lawyer was at a loss for words.

Brother Peter was sitting behind the desk, his feet up on it. A tastefully framed picture of the Last Supper hung behind him. Mitch studied the young man and thought about the world according to John. Imagine the world without religion. From Belfast to Beirut. No reason to kill or die for anything, except oil and fresh water.

The Christian Reformed were so full of contradictions. But so were most religious zealots of the world, except maybe the Amish, who appeared to practice what they preached and never hurt anyone in the name of anything. But he had never known the Amish. Not up close like the CRs.

He had grown up with CRs. Mitch's earliest memories of CRs dated back to his childhood days in Grand Rapids. His first best buddy was Billy Koistra, who lived next door. Billy went to a CR elementary school. Mitch went to a public elementary school. On Saturdays they would play until they dropped.

Saturday was fun, but meeting the family on a Sunday was a different story. Twice each Sunday, little Billy, his three sisters, and his parents would walk by on their way to church. Always they would walk, never drive. Grand Rapids was a quiet place on Sundays. If, God forbid, Mitch and his dad were raking leaves or painting a fence, the Koistras would not speak. They would just look the other way. Mitch's heart would be still, until Billy would sneak a wave.

"You aren't a Hollander, are you?" Peter asked.

Mitch shook his head.

"I wonder why my Reverend father didn't hire the church lawyer?" He paused. "Probably cause the case is too big."

Mitch figured he could grow to dislike this client, despite his nice-looking sister. Big cases had bigger files, even at this early stage. There was nothing in this file other than Calley's intake note. No complaint, not even an accident report. All Calley's note stated was name, address, date of accident, and the phrase, "fender-bender."

Before Mitch could ask, "What big case?" Peter blurted, "Do you think I will go to Hell for this?"

The transformation was dramatic. The earlier cockiness

had gone out of his voice. Peter had even removed his feet from his father's desk.

Mitch looked at Jesus sitting in back of Peter. Personally, Mitch wasn't into Hell either — that was the Old Testament. Forgiveness was New Testament. With compassion, Mitch offered, "You won't go to Hell for a rear-end collision."

The boy looked relieved, but not totally satisfied. He had one more question to ask.

"What about the baby?"

Mitch looked back up at Jesus and frowned. If sex was involved, questions about Hell and forgiveness were back on the table. "What baby?" Mitch asked.

I'm from Milwaukee and I ought to know,
It's Blatz fresh draft beer, wherever you go.
Smoother, refreshing, less filling that's clear,
Blatz is Milwaukee's finest beer.

Rick thought those were the best pop lyrics to ever come out of Wisconsin. But who's to say things couldn't change?

Jeff Austin was a small-time booking agent. Of course, promoters from Chicago booked most of the big concerts in Milwaukee, but Austin managed to make ends meet, if barely. In the summer he did bookings for north-woods Wisconsin resorts, from Door County sticking out into Lake Michigan to Rice Lake, not far from Minneapolis. In the winter when things slowed down, he taught guitar to blind kids in the public schools.

The usually calm Austin had been frantic when he called Rick the week before Thanksgiving. "I found this great group, man."

"Polish-American Vets doing the 'Proud Mary Polka'?" Already in his young career, Rick had grown tired of the "Hey, I heard this great band" pitch, but his quip to Austin was without edge.

"Straight up, man. They got this idiot manager who keeps telling them a record deal is just around the corner. But he doesn't know shit from shinola. They got a really tight sound.

You got to hear these guys."

"Send me a demo," Rick said.

"Their manager won't give out their demos. He's afraid someone will steal them away."

Dubious, Rick nevertheless knew Austin's opinion deserved consideration. Besides, it was a chance to visit the Harley-Davidson factory to check out the Heritage Soft-Tail he had on back-order. It was a pilgrimage to an American shrine. A city on Lake Michigan that made lots of beer and the finest motorcycles on the planet was worth a visit now and then.

The Northwest captain's landing announcement lifted Rick out of his airborne winks. For most people, FAA erect seat-back regulations would have discouraged sleeping on this short hop. But Rick did not need his seat-back reclined to doze on a plane. He had fallen asleep before takeoff.

He peeled open his eyes and looked down from the plane. Through an occasional opening in the clouds, the lake was all whitecaps. Canadian winds were making their annual late-fall attempt to stir up the huge glacial bathtub known as Lake Michigan.

He thought about his last outing to the dairy state. He could picture Austin, Rick, and Eddie, there on the third hole. Or was it the sixteenth? It was hard to tell. They all looked alike: perfectly white and frosted, like an immense wedding cake — with occasional flags instead of candles. It was the snow drifts which distorted the lay of the land. Even Austin wasn't sure, and he had played that course many times.

It had all started after the big concert, back at the hotel bar. Austin and Eddie were talking about golf with an earnest

"D-Day, you name the beach, we will take it" passion. Austin was lamenting how short the golf season was in the north woods.

"But hey, we could play in snowshoes. I mean, up at Lake Tomahawk they play softball every summer in snowshoes," Austin offered. By the time they closed the hotel bar, it made perfect sense. But Austin's speech was seriously slurred. So Rick figured it was just happy talk.

And why not? It had been a stellar performance to a sold-out crowd. They had all made money and Rick had an earnest groupie plying her tongue to the nape of his neck all evening long. Who in hell was going to get up early on Valentine's Day to play golf in Wisconsin in the snow?

Mary Widow. That's who. The mascara-laden rocker was still rocking. Perhaps it had something to do with global warming after all. In any case, Mary the rocker at night was Eddie the golfer by day. The allure of playing a round in snowshoes was too intriguing for either Mary or Eddie to resist.

Rick had opened his hotel door to find Eddie and Austin standing side by side in the hotel hallway. They had on snow-mobile jumpsuits, ear muffs, and matching plaid scarves.

"Tee time," said Eddie, barging past Rick into the room as the groupie from Wauwatosa slid under the well-used sheets.

"We even brought you a set of sticks," said Austin, close on Eddie's heels. He carried a skinny, grass-stained old canvas bag that could have been Ben Hogan's first.

The rock star had had a fabulous time that Valentine's Day, one he would never forget. Neither would Rick. There had been no snowmobile suit for him. His buns had taken days to thaw out.

"I hope this band is good," Rick said to himself as the plane bounced down on Mitchell Field. It was time for a brew.

❖ ❖ ❖

"Kling Wrap."

"Kling Wrap?"

"Kling Wrap," Peter repeated, wondering if his lawyer was deaf.

"That's what I thought you said."

There was nothing wrong with that answer, assuming what Mitch had just asked was something like: "What does your mother use to cover a fruit pie when she puts it away in the refrigerator?" But that had not been the question. It wasn't even close. The question — could we please have the court reporter read it back? — was:

Court Reporter: "'What baby?'"

Attorney Miller: "No, after that."

Court Reporter: "'What did your parents say?' And then the witness said, 'My mother cried a lot.'"

Attorney Miller: "Much further on. After I asked him, 'Are you sure the baby was yours? Did you do it more than once?' Before I ask him about the miscarriage."

Court Reporter: "Here we go. 'Didn't you use a rubber?' Answer: 'Kling Wrap.'"

Attorney Miller: "Okay, back on the record."

Of course, there was no court reporter present for this interview. Just little Peter, Mitch, and Jesus. Peter had become defensive during the pregnant pause while his lawyer reconstructed his earlier answer, so he added, "A lot of guys at school were doing it that way. It's not like I could ask the Reverend to buy me some condoms."

The kid had a point. Too bad people wait so long to seek legal advice, Mitch thought. If he had come to me sooner, I could have let him borrow the Trojan I'm presently sitting on in my billfold. Unless it's petrified.

"How hard was the impact?" Mitch asked. "Have you got any pictures of her car?"

"Her dad took some pictures after they found out about the baby. Dusty told me her dad's either going to kill me or sue me."

"Peter, no one's going to kill you. That's not how we do things in this country. That's why we have juries."

"Will the jury kill me?" Peter asked suddenly, remembering how his father had crucified him for a failing grade in government.

"Of course not. This isn't a criminal case," Mitch said, managing to feel pity and anger for his client at the same time. "What about your car? How much did it cost to repair?"

"There's a little dent. You don't even notice it."

Peter lowered his head. Tears began running down his cheek. "Dusty used to say I was the only one who could ever teach her."

Mitch was wondering if anyone ever got married at sweet sixteen if someone wasn't pregnant, when suddenly the door to the library swung open.

There stood the Reverend. The man was the spitting image of Gary Cooper or Lou Gehrig. Either image would do — most people today don't know the difference.

"Father," Peter Junior said, as he jumped like a cat out of

his father's chair.

The Reverend moved over to his credenza and covered up some blue architectural renderings, which Mitch had glanced at. The grandfather clock made in Zeeland, Michigan, probably by a shirt-tail cousin of the VanderHooks, struck twelve. It was high noon.

❖ ❖ ❖

The Milwaukee alley was pure *film noir* — black-and-white and underexposed. Matching wrought-iron fire escapes clung to the two warehouses that formed either side of the alley. A noisy line of young, bundled-up people wound down almost to the far street at the other end.

Austin nodded to the burly bouncers at the door, who promptly ushered him and Rick in, to the grumbles of the people in the front of the long line.

"Hey, why do those guys get to go in?" protested a would-be entrant.

"That's a big-time manager," said the head bouncer, not sure at all who, and not really caring. Even bouncers know well enough that this year's big-time was next year's bomb.

Rock was tricky that way. Producing a winner was not easy. You needed an ear and incredible timing. As a manager, you didn't want to sign a band too early. Otherwise, all you got was a chance to feed them while they waited for stardom, only to see them run off and sign a management deal with someone else if they ever made it big.

And now the entire music industry was in a slump. In the post top-40 era, pop music was segmented by the same cultural tribalism that was fragmenting society as a whole. Rock music was living on its old catalog and its aging legends, who were still being recycled because they were the only ones who could still fill the sheds and the stadiums.

Rick had been searching a long time to find an act that would take him up to the next level. At age twenty-five, he had already paid a lot of rock 'n' roll dues. And although he was probably making better money than his new neighbor, without having wasted the best hormones of his life in a dusty law library, Rick's career was stalled. He needed to find and sign that mega-group. He was beginning to question whether he would ever become a giant in the industry, like an Azoff, Ertegun, or Geffen, men who had helped carve rock 'n' roll legends.

"Give me a Sprecher Special Amber," Rick said to the bartender.

Rick looked at the name on the bass drum, which dominated the stage set. "White Lies?" Rick said, in Austin's direction.

"You can always change the name," Austin replied as the band took the stage. Austin wanted this to work. He knew Rick would give him a little over-ride if this band ever took off.

Rick guessed that the Wisconsin band's name had a double meaning, relating to race — a liberal apology to Native Americans. On the other hand, White Lies could just as well be an allusion to golf played in the snow.

The opening chords of the first song bounced around the rafters of the old brewmeister's warehouse.

White lies, telling me what you want to hear.
White lies, it's your disguise.
White lies. White lies. White lies.

The crowd went nuts while the drummer wrapped the song with a furious drum riff. These guys could pack them in and work them over in Milwaukee. But what about a bigger venue?

Austin looked at Rick, waiting for his reaction. "Well?"

Rick gave him a nod. It was a seasoned gambler's nod. It said: maybe yes, maybe no. Rick had learned it from his Irish grandmother, also known as Nana. She was known throughout the elderly card tables of Rockford, Michigan, as a devastating cribbage player. In fact, her pink granite tombstone in the old Catholic cemetery contained words to that effect. "The hand you dealt, I played it well, Please Lord, commend my soul ... to heaven." She had composed that epitaph herself. And at her Irish wake, right before they sang "Good Night, Irene," everyone debated which was better, her card playing or her sense of humor.

Her legacy to Rick was to teach him all about facial expressions. She had sensed that her grandson would someday abandon cribbage for bigger games, so she taught him "the nod." The nod always bought Rick time to think, in circumstances like these. What he was thinking right now was how to get rid of the manager of this group, who was working his way towards him and Austin from the other end of the bar. If the dolt didn't know what he had, he didn't deserve a piece of the action to come.

❖ ❖ ❖

"What a great 'products' case!" Cheer Cheer was pumped.

Mitch gave him a puzzled look. "What are you talking about?"

"It would be a great products liability case."

"I don't think the manufacturer ever intended Kling Wrap to be used as a prophylactic."

"Failure to warn. Failure to warn," chimed Cheer Cheer. "And he's a minor, too. Hey, so is she. It's perfect. They should have had a warning on the box or some kind of package insert. I bet all food wrapping products have to be approved by the FDA. The box should have warned: Do not use as a rubber."

"Or how about: Don't wrap it ... bag it." Mitch hoped sarcasm would divert Cheer Cheer. Not a chance.

"402-A, *The Restatement of Torts*," boasted Cheer Cheer, always the first lawyer in the crowd to drop a citation.

"You're suggesting sex was a use the manufacturer should have contemplated?" Mitch asked.

The day's events had made Mitchell anxious. Preacher. Preacher's daughter. Preacher's son on an emotional rollercoaster. The Little Big Case. A mix of business and pleasure. Where was this going to go? His thoughts wandered. "Sure, Mrs. VanderHook, I'll take a smidgen of your pie. Sure, Sarah, I'd love to come to church with you on Sunday. Will God be preaching? Or just your father, who art in the other room having excused me to have a few choice words with your brother?" Mitch looked at his watch. He had stopped back at the office just to check his Friday afternoon messages before heading home.

Cheer Cheer continued unabashed. "He said he wasn't the only one using the stuff. That is proof that the use was reasonably foreseeable. If you believe the kid, his entire junior class was wrapping with it. You've got a class action, man!" Cheer Cheer started doing the wave, as best a single person could. "Give me a T. Give me an O. Give me an R. Give me another T. What does it spell ...?"

"You're crazy."

"Not as crazy as you. Wanting to go out with your client's sister. Actually our client's daughter. You better talk to Mr. Calley, he's involved in this one. We can all retire on the deal he's got going, if we play our cards right."

After Cheer Cheer finished haranguing Mitch about the dangers of dipping his pen in the company ink, Mitch suggested a change of venue. "Speaking of cards, let's go check out Beaver Sands this weekend."

"That casino up north?" Cheer Cheer asked.

"That's the general direction," said Mitch.

"Have you ever actually been into one of those Indian joints? There's people without any teeth playing blackjack," Cheer Cheer said with a righteous tone.

"Hey, there's a reason the Indians call the gaming crowds 'the New Buffalo.' I read they used to use every part of the buffalo. The tongue. The tail. It only stands to reason they would use the teeth, too."

Cheer Cheer didn't even crack a smile. "When Calley gets

the ballot proposal passed, our casinos will be world-class, with unlimited stakes. Plus big-name acts like the ones they get in Vegas and Branson." Cheer Cheer was getting agitated.

"Our casinos?" Mitch asked.

"Calley has cut a great contingency deal with Malone and the Indians. We aren't working on a hourly rate on this one. Instead our firm will own a piece of the gambling action," said Cheer Cheer.

"You're talking crazy. That's nuttier than that stupid Texas fruitcake you just mailed your girlfriend at Purdue. Don't start counting your money, yet. The referendum's not going to pass. It's not even going to come to a vote. It's not my specialty — as I'm sure Calley would point out — but no decent judge is going to certify it for the ballot. There's some law somewhere that prohibits two separate issues being posed as one referendum. And water and gambling don't mix."

Cheer Cheer frowned, but Mitch was just warming up. "Look, the way I see it, Malone's political advisors were idiots to combine the two issues. It unites two totally disparate groups against it. Sure, the religious right could care less whether Lake Michigan water gets sold to Nevada or pissed in. I know those Bible thumpers, Cheer Cheer. They believe that every word in the Bible comes from God's lips straight to their ears.

"And what they read," continued Mitch, in rising passion, "says the world is going to come to an end. And sooner, rather than later. The Book of Revelations makes it a sure bet. So, in their one-track minds, things like conservation of natural resources is senseless. It only delays the inevitable Judgment Day, when they get raptured to Heaven and the rest of us go straight to Hell."

Mitch was waving his arms in his own ecstacy. "But shooting craps in a casino? That gives them conniptions. You can gamble with God's water, but don't touch the Devil's dice. The religious right will oppose the gambling part of the referendum.

"And then you're up against the environmentalists. Sure, they may not mind a little state-sanctioned casino action. Casinos create employment that is a lot more friendly to the environment than factory jobs. And if gambling is good for the economy, then we can afford to invest more in protecting natural resources. So the tree huggers — and the Joe Six-Packs — won't mind the gambling part. They might even line up together to get a shot at doubling-down in blackjack or drawing to an inside straight in poker. But the people," Mitch was not really sure who he meant by "the people," but he was on a roll, "a lot of people are sure to go bonkers when it comes to wasting fresh water. And when our fellow Midwesterners hear it's for a corporation in Nevada ..."

Cheer Cheer was not fazed in the least. "Mitch, Mitch, Mitch," he said gently, to calm down his heated colleague. "Three things. Number one. Don't ever underestimate Calley's commitment to this ballot proposal.

"Number two. You knew we solved environmental-law problems on behalf of corporations when we hired you. You said you wanted to get your feet wet. Well, here's your big chance."

Cheer Cheer radiated confidence. "And number three. I'm hand-delivering the fruitcake this weekend."

Giovanni's plastic milk-crate full of classic rock albums was sitting out in the center of Mitch's living room where he had left it. Mitch walked over and knelt in front of it to review the selections. He was looking for something black or blue. Giovanni's taste was fully integrated, with Jefferson Airplane, Creedence, Seger, and the Stones squeezed in jacket to jacket with the Tops, the Temps, Smokey, and Diana. Mitch finally settled in on his sleeper sofa to the sounds of Al Green, who had been resting next to Cream's *Disraeli Gears*.

He looked out the sliding-glass windows at bare trees with wet trunks. He always thought of Nathaniel Hawthorne when he saw wet trunks in the fall. He could not remember whether it was something Hawthorne wrote, or if he had been reading Hawthorne in Ann Arbor in the fall when the trunks were wet.

Mitch got up and walked into the kitchen. He opened the drawer containing two tube-length rectangular boxes, and picked out one. If the Kling Wrap had been empty, would those kids have tried aluminum foil? Was Dusty the kind of girl who would have said, "Peter, put on your mask before you give me your silver bullet"? Mitch put the foil back in the drawer. What was sex really like these days for a sixteen-year-old kid? For that matter, what was sex really like for a young single lawyer living in Grand Rapids?

He picked up the other tube-length rectangular box and carried it into his living room. He sat down on the sleeper sofa. He looked closely at the label. Pow Chemical. Giovanni would have asked, "Didn't they stop to think that little gook children would be tortured and maimed by their napalm? Maybe they were just focused on various ways to prevent babies, after all." Mitch imagined Giovanni's voice shaking with anger.

He tore off a sheath of plastic wrap and was just pulling down his Jockeys to see exactly how this homemade condom would have worked, when the phone rang. He stood up in startled attention and stumbled in his embarrassed haste to grab the phone. Trying to catch his balance, he launched the roll of plastic wrap halfway across the living room, while the free end of the plastic sheet was still caught in his underwear.

"Hello." He hoped it wasn't his mother.

"What are you doing down there?" asked the girl with blue eyes, nipples, and beautiful skin who lived above. Sort of like an angel, he thought.

"Just working on a case," he gasped, quickly pulling up his shorts. He looked out the window. No one could see him.

"You sound out of breath."

"It's an exciting case."

"I wish I had something exciting to do. Rick's gone all weekend to Milwaukee."

Mitch had been naive. It never dawned on him that Laura had teased him the first time they met. Mitch had just assumed that his let-down had been the fault of his own wild fantasies. He had yet to learn that his fantasies were mild compared to the rest of the world.

Mitch had confessed to Laura on the phone that he wasn't really dressed.

"It's only up the stairs. Don't you own a robe?"

"No."

"Just streak up."

"Streak up?"

"You can wear one of Rick's robes. You're slender. You can wear one of mine. Come up right now before it gets cold."

He hung up the phone.

She was referring to a late-night snack. She had to be. He repeated that thought out loud, as he wondered what not to wear. "She was only referring to food." He wasn't going to let himself have great expectations like the last time she asked him up for a meal. And he certainly wasn't about to streak up. He might move with swiftness of foot, but he would not expose himself.

He dashed into his bedroom. Blue jeans. He started to put the jeans on. He pulled them down. He whipped off his Jockeys. He again hitched up his jeans. No shirt. Stomach in. He looked at his wallet on top of his dresser. He pulled out the blue foil insert and stuffed it into his jeans' pocket. He halted. He pulled it out again. "She was only referring to a snack." He flipped it back on top of his dresser.

He swung into his bathroom to look in the mirror. He exposed his teeth like a horse anticipating an apple from a hand. Make that the original apple. Make that a stallion. There was an increasing fullness behind his zipper. How rough denim could permit that to happen to such sensitive skin was beyond him. Especially with those lingering early boyhood memories of being caught in a zipper. He ran back and grabbed the condom. Just in case.

In a flash he was at her door.

He knocked. The door was open. "Hello?" he asked softly, as he pushed the door all the way open. There was a huge white towel lying in the hallway. He walked to it and lifted it up. It was a bath robe with the monogram, RGL.

Stu, his roommate at law school, use to say that an erect penis had no conscience. At least that was how it translated from Yiddish. This saying was rooted in folklore and not science. Take Mitch, for example. He had thoroughly considered RGL before heading upstairs in a heated rush. His conclusion: RGL was probably having his own debates with conscience right now somewhere out of town. In Milwaukee, far across the big lake.

Mitch cautiously walked towards the kitchen, waiting for the smell of something cooking to smack him in the nose. There was no such smell. Well, a simple snack would be fine. Finally committed to breaking the silence, Mitch called out, "Laura."

"Close the door behind you," she called from upstairs with even more authority. "It is getting cold in here."

Yes, ma'am, he thought, as he hurried back to do just that. Mitch couldn't see the blue-eyed lady sneaking a peak of him from the loft. Her eyes were smiling as she watched him standing there at the foot of her stairs. One side of her had guessed that he wouldn't streak up; the other side had bet that he would. Since the lawyer was half dressed, they were both half right.

"Come on, we're going to eat up here." Laura again ordered.

Mitch completed all the assignments Laura gave him that night, though the first really important one he turned in a little early. At least he took direction well. And Laura had concluded that he was a decent understudy to her Rick.

❖ ❖ ❖

"Praise God from whom all blessings flow ...." Hey, our tribe sings that same song, thought Mitch. Maybe the CRs aren't so different. The hymn finished with a lusty "Ahhhh ..." like you're showing your tonsils, "... mennnnn."

They all sat down. Sarah seemed to move closer to him. Mitch suddenly felt claustrophobic. Why did I come here? Cheer Cheer was right. I should not be socializing with my client's family. I have no business being here.

Mitch grabbed for his tie and the button behind it. Is it hot in here or is it just me, he wondered? He had taken two show-ers that morning after the night spent at Laura's, not counting the one with her. He still felt sticky from guilt.

There is only one sure-fire way to get over guilt feelings from an illicit affair and that was to get horny again. But that would never happen. He had been so completely released and fulfilled by Laura that there would never be a need for sex again. Sex had simply gone from him, expurgated from his body. Such joyous relief.

Peter VanderHook, Sr. rose to the pulpit. Mitch watched the black robe flowing behind the Reverend as he ascended. Judges and preachers —there were a lot of similarities under those robes. The Reverend quoted words from Job, something about loathing his life, and then moved on to the topic of his sermon.

"The time has come to conquer Sodom and Gomorrah,"

he began cautiously, looking up and down the aisles. "We all know too well that the wages of gambling are eternal damnation. We also know that the Lord speaks in mysterious ways. I have been visited by a vision," said the Reverend.

Mitch thought this was getting heavy. Sarah was sitting erect on the edge of the pew, looking alert and somewhat surprised.

"I have seen a vision of a place where sinners will be relieved of the wages of sin. Where, after plunging to the bottom of the pit of hopelessness," he modulated his voice to a new level, "they will rise again! To be baptized and sent afresh out into the world. Only by working with the poor, the downtrodden, the lechers and the sinners, will we be able to find the crystal doorway to a better place.

"In my vision, I have seen such a place, a vast house of shimmering beauty on the edge of a great inland sea." His voice slowly swelled, like powerful waves ready to crest on the shore. "Here, people will come to be cleansed by the waters, and to break the chains of material wealth.

"Yea, I say onto you!" his voice boomed. "Only by learning to break the mighty chains of material wealth can we learn to live as simple people in the eyes of God."

He paused and looked at his congregation. "I have been told to lead you to a place where we will build a magnificent cathedral of clear waters, to baptize and minister to the unholy flocks."

He raised his arms in triumphant glory. "In my vision, I have seen such a place," he thundered, "and now, I want to share it with you!" Whereupon, the Reverend walked over and pulled a large white sheet off an easel standing erect on the dais. Underneath, in acute, upswept angles was revealed an architectural rendering of a massive sandstone-colored edifice, titled in bold letters: The Water Cathedral & Casino.

To Mitch, and probably to the others, it looked like a mirage. Just then, the heating system kicked in, and warm waves of heat spreading out from a duct under the dais made the colorful drawing shimmer in its spotlight.

The Reverend explained the eminent technology behind this remarkable vision. There was not a funicular truss in sight. This was nouveau organic architecture. The most remarkable feature: the buff-tinged, quarried sandstone walls were open at the top. There was no roof, at least not a solid one. The building looked like it was open to the heavens, but with a strange translucent film, drawn on the rendering with a lightly shaded blue pastel.

The roof of the cathedral would be water. Yet it was designed to be completely waterproof. With powerful pumps, great volumes of water would be forced up in pipes laid into one of the sandstone walls, up into stainless steel abutments running across the top of that wall. Employing the latest in hydro-technology, millions of micro high-speed jets would create a sheet of water, which would arch out and across the open roof, cascading down beyond the far side. There, it would be collected in catchment toughs, to be piped around and recycled back up to the roof of constant water.

The high-powered jets were designed to beam out non-stop beads of water with a blistering velocity. The water would be shot across the opening with such speed that any dust, any outside rain or hail or even bird-dropping — the bane of many a majestic cathedral — would be deflected, launched off the far side of the building. Underneath the building was a system of tubing, pumps, and a massive intake valve to draw in water from the nearby lake.

From the inside, a computerized lighting system would

enable the projection of celestial images up onto the watery ceiling of the cathedral, in concert with any sermon or organ music. Filtered natural light would flood the cathedral by day. Golden sconces and swirling neon patterns would light the visionary edifice by night.

The main floor plan was to be filled with gambling devices — slot machines, blackjack tables, roulette wheels — all the trappings of a Las Vegas casino. But there were a few other odd features unlike a traditional gambling establishment. Perhaps the most intriguing design feature was the opportunity to baptize anyone who came in the door. There were special areas designated for baptism ceremonies, strategically placed throughout the building.

Towering above the sandstone cathedral was a campanile, whose bells were programmed to ring twenty-nine times whenever a soul was saved — or a big jackpot was hit. The synergism between gambling and water was dynamic.

There were gasps from a few of the older members in the congregation. Quickly, the Reverend VanderHook reminded them that the Catholics down the street at St. A's had been playing bingo in the basement for years.

"A very enlightened messenger has brought this opportunity to me, to our congregation. He could have easily gone to some other church in our denomination. He could have gone to one of those televangelists, like those Rolex-adorned folks from Louisiana, who have caused our denomination not to grow and multiply as quickly as others who market their good words and deeds in the mass media. If we build this new cathedral and hall of chance, our power will carry far across the land."

Mitch again looked over at Sarah. She was shaking her head no. On the other hand, farther down the pew, Sarah's mother was shaking her head yes. There was an honest difference of opinion going on here, as parishioners' heads nodded up, down, sideways, or were frozen in awe at the immensity of this presentation.

It looked like VanderHook's congregation would soon be splintering in two, much like the Reformed and Christian Reformed had split a long time ago. The question was: Could the maverick Reverend VanderHook lead his flock — hopefully to be followed by the rest of Michigan's religious fundamentalists — to support big-time, unlimited stakes gambling?

Malone and his Desert Development Corporation were laying odds that he could.

From the Rocky Mountains and beyond, all the way to the Pacific Coast Highway, the landscape is dry, dry, dry, baby. Dinosaur-bone dry. Dry like Xerica, the Greek Goddess of dry. Dry like Ronald Reagan and Twenty Mule Team Borax.

Even before you get to the Rockies, the western desert starts as the plains rise up a mile high to the foot of the Front Range. With a minuscule annual rainfall, there are not many places they can grow crops from there to the Pacific without irrigation. Most of the territory of the western United States is nothing but a big, thirsty desert.

"There's a good view of Denver coming up on the right side of the aircraft," the pilot volunteered.

Cheer Cheer looked out the window of the plane. There were cottonwoods growing along dry creeks leading to the metropolis, which sprawled from Colorado Springs almost to Cheyenne. But the majority of the green trees of the "Mile-High City" 35,000 feet below were all imported. And the grass? Some of the golden-brown grass was native. But the well-fertilized Kentucky bluegrass? Just window-dressing. Stage props put there by an army of weekend greens-keepers and maintained by perpetual irrigation.

Even after the Denver Water Board built a series of reservoirs in the mountains, Colorado still wanted to suck water out of the North Platte and the underground aquifers of western Nebraska. This was most easily accomplished on Saturdays during Cornhusker home football games, when everyone in Nebraska was either in Lincoln or looking in that direction.

Ken Calley had taken this flight to Las Vegas once a week since being retained to represent Malone's corporation. But this was Cheer Cheer's first flight west.

"You like to bet on football? In Las Vegas, you can bet on anything. It is truly the All-American city. You've never been here, have you?" Like a good lawyer, Calley was only asking questions he already knew the answers to.

"How did you meet Mr. Malone?" Cheer Cheer asked.

"We go way back," said Calley. "I've been his lawyer through three wives. The last one tried to wipe him out. Ran off with a blackjack dealer from the old Circus Circus Casino. She was a good-lookin' broad," said Calley.

"Was? Did she die?" Cheer Cheer asked.

"She was in a tragic accident. Steering failed while she was driving out in the desert," said Calley.

"Sounds like a good 'products' case," said Cheer Cheer.

"I'm sure it would have been, but everything was burned beyond recognition," said Calley.

Cheer Cheer didn't want to leave the airport. He couldn't decide which one to pick. They were all so darn cute.

"You can only have one. For later tonight. They are very expensive," Calley whispered in his ear, after the three young women who looked like cheerleaders performed a marvelous curbside routine for the two lawyers by the waiting limousine. "Hurry up, they're stopping traffic."

"They're not prostitutes, are they?" asked Cheer Cheer, with considerable disappointment in his voice after finally picking the perky redhead.

"Of course not," said Calley, wondering for the first time whether his associate really had what it took to be an HD&H partner.

Before heading out to the Malone ranch, Calley played tour guide for his young charge. He diverted the limo through The Strip, driving slowly past a flood of sights that looked so different in the light of day. Cheer Cheer was all eyes and ears.

"I'll be opening up a Las Vegas office after the election. You could be my right-hand man. There will be one mother lode of a jackpot when the pipeline gets hooked up. Water is the only thing stopping this town," said Calley, as the limo drove by the fountain in front of the Mirage, which ruptured up like Niagara Falls in reverse. "They're going to run out of water in less than seven years," said Calley.

"Seven is an unlucky number," said Cheer Cheer.

"It's lucky for us. The closer it gets to the end, the more they'll pay. They'll pay anything," said Calley.

Gargantuan hotels, casinos, tiny wedding chapels, and everywhere, the ghost of Elvis, soon gave way to condos and miles and miles of suburban tract homes. Eventually the limo rolled on into unliberated desert. Green turned instantly to brown.

At the guarded gatehouse to the main entrance of the Malone ranch, a barbed-wire fence extended to either horizon. The limo was waived through. A few minutes later, Cheer Cheer had his first glimpse of the Malone compound and Malone himself, who was barking orders to his ranch foreman, Clint Walker.

"Triple darn it," Malone screamed.

"But Mr. Malone, sir, when they make it in Tahoe, they

got freezin' temperatures workin' for 'em. Even then, they don't make true powder. Powder only comes from the sky. I know what you're trying to achieve here, sir. But I ..." Walker, the foreman, caught himself just in time. Better to say, "Your Excellency, you got spinach between your teeth and pungent gas," than to say the word "can't."

Walker knew what not to say, but he was exasperated. It had been raining slush off and on ever since Thanksgiving at the Malone compound. The only thing he could show for it was a deeper shade of green on the big lawn, *secate grande*, as it was called by the illegal Mexican aliens who tended it.

"Walker. You got all the water in Nevada. Get the cold too. Do whatever it takes. There's got to be a way. Get some factory-sized refrigeration units from my friend at Nellis Air Force Base. I don't care if it takes two hundred of them, and costs a million dollars."

He paused for a second. "And fans. Get some airplane-hangar fans. That should do the trick, if we just set them up right. We can make a lot of cold air and the fans can circulate it to where we want it. It's just a matter of the will to do it. Let's not hockey puck around here."

Malone didn't own a National Hockey League franchise, yet. Nor did he like to "hockey puck around," not since he had found the Lord, recovered from alcohol, and married his third wife. To his acquaintances — like Calley, who had known Malone before his transformation — such quaint phrases seemed a bit anachronistic, if not feeble. Back in the old days, Malone would think nothing of feeling up his most recent chorus-girl with one hand, throwing back Maker's Mark bourbon with the other, and machine-gunning orders with four-letter expletives on the speaker phone to Clint Walker without losing a beat.

In spite of giving up profane language, his employées still responded promptly to his new-found euphemisms, except the illegal Mexicans. As everyone knows, swear words are one of the first things you learn when you study a foreign language. However, "not hockey-pucking around" did not translate easily.

Cheer Cheer stepped out of the limousine into a pile of slush up to his ankles and swore. On the other side, attended to by the chauffeur, Calley emerged with a little more grace. Both men could now see hoses, pipes, and compressors strewn around the vast green yard, part of a grand and as yet unsuccessful snowmaking enterprise. While foreman Walker obviously looked fed up, the Mexicans were taking great joy in their wet job. It was welcome relief from the desert heat.

"I promised Tammy that her mother would have a white Christmas. Can do. Can do. That's all I want to hear," Malone was hammering at Walker.

Tammy, Calley had explained earlier on the airplane, was a former chorus girl with outstanding physical attributes. She also clung to stronger family values than either of Malone's other wives. After they got engaged, Tammy made Malone meet her parents back in her hometown of St. Ignace, Michigan. He didn't want to go, but she insisted.

St. Ignace sits at the Straits of Mackinac on Michigan's Upper Peninsula, facing the cool waters of Lake Huron. It was on that fateful trip that this son of a western-desert pioneer got his first glimpse of not one but two great lakes, Michigan and Huron. Along with their sisters (the lovely Superior, Ontario, and Erie), the Great Lakes hold one fifth of the world's fresh water. It was one thing to know the statistics; it was another to see such an expanse of fresh water in person. The man from Nevada was impressed.

As Malone had gazed out at the place where the Mackinaw Bridge spans the two peninsulas of Michigan – where the sibling rivalry between Lakes Huron and Michigan makes the water in the passage rough and treacherous — a thought struck him. "This is not the place!" he yelled, a kind of converse echo of the words Brigham Young called out enthusiastically upon seeing the Great Salt Lake on his pilgrimage west.

Malone had always been as conflicted as he was complex. Even when he was drinking a bottle of bourbon a day and telling Calley and his divorce lawyers that "the second bitch don't deserve squat either," Malone had harbored visions of a Brigham Young-like grandeur. He had just needed Tammy to bring sobriety and clarity to his life in order to realize those visions. It was Tammy who brought him the Word.

Small gambling casinos in Las Vegas like Malone's had taken a hard hit lately from the mega-casinos. And then there was Atlantic City and all those state lotteries, not to mention those darn Indians everywhere with their two-bit gambling joints. On the verge of cashing in his chips, Tammy had appeared, calling upon higher powers to console and comfort him. She had explained, better than the Christian right-wing ever had, exactly how Jesus of Nazareth was a laissez-faire economist at heart.

"The Scriptures say do not give the shaft to your wheat," Tammy had spoken with garbled conviction. "Besides, over in Colorado there are God-fearing folks who brew beer, but drink nary a drop. And there are Mormons in this country who sell liquor in their hotel bars, but tithe generously to their church. Honey, what is the difference between drinking and gambling? Personally you have given up both."

Raison d'être! With those words Tammy had sparked a renaissance in her man. He had come up with the brainstorm, which had quickly grown overnight into the Malone Desert Development Corporation.

"How the hockey puck are you?" Malone's voice boomed when he finally spotted Calley picking his way across the slushy courtyard, with wet-footed Cheer Cheer not far behind.

The evening weather forecast had promised snow. Mitch pulled back his drapes with hopes of reviving memories of John Greenleaf Whittier and Robert Frost.

But there was no blanket of white. Just low-cloud November gray.

It had been exactly two weeks since he hopped had into bed up the stairs. His subsequent re-dedication to the practice of law had been intense. By last night, he had billed one hundred and forty-nine hours. But he was starting to get bored. He was feeling restless. As more and more of his human existence was accounted for in hourly increments, he began to question the value of it.

As an Assistant U.S. Attorney, he would never have had a chance at owning a forty-foot sailboat on Macatawa or Spring Lake. But he had enjoyed a lot more satisfaction than in his present clock-punching situation. Sending bank robbers to prison — or better yet, crooked bank vice-presidents — was something worth doing. Now, Mitch found some of the assignments at HD&H to be downright distasteful. "Just give it some time," his old law-school roommate Stu had counseled in a recent telephone conversation. "And time and time and time."

But his free moments were overwhelmed by images of the night he had spent with Laura.

Little gusts of wind stirred up a few oak leaves outside

his sliding glass window. He pulled it open to let a rush of cold air refresh his face. The temperature was dropping, but he would not be snowbound this Saturday morning. He shut the door and walked over to Giovanni's milk crate and began flipping through the classics. For the first time, he couldn't find a tune that suited him. He only wanted to hear Laura's voice.

"Did you pitch any of my songs?" Laura asked Rick, who was lying in bed next to her. He didn't answer right away. She sat up in bed and looked at him. "You did give my demo to the guy at the label?"

"Honey, it was so crazy there. Sixteen-hour days. I produced all the White Lies tracks myself. You know what that's like," said Rick.

"No, Rick, that's the problem. I don't know what that's like. I've never been in a studio, making a record," said Laura. She threw back the sheets and got out of bed. Immediately her fully exposed body was attacked by thousands of goose bumps lurking in the morning chill.

"Come on back to bed. I haven't seen you for so long," Rick pleaded.

Laura yanked open the metal folding door of her closet. The accordion door came off the runner. A brief struggle ensued, until she was able to jam it aside enough to access a bulky sweatshirt and sweatpants.

"I can't believe you didn't care enough to hand my demo to him. To just hand the damn thing to him," Laura was fuming, her blue eyes ready to blow Rick out of bed. Dressed, she turned back to look at him. "To just hand it to him. Here, Mr. Geltman, this is my girlfriend's demo. She can't sing and her material is not very original. But she put her career on hold for me, so I could go out and discover the great American band for the 21st century. She really is a great lay, so I feel like I owe her this much."

Laura walked down the stairs from the loft. Rick remained in bed looking at the ceiling, but his voice trailed her down the stairs. "I'm planning on having you open for White Lies, when they tour back here. What do you think of that?"

White lies, thought Laura. That's what she thought — and had ever since they first met. It had been a Presidents' weekend holiday, a senior-year ski break for Laura and her girlfriends from Interlochen. Rick had been plunking at the piano in the lobby of the Perry Hotel in Petoskey, while waiting to register. The old upright was just supposed to have been furniture against a wall. It sounded so out of tune. But it all seemed so perfect. He, a handsome young rock promoter just old enough to have legal ID. She, with a beautiful voice that had rock 'n' roll promise all its own. She just walked up and sat down on the bench next to him. Soon they drew a crowd from the bar across the Victorian lobby, and her girlfriends didn't need to buy drinks either.

Laura now sat at the bench in front of her electric Yamaha, an angry young white female vocalist in the vein of Crowe, Morissette, and Osborne. She lit the organ and began to play.

Rick didn't recognize the tune. There were a lot of them that she had written which he had never heard or, worse yet, never taken the time to listen to. It didn't matter, he knew too well, if she wrote a good melody or had anything to say. The music business was no longer about some Carole King songsmith writing a ditty about tomorrow's love and pitching it down tin-pan alley to an A&R guy. Maybe the boys in Nashville were still doing it that way on 16th Avenue.

But in rock, it was about EBITDA — Earnings Before Interest, Taxes, Depreciation, and Amortization. It was about big business. It was about packaging. Laura sounded good. But she wasn't packaged. She needed a marketing hook.

As the music came down through his ceiling from the apartment above, Mitch didn't recognize the tune either. But he sure did love that voice.

❖ ❖ ❖

For Calley, the thrill of the deal counteracted the jet lag from yet another trip to Las Vegas. He brightly did the introductions. "Reverend, come on in. You and your son have met Mr. Miller. This is Mr. Lattisaw, the claims representative from Great Lakes Auto and Marine."

Some judges and preachers looked much smaller without their robes. Not Peter VanderHook, Sr. As he shook hands with Mitch and the claims rep, he still looked a lot like Gary Cooper.

The Dutch who settled in West Michigan tended to be tall, angular people, with blond hair and blue eyes. Pretty was not a word that would usually come to mind, not like a heart-stopping sixteen-year-old Florentine school girl cycling past the map in your hands while you stood in the Piazza della Signoria. Nevertheless, the Dutch could modestly claim handsome and wholesome as an identity. Of course, in Grand Rapids and throughout the Grand River Valley, where they were the dominant religious and political force, bumper stickers often proclaimed more: "If you ain't Dutch, you ain't much."

The Dutch did have a lot to be proud of. Most of what was good about Grand Rapids was because of them. Having come to America to avoid religious persecution, they were industrious to a fault. They didn't go on welfare. They placed a high value on education. Their children were studious, well mannered, and didn't spray graffiti on public walls. However, like more recent immigrants, the Dutch did exhibit gang-like behavior. This was most evident on Sunday when walking to church, as they scorned neighbors who were cutting grass, raking leaves, and so forth. Also, like recent immigrants to America, some of the boats bringing them here had sunk en route. Such was the ancestry of the VanderHook clan.

It had been known as the Society of Christians for the Holland Emigration, the group which helped to locate good land for the Dutch Reform immigrants along the western and eastern shores of Lake Michigan. In response to the promise of freedom and land, one boatload of immigrants set sail from Buffalo on November 11, 1847. On its last voyage of the season, the *Phoenix* was filled with Hollanders, thronging on deck in their wooden shoes even as the boat left a sunny Lake Erie and plowed north towards Lake Huron.

On November 21, having made the horseshoe turn at the Straits of Mackinac and taken on wood for fuel in Manitowoc, the *Phoenix* and its load of three hundred hopeful people seemed ready to endure any blow Lake Michigan might offer. But it was not the gales of November which came calling. It was fire.

No doubt there were both heroes and villains making life-and-death decisions as a few overcrowded life boats were lowered from the burning decks into those icy waters off the town of Cheboygan. Suffice it to say that Peter VanderHook came from strong, aggressive stock.

"I've read the demand from the girl's lawyer. It seems to be a reasonable way to resolve this," said the Reverend VanderHook. He was looking at Calley, but Lattisaw answered.

"It's outrageous. My company has no intention of settling for anything like that." Lattisaw was a local claims representative and a young one at that. His settlement authority only went up to thirty-five thousand dollars. On this case, he took marching orders from the home office in Lansing. He continued, "We are going to have to fight this one unless the plaintiff gets realistic."

The Chevy Lumina which little Peter had been driving when he rear-ended Dusty belonged to the church, and had a relatively large policy. The demand made by the opposing lawyer, hired by Dusty's father, had been for the full policy limits: three-hundred thousand dollars.

"No jury in conservative Kent County is going to award anything even close to three-hundred thousand for some knocked-up teenager with a phony sore neck and a dead fetus," Lattisaw volunteered with a complete disregard for the feelings of those present.

Mitch could not believe his ears. He looked at little Peter. Peter looked at his father. His father looked at Calley.

Little Peter's head was bowed, probably in prayer.

But the Reverend's head was high, his temper simmering, about to boil over. The last couple months had been tough on him. The Reverend had managed to keep the dark secret of Peter's accident from even his most supportive Elders. All they knew was that there had been a minor fender-bender involving the church's Chevy.

Calley kept his cool. He and the Reverend had much bigger fish to fry than this overworked and underpaid claims rep. In fact, Calley was looking forward to see how the Reverend would handle a little friction.

Lattisaw's crude remarks ignited more than a little friction. Friction was just a matter of skid marks, surface condition, weight of the vehicle, and speed. The real problem in this sticky case was the unholy mix of sex and religion. To a Christian Reformed congregation in Grand Rapids, that would cause an explosion.

The Reverend had struggled to maintain his self-righteous and pious attitude ever since he got the unbelievable call from Dusty's father. "Your son rear-ended my daughter. And she just miscarried in my toilet," screamed the irate father who the Reverend had never met. It had been almost three months since Peter VanderHook, Sr. had received that call on the second Wednesday in September — at 6:59 pm to be exact; just before his monthly men's Christian fellowship meeting.

Now the Reverend VanderHook glared across the room at Lattisaw. "Fetus, Mr. Lattisaw? Fetus?" Between the first "fetus" and the second, the pitch in the Reverend's voice had increased an octave.

"That was no fetus. It was a life. A baby. With arms and legs and eyes. Invested with all the God-given glory of human life. Sacred life."

Just then Calley's secretary walked in with a pitcher of water. I have already been baptized once, thought Mitch. His mother had shown him the old picture of himself as a baby boy in a white-lace christening gown.

"Who do you presume to be, to come in here and tell me that the value of that child is anything less than infinite? Only our Creator knows what was in store for this precious life."

For a second, Mitch thought he heard a choir humming Monty Python's "Every Sperm is Sacred."

"It is not for me and certainly not for you, Mr. Lattisaw, to say what a jury in our town will find in this case. We are not the lawyers. But I have lived in this community all my life and I do know that you will find citizens on a jury who will look to the Lord in their deliberations."

Little Peter had raindrops, so many raindrops streaming down his cheeks. Mitch thought the father's words were unfair to the one child in the room who was, according to anyone's religious theology, clearly not unborn.

"What is your opinion, Mr. Miller? How much do you think an unborn life is worth, young man?"

VanderHook's question caught Mitch off guard. From the outset, the Reverend never seemed to pay any attention to him. VanderHook wanted Calley on the case — and he wanted Mitch kept away from his daughter. Calley had assured his client that he himself would handle all critical aspects of the case, and that his young associate had simply accepted Sarah's one invitation to worship in all innocence.

"Under Michigan law, the loss of a fetus, a baby, is compensable to the mother as mental anguish." Mitch spoke in a slow, measured monotone. "The plaintiff will need an obstetrician to testify that the impact caused the miscarriage. The uterus is a very thick muscle, especially during the first trimester. There is a serious question whether a slight impact ..."

"Mr. Calley, you must have an opinion," interrupted the Reverend.

"The sky's the limit," pronounced Calley. "This claim should be settled forthwith."

Once again Mitch looked around the room.

Lattisaw looked converted.

The Reverend looked vindicated.

Calley looked extremely pleased with his worthy ally.

Little Peter looked suicidal.

❖ ❖ ❖

For anyone from out East, the first time they saw Christmas lights on palm trees, it seemed weird. It did to Rick. He had been to Los Angeles many times, but never in December. A smogless yellow December sun was just setting on the Boulevard. Before the white man came, this place must have been as pristinely beautiful as Michigan. Maybe even as recently as 1958, when Orange County still deserved its name, and you drove through grove after grove to get to Disneyland.

He stood on the rooftop of Le Parc, a little West Hollywood hotel at the foot of the Hollywood Hills. This was his new base camp. From here he would make his assault. His previous forays into those Hills had been unsuccessful, but now he had struck a record deal for the hot band from Milwaukee. Now he would soon be one of them, and not just a Midwestern small-time promoter coming to visit the deliciously opulent candy store.

Rick had argued for a top producer, but budget and schedules didn't permit. So he settled for more studio time, which was easy to get in December. "Fine. I'll just produce the record myself," Rick had told Geltman, vice-president of the record company.

Still scanning the Hills and mapping his plans for conquest, Rick hardly noticed as a waiter brought a tray and set an ice tea and a cappuccino on the table by the rooftop pool. Then, a hand with well-polished nails was thrust in front of his face.

"My first Rodeo Drive manicure," said Laura as she gave him a quick kiss on the cheek. "Is that what they call packaging?" Laura asked with mocking affectation. "Can I be a star now?"

"You're already a star," Rick smiled. He had finally coaxed Laura away from her keyboards that gray Saturday morning with a promise that she could come to L.A. and meet Geltman herself.

Rick cupped his palm on the black leather knob and pushed her into second. He loved driving these Hills when he had no particular place to go. Tonight, however, they had a printed invitation. Geltman's house was somewhere off Mulholland, on the way over to the Valley. An avid fan of military history, Rick wondered which route Hannibal would have chosen to reach the top of the Hills to conquer them, as he and Laura wound around endless curves in the rented BMW.

Rick was pleased and Laura impressed as he found the road to Geltman's without turning around once or asking for directions. Of course, he did miss the final turn by a few yards; leave it to the BMW to make that tell-tale spinning sound of reverse gear as it retraced thirty-plus feet of fresh skid marks.

"There's a dead skunk in the road," Laura commented.

"There's a lot of wildlife up here," said Rick, trying not to sound metaphorical. "There's deer. Lots of deer, coyotes, you name it."

They did not spot any deer as they drove up the driveway, but cars. Fast cars that most men and boys only dream of were parked along both sides of the road at various angles of intoxication.

"Rick, I am glad you could make it, buddy. Greetings of the season," said Geltman, at first only half-noticing the two of them, because he was talking to several other people at the same time. "And who is this gorgeous arm-piece?"

"This is Laura," Rick said.

"Tell Laura I love her," Geltman yucked loudly, hoping that a few of the holiday party revelers bumping by him might also catch his wit.

Laura hated when people played with hooks like that. It trivialized them — the lyrics that is. Mildly disgusted, she immediately pumped her twelve-gauge and blasted Geltman with her very best party-girl response: a bright sly smile, with just the tip of her tongue, and a look that said, "Come on down to my boat, baby."

It worked. Geltman was visibly impressed by the blue-eyed one. "Rick, go help yourself to a drink. We have pink champagne on ice. Let me introduce Laura to some people she needs to know."

❖ ❖ ❖

"I heard this used to be quite the office party. Until three years ago, when the wives insisted that they come," said a sodden Cheer Cheer. He had just broken the news that his girlfriend, Stacey, had met a trader from the Chicago Board of Trade and was quitting grad school to move in with him. "And he's got a two-million-dollar brownstone on North Dearborn."

Mitch knew the Chicago neighborhood. This was bad for Cheer Cheer, though it showed solid upward mobility for the Golden Girl from Purdue.

"So I take it she wasn't impressed with your fruitcake. You know, lawyers are good at finding creative ways to use the law as a shield or sword for their clients — but fail miserably when it comes to gift-giving ideas," said Mitch. "On the other hand, I must admit that I was wrong about something — the chances for the ballot proposal. There seems to be more support for the gambling part of it in places I never would have expected." He recalled watching the members of VanderHook's congregation receive the minister's vision of a gambling casino with interest.

Cheer Cheer shrugged. "This is serious, Mitch. I planned on marrying Stacey."

Under his shoulder pads, Cheer Cheer was a sensitive guy. At least Mitch assumed so. No doubt Cheer Cheer had known all along that the conservative VanderHook was on board with the combined gambling-and-water initiative. By now, Mitch had also figured that Calley had handpicked Cheer Cheer for some high-level operations regarding the ballot proposal.

"Is VanderHook getting a piece of your casino, too?" Mitch asked.

"Mitch, it's our casino, if you're still on the HD&H team."

"I am loyal to thee, Oh Holland, Dawson and Hager. I just want to know what's in it for the Rev. Is it the Water Cathedral?"

"There's something in this for everyone. Yourself included, if you stay cool," said Cheer Cheer.

Mitch was about to say something, but Cheer Cheer was on his own track. "She'll be sorry. I'm going to be richer than that asshole trader."

"What does he trade?" Mitch asked.

"Soybeans," Cheer Cheer spit out.

Cheer Cheer wasn't totally drunk yet. Maybe he wouldn't cry, if they left soon. He sure looked pathetic — almost as pathetic as little Peter VanderHook, Jr. had looked at his recent funeral. Peter's Thanksgiving Day swan-dive off his father's church roof had been a terrible shock to the VanderHooks — and did not go down well with Calley, either. Calley was furious at Mitch, somehow blaming him for the suicide. The congregation was stunned, of course, and VanderHook the elder was now engaged in major damage control.

The sight of Cheer Cheer sitting there stirring his beer with a plastic swizzle stick temporarily lifted Mitch's spirits. It was odd how someone else's misery could help lift you out of your own.

Mitch walked across the room giving a few nods to young comrades in attendance. He avoided a circle of senior partners, which included Calley. The secretaries and their husbands or boyfriends seemed to be having the most fun, soaking up the holiday ambience. There was a long table where the food was laid out.

Mitch looked at the spread with its plates of decorated green and red cookies. As the first buzz of wine hit him, he started to feel a major case of wallowing coming on. It was mistletoe wallowing, the worst kind in the Judeo-Christian tradition. Some years back, at a law-school Christmas party, Mitch had learned from Stu that Jews could get melancholy at Christmas too. But for different reasons, of course. "About six million," Stu estimated.

"Is that all they had left?" Cheer Cheer turned his nose at the sight of the raw vegetables that Mitch had piled on his plate. "Why didn't you get some potato chips and pretzels?"

Mitch looked at the vegetables. Cheer Cheer may have had a point. The vegetables at the HD&H Christmas party did not present well. The carrot, which Mitch was now holding in his hand, was flaccid.

Laura was probably eating turgid vegetables in California right now. Probably on the beach with Rick. Giovanni's complete Beach Boy collection had so ingrained the beach image into Mitch's mind that he never considered any other location for fun in California.

Cheer Cheer got up to get another beer and some fried food.

Mitch held up the wine to the banquet room's fluorescent light. He searched for body inside the clear plastic cup, like Laura had shown him that first night with her fine crystal.

There was some unsteadiness in Cheer Cheer's gait as he returned to the table.

"Let's get out of here while we can," Mitch ordered.

❖ ❖ ❖

Sure, when it comes to sunflowers, or maple leaves in autumn, yellow is fine. But the truth is that yellow is the least appreciated color in the spectrum. Particularly in commercial applications. Take Rick's first car, for example, a yellow Camaro that he had left lying on its axles in the middle of Plainfield Avenue. As a teenager, Rick had been on his way, a little late, to pick up his prom date. Of course, it would have been less concern if he had been old enough to drive. Luckily the cop bought his fake ID.

As Rick brushed through the party crowd in Geltman's well-appointed cliff dwelling, Rick was reminded how successful people in the entertainment business kept in touch with all their Crayolas. Rick found the dining room, for instance, to be a perfect example of yellow at its best. A multitude of candles, perched high on Spanish wrought-iron, splashed yellow hues and shadows on the textured walls. Only a candle could make light that seductive. Everything looked edible.

"Try the tartar." The woman shoved a toast point, covered with raw beef laced with caviar, into Rick's mouth before he could say "vegetarian."

"Do you like it?" she cooed.

For a split second he thought he would choke, then he saw the silicone sister and decided to chew. A different division of Pow chemists had turned their attention to giving humanity an uplift.

Dante and Milton would have agreed that, in the scheme of things, the dining room and the living room of Geltman's house should have been located on the top level. In classical tradition, the bedrooms then would have been the Middle Kingdom, due to their proximity to both Heaven and Hell.

Neither poet would have had any quarrel with the location of the basement, with reference to what was happening there. It was hotter than Hades. There were half-clothed peopled sweating and writhing in painful convulsions to steamy hip-hop. It was pure Hell — with one glaring exception. It was a walkout. Sliding-glass doors led outside to a patio. That intriguing prospect would have preoccupied Dante and Milton for eternity, if not completely blown their minds.

It was to that walkout basement where Geltman escorted Laura, saying, "You make me feel like dancing."

Laura mounted the throbbing beat of the bass without missing a step. Geltman's heart, which was now only an inch below his belt buckle, soared with Laura's every gyration. "Rick tells me you're a singer-songwriter," Geltman tried to shout above the Foxy Brown hip-hop hit.

Laura ran her hand down the short length of the skimpy skirt to her silky thigh. Geltman's pulse raced. She didn't stop there. She reached into the top of her black suede boot which came to just below her knee. A stiletto to cut out his heart? No. It was Memorex. She plucked the cassette and slid it into the pocket of Geltman's three-thousand-dollar holiday jacket, which he had just picked up at Max's that afternoon. "I hope you like it," Laura said with all the charm she could muster.

"I can already see the video in my head, baby," said Geltman. "You know I'm plugged in big-time to MTV. Developing a pilot for them right now. It's got attitude. Surveyed twenty fifth-graders at an Elementary School in Encino. Asked them which color they would use to draw strobe lights. The results: nineteen out of twenty picked black-and-white," said Geltman as he made a move to grab Laura by the ass.

And a tight little one it is, thank you, thought Laura as she artfully moved out of his reach. "What about the twentieth kid?" she said to Geltman, who was visibly disappointed that his advance had been so gracefully thwarted.

"What?"

"What about the last kid?" Laura asked, while looking around the room. Where had Rick gone? Was that Michael Stripe over in the corner? The guy from the rock group R.O.M. who had said Lennon and McCartney wrote elevator music? She wondered if she would have to sleep with a creep like Geltman for her music to ever have a chance of making it in an elevator.

"Something about advanced periodontal disease," yelled Geltman, trying to re-direct her attention.

"What?" asked Laura.

"The kid never responded," said Geltman. He made another move towards Laura.

❖ ❖ ❖

It pained Mitch to even think about singing it. He was not exactly a Notre Dame fan. Just the mere thought of touchdowns for Jesus bothered him. Unless you were playing against Moslems in the Crusades Bowl, it didn't seem fair for Jesus to gang up on anybody.

Besides he doubted that Jesus was all that interested in football. There simply weren't that many Jews who were great football players. Benny Friedman, a Michigan quarterback, was probably the best, but that was way back in the '20s, when football was an incipient American religion. Even Stu conceded this point one lonely Saturday night in the law school library, but only after talking about Sandy Koufax's fastball for an hour. And reminding Mitch that it was not a gentile who postulated the theory of relativity.

Mitch did have to admit that Notre Dame had a great fight song. The Wolverines, the Badgers, and the Catholics had the three best fight songs in the whole world. Mitch had a theory that it had something to do with the three schools' proximity to the Great Lakes; the well-known lake effect. If Lake Michigan could affect weather so dramatically, why not music too? The French had a pretty good fight song, too, and Paris was about as close to weather-changing water as Ann Arbor, Madison, or South Bend. However, given their lousy defense, all those losing seasons against the Germans, Mitch saw that as punching a hole in his theory.

Reluctantly Mitch burst out loudly, not really singing, "Cheer, cheer, for old Notre Dame. Wake up the echoes. Something, something — calling your name. Dah, dah, dah, dah, dah, dah, dah ..." Cheer Cheer didn't even look up. His face was fixed on his beer glass in despair. But the older couple in the next booth turned around and smiled. Mitch stopped singing. "Come on. How's it go? Help me out here."

Mitch was starting to get more than a little perturbed with Cheer Cheer. If the Latin root of "con" means "with," as in "Scotch con aqua," then it would be fair to say that Mitch had been having a "versation" with himself ever since they got to the Copper Top Bar.

Mitch knew that Cheer Cheer's head was probably feeling eight miles high by now and could ill afford to touch down. Mitch dug his cleats in. Not his baseball cleats; he was always afraid of getting beaned in the head. He dug his football cleats in and went into a four-point goal-line stance. He felt the wet muddy sod on his knuckles, and he could smell it too. That smell of wet Michigan grass was always the best part of the game anyway. This was collegiate intramural tap football at its roughest.

"What would Knute say?" pressed Mitch. "The Four Horsemen, Paul Hornung, Joe Theismann, all those black Irish running backs —would they quit? Would they let some woman mess up their game plan?" Mitch was grasping at straws, obviously weak in all but the most common Notre Dame sports trivia. "Ah-hah! Red Grange. What would he do?" It was a desperate Hail Mary fourth-down play, but it worked.

"Red Grange went to Illinois." The sphinx sitting across from Mitch, crying tears in his beer, finally broke his silence. A cheer went up from the couple in the next booth.

Laura was pissed as the sun came around to her cloudless day on the West Coast. She was going to kill him. She would stuff the papaya, which she hadn't ordered, down his throat and push him in the pool.

The waiters wouldn't understand, but they would smile and nod their heads. The tourists having breakfast a few tables over were from "down under." When she was first seated, she overheard the tourists telling some other visitors from Iowa that they were on holiday from Auckland. They had a map of the stars' homes. If they were in search of that America, then a little murder for breakfast on the hotel's rooftop lanai would be a special way to start their day.

Rick had abandoned her to Geltman for most of the night. She never saw him with the attractive woman who had offered him raw meat. If she had, she would have known that her fantasies about papaya and drowning were pedestrian, which is to say unimaginative — a bad thing to be in a town which effectively banned all pedestrians.

All she had heard from Geltman was what a big shot he was in the music business, as he tried to feel her up. She had been sincerely debating whether she should let Geltman advance her career, when a short but very high woman spilled her wine all over Geltman's new holiday sport coat. The woman, whom Laura thought she had seen on the cover of some magazine in the grocery store check-out line, promptly ushered him off, all the while making profuse apologies and offering to make it up to him. Laura never saw Geltman the rest of the night.

"Morning."

She didn't answer.

Rick sat down at the table. He looked up to the Hills,

green and lush this time of year. "No smog today," Rick said as he waived the waiter over. "Can I get some orange juice and some fruit?" He looked at Laura. "That was great food last night," said Rick, who had finally come looking for Laura after midnight at the party.

She still didn't speak.

Rick looked at his watch. "If we leave by eleven, we should be okay. Your flight's at one. The band's in at two. Traffic shouldn't be too bad."

Not a word.

Most men panic in a situation like this. They just can't bear the silence. Rick, however, figured why ask if you already know the answer? Asking questions only puts you on the defensive. He was just doing his job last night. It's not like he didn't drive her back to the hotel. If she's going to act like this she can just stay home next time, he thought.

Laura stood up. "I better go pack." She walked down the steps past the pool and towards the door to the elevator.

Rick reached for the *Los Angeles Times*, which was lying on the pool lounge-chair beside him. He didn't even bother to watch her walk away. Leave the tourists from New Zealand to view her fine posterior and wonder if she was a movie starlet.

The heated pool was clear blue without a ripple. Nobody was swimming or drowning.

❖ ❖ ❖

There was not any critical reasoning involved in Mitch's homecoming to Michigan. He had not engaged in any real analysis of this place versus that, like he did his senior year of law school. Back then he debated and debated which offer to take. It had been a dead heat, until he considered the patriotic issue: private practice with Horton & Everly in Chicago versus public service with the United States of America and the Republic for which it stands, one nation, under God, indivisible, with liberty and justice for all.

Any good lawyer knows that how you frame the question can often dictate the answer.

His homecoming had been purely instinctual, a migratory bird's pilgrimage, like a swallow to Capistrano or a buzzard to Hinckley, Ohio. There was something primal at play. Perhaps if he had somehow been able to trace the real origins of his call to North American Van Lines, he might have noted how two ballads of the lake country, each by Canadian pied-pipers, had beckoned him with their siren songs. Neil Young's "Helpless" and Gordon Lightfoot's "Wreck of the Edmund Fitzgerald" formed a persuasive duet for his return to the Great Lakes water wonderland.

Mitch drove along Lake Macatawa where docks were stacked by cottages and boathouses. The guardhouse at the entrance to the Ottawa Beach State Park was unattended. Where just three months before, campers in tents and pop-up trailers had swarmed, now there was only one parked car. Three teenage boys stood smoking around that car. Reflexively, they hopped back and forth on their feet in alternating motions as if they were standing on hot sand. But the sand had not been hot since the campers left. The boys shivered, faking an occasional nervous laugh.

A plow had been through the parking lot since an early December snowstorm. Snow piles had been curled up, like melting vanilla ice cream scraped to the side of a carton — but then someone left the carton open and put it back in a windy freezer.

Mitch had returned to see the lake. He had not seen her since he graduated from law school. For him, it had been a long time. For Lake Michigan, three years was far too short to measure. She had been there for ten thousand years or more, ever since the glaciers melted. As far as Lake Michigan was concerned — and she could probably speak for her four sisters, too — there was no need to take it personally.

Mitch was certainly not the first man to ignore her or try to exploit her patience. Many men had been trying to get in her pants for a long time. The heavy metals were a toxin in her, but besides cruising over her surface, man had yet to invade her inner space.

In law school in Chicago, he would watch her everyday. Looking down from nine stories above Lake Shore Drive in his heated dorm room, he would feel a chill as winter waves crashed wildly over the concrete dikes and leaped onto the pavement. From Superior Street to Oak Street Beach, driving could get hydrological. Some days, windshield wipers were needed as much for lake water as for rain from the heavens.

Mitch walked over frozen crunchy ground towards the shore. During the rock 'n' roll ice age, which Giovanni calculated had begun to recede sometime in the winter of 1967-68, the lake would freeze over for miles out from the land, even this far south. Up north, she would freeze over all the way to Wisconsin.

Today, there was ice and snow along the shore, but her water moved freely, if sluggishly, less than thirty feet away. With only a slight breeze, it was still colder than a witch's tit. However, it was a colder chill that penetrated his soul when he imagined her depths, where so many boats, large and small, rested in a lasting embrace. That chill came without reference to Fahrenheit or Celsius.

Mitch took out a small brown plastic bottle and squeezed the lotion into the palm of his hand. He rubbed it on his face. He assumed a wide stance, and dug in as well as he could with his old college construction work-boots. He spread his arms like the man on the cross. He was not totally crazy, only a little touched, so he did not unbutton his coat.

Like a mantra, he chanted to himself, "Summer. Hot sun. Summer hot sun." It seemed to work, if only a little. He kept it up, visualizing the sky, not the hazy kind, but deep blue. The beach was becoming crowded with people, with kids and blankets and competing radio stations. His friend Terry selects a prime viewing spot for them. As he slowly lowers himself onto the beach, warm grains of sand stick to the lotion on his skin, but he doesn't care. He loves the smell of Coppertone and all its connotations. As he settles into the beach, he gets the stubborn lumps of sand re-arranged under his towel so that his maleness can be comfortable should arousal occur.

And boy, does it. Young, hard female bodies are all around. Walking, running a few steps, laughing. Their swimsuits are fascinating, the way the material hugs and surrounds their smooth skin, so brown, so white in parts. Terry actually wants to get up and talk to some of them. The guy is totally amazing; he can actually think of things to talk about. Mitch stays on his towel and watches with admiration as his friend makes the moves. The girls on the beach are all within reach. This time Terry will get one for me.

Mitch opened one eye, slowly. It was working. Images of the foundering *Fitzgerald*, the *Bradley*, and a hundred other wrecks were gone. Along with one personal shipwreck memory, an unforgettable burnt-in image of himself, tossed into the water, thrashing in panic, trying to reach a capsized catamaran in East Traverse Bay, screaming for his life. Even that was fading.

Mitch knew that he was singing out loud, but he had to. It felt like Handel's "Hallelujah Chorus" as he launched into the Beach Boys' "I Get Around."

"You okay, mister?" A voice called.

Mitch's daydream was interrupted. He looked around. His arms were still hanging on the cross. It was one of the three boys, a sandy-haired kid. He looked Dutch, but he wasn't in church. He must be "Jack Dutch" — like "Jack Mormon," what the Mormons call their lost sheep. The other two kids stood back behind him.

"You on a bad trip, man?" the kid with sandy hair asked.

"No. Just thinking about summer," Mitch said as he lowered himself from the cross.

"What's that white stuff on your face?" Whether he knew it or not, the kid sounded like Bob Dylan when he pronounced face. "What's that on your face, you look out of place, in the human race ..."

"Suntan lotion," Mitch answered candidly, still tangled up in memories of blue.

"That's different." The kid looked up at the gray sky and

then imparted his own insight. "You can never be too careful."

"That's true."

For a few respectful seconds, Mitch and this kid from the next generation shared a view out onto the big lake.

"Winter's a major bummer," the kid offered. "Well, be cool, man." The kid turned and started walking back towards his buddies.

Nice kid. His language was so '60s. "Hey," Mitch yelled. "What do you think about people selling water from this lake and pumping it to Las Vegas?"

The kid turned back around. "Never been to Las Vegas. But my uncle goes there for conventions all the time. Says they got these big indoor amusement parks that are cool as shit," said the kid.

This wasn't exactly a Gallup poll, but to Mitch it wasn't a good sign. "I heard that too," Mitch said sadly. Mitch looked at the kid's Motorhead T-shirt. He decided not to query the kid about the coincidence of global warming and the decline of rock 'n' roll.

Mitch's disappointment seemed to register with the kid. He took a final drag on his cigarette. Then tossed it on the beach and walked back to his friends.

Steketee's was one of the last of those downtown department stores that still had some original wooden floors on the inside and some architecture on the outside. It was a mini-Marshall Fields without the Walnut Tea Room. Outside the heavy brass-plated doors, Mitch threw some change into the red Salvation Army bucket. The uniformed Christian soldier nodded a thank-you and kept on ringing.

After meeting the ever-elusive Maggie out east, who had so easily avoided his romantic intentions, he had bought a Christmas present for her every year since. Since it was a rather masochistic venture in the first place, he always went shopping on the day after Thanksgiving to buy it. Then, he would mail it to the address in Redondo Beach, and wait for her to call and thank him — hoping she would invite him down to East Lansing for a day when they both were home from their respective coasts to see their families for Christmas. Every year it had worked, because her mother liked him.

Last year he really outdid himself. He bought her this little pendant at Strawbridge's in Philly. The sales clerk said it was a semi-precious stone. It wasn't cheap and it didn't look cheap either.

"Do you think she'll like it?" Mitch questioned.

"I sure would, if you bought it for me," said the sales clerk, who was not on commission and spoke from the heart.

The clerk was right. Maggie invited him for a sleep-over

at her parent's house. Of course, he didn't get to sleep with her, because her parents and her two brothers were home. He got something almost as good — a midnight stroll through the red brick part of the Michigan State University campus.

A light snow had fallen. Hand-holding had escalated when Mitch laid on the ground and made a snow angel. Surprised by his spontaneity that night, Maggie had followed suit. After a few chilly seconds of jumping jacks on their backs, he had rolled over and kissed her right there on the banks of the Red Cedar.

Mitch thought of that midnight stroll as he presented his sales receipt for this year's gift to the Steketee's clerk.

"No, there's nothing wrong with the sweater. It's just that the person I bought it for won't be coming home for Christmas this year," Mitch told the clerk. Hopefully, the clerk would give him a cash return —after all, it was Christmas Eve — without making him read aloud the "Dear Mitch" letter which had accompanied the returned sweater. The letter was there in the pocket of his parka — the same parka which had been pressed against her parka on the MSU campus almost 365 days before.

Mitch was surprised at his own calmness when he said, "She won't be coming home for Christmas this year." No wallowing. There would be no blue Christmas for Mitch. Maggie's new west-coast boyfriend, whom for some perverse reason she had felt compelled to write Mitch about, wasn't even an ex-football player from UCLA. He had gone to some-place called Pepperdine; it sounded like a culinary institute, not a college. But the guy had been captain of the volleyball team there.

"Take this slip to the cashier on the second floor by the lingerie department. And Merry Christmas," said the clerk, who had enough presence of mind to realize this return was even less enjoyable for her customer than for her.

Receipt in hand, Mitch rode the escalator to the second floor. Out of the corner of his eye, he started looking for lingerie — in other words, women's intimate apparel. He held the yellow Steketee's receipt out in front of him like a blind man holding his cane, so his fellow shoppers would know that he was not really there to buy anything.

He spotted the "Cashier" sign on the wall above an archway, but first he had to negotiate a maze to get there. He was standing by a number of tall round racks, festooned with big, bulky bathrobes, which partially obscured an aisle. This route looked safe. He started down the aisle brushing past the canyon of bathrobes. Suddenly he found himself trapped, surrounded by bras and panties. He felt tense, claustrophobic. It wasn't that he couldn't enjoy these items, given the right woman, like that lacy black thing over there.

"Mitch!" the right woman yelled.

Jerry Lewis was funny, even the French appreciated him. Mitch, however, was never wild about physical humor, preferring more cerebral laughs. Nevertheless, at the sound of his name, a startled Mitch managed with just one jerky backhand to de-rack an entire shelf of panties on hangers and, falling, landed spread-eagle on the floor. There were panties everywhere. As he floundered trying to get up, it looked like he was trying to make snow angels in their multi-colored silkiness.

Laura was laughing so hard she could hardly manage to assist her beet-red neighbor, as they both knelt on the floor and tried to put the displays back together again.

"You look so ... you look so ..." Laura repeatedly tried to speak, but the only thing coming out were tears rolling down her cheeks. Mitch still had a pair of extra-large panties perched on his head.

❖ ❖ ❖

In the middle of America, there isn't any more fertile piece of urban real estate than Michigan Avenue around the Water Tower. On a good day, like one of those spring days when the radio towers on top of the Hancock Building could be seen sprouting to the clear blue sky, Mitch could fall in love, marry, and have children with as many as three female passers-by before he reached the gothic entrance to Ole Northwestern at 357 E. Chicago.

Later, at night in the library, when even Environmental Law polluted his desire to be a lawyer, Mitch would desperately try to recall the pretty face, nose, eyes, lips of any of the women he had truly loved in passing that day. If only they would let him take a Polaroid so he could preserve their image for the long hours of those library nights. He longed to be able to remember those few seconds of falling in love.

He felt that kind of longing now. Even though this memory was barely at arms-length.

Laura and Mitch sat at a little round table for two in front of a framed window. Each had a mug in hand, a cappuccino for Laura, hot chocolate with marshmallows for Mitch. Last-minute shoppers laden with sacks and bags hurried by on the sidewalk outside.

She sipped her steaming drink. For the first time in the last ten minutes, her face was not contorted by convulsive laughter. Mitch checked his memory of that face from their one-night stand a few weeks earlier. It seemed like years had passed. But for once, his memory had served him well. Her lips were definitely fuller than Maggie's. And those eyes, still blue, deep, and smiling.

That night they had shared, he had been summoned and examined. He had been all object; she had been all verb. His actions had been directed or encouraged by blue eyes and eyebrows. And by her hands, as when he first was granted permission to touch her nipples, a source of wonder since they had beckoned him from over Robbie Joe's textbook.

"How is your law practice?" Laura asked. Mitch had eyes, too, and Laura could also read. She wanted to change the unspoken subject.

"I'm quitting the firm." Mitch said, with such nonchalance that even he was surprised. Without losing a beat, he added, "I've thought about you everyday since that night."

In a way, both sentences were answers to her question about his law practice. Laura could sense this, and it made her anxious.

She didn't have to dig deep to know that Mitch had been very different from the other men she had seduced for sport. Perhaps because he was only a boy in a man's body. She recalled how, when he had reached the top of the loft that morning and seen her naked on the bed, he had stopped, like the Tin Man of Oz in need of oil. She had to lead him by hand to bed. He never would have made it by himself. Except for his spasmodic finish, which she thought for awhile would never cease, Mitch had waited for permission for everything. And yet once granted permission, the man-boy had touched and kissed with such sweet, slow tenderness that it had tingled and aroused far beyond her mechanical expectation.

"You're not really quitting your law firm? You just started."

Mitch could see that Laura was not going to talk about that night. More significantly, her eyes were not going to betray the tingling she had felt, not this day anyway. He saw no hope of ever being wanted by her. He added her to the women of Michigan Avenue and Maggie. All the more reason to have a job he could love. Thus, his response was mildly indignant.

"I'm tired of the hourly bullshit. That's all they talk about. How many hours did you bill this week or month or year? No one ever talks about the consequences of what we do. Whether things are right or wrong for the world. No one talks about helping people, unless it's doing a driving-while-intoxicated case for one of our alcoholic clients." Mitch was just getting warmed up. "I don't want to measure my life's work in hours. If I wanted to do hourly work, I could have gone on the assembly line at Fisher Body.

"If that's not bad enough, one of the partners trashed the medical records on one of my cases the first week I was there. And they're working to drain the Great Lakes. I should have quit before I started."

Mitch paused, as thoughts of all those lonely nights stuck in a library with Stu and his other law-school buddies blitzed through his brain. He leaned forward and looked straight into the blue eyes across the table. "If this is the best the law has to offer, I shouldn't have spent one single Saturday night in a law library. I should have been out searching for a girl like you. Before all the good ones got away."

Laura wanted to say, "You're a nice guy." But she knew where those guys finish. She believed that Mitch deserved better from some woman.

"I'm sure somewhere there's a good woman waiting for you," she said.

❖ ❖ ❖

In the low, knee-high basement window, only two feet above the sidewalk on South Division Street, were the orange and black bold letters which read "Native American Legal Services — The Ottawa Nation." Below that, just inches above the concrete, Mitch had spied the cardboard "Office for Rent" sign resting on the window sill.

The sign had caught his eye. It wasn't exactly what he had been looking for when he decided to go out on his own, but it was all he could afford. And he had instantly discovered some common ground with the red men of the Ottawa Nation, which he had never felt among the forked tongues at HD&H.

Mitch looked around his new surroundings, subterranean and windowless. It was amazing what it cost to furnish a new office, even one without thick carpeting and walnut wainscoting. Except for Robbie Joe's text and a few other books, he didn't own much. He had emptied his savings from his government job to purchase a new computer and printer, which were supposed to arrive that week. The metal desk, and the broken secretarial chair he was sitting in, belonged to the tribal legal-services office. The good Indians. Mitch's new pencils, which read Beaver Sands Gaming Casino, belonged to what the good Indians called the bad Indians. The intra-tribal relationships were complex. Mitch was only beginning to figure it out.

Mitch heard the bells jingle above the front door of the office. He was alone, covering the office phones, which had not rung once. All the staff had gone over to the Federal Court for a big pow-wow with Judge Double Chin, also known as Judge Alkema, who was appointed many, many moons ago by powerful Commander-in-Chief Watergate far away in Washington.

Mitch hurried down the hall to greet or thwart whoever had rung the bells. David Wasaquom was walking towards his office carrying a suitcase-sized briefcase.

Jim Thorpe, the great Indian athlete from Carlisle. That's who Mitch had instantly thought of the first time he met his new landlord. David Wasaquom's physical size lived up to his surname, which in the Ottawa language meant "Thunder and Lighting at the Same Time." It was a powerful name, greatly respected among the Ottawa. It did not sound like a name of someone you dared to cross, in the courtroom or any-where.

Wasaquom was tall, broad-shouldered. There was not a trace of age at his waistline. He wore a black flannel blazer and a bolla string-tie held together with a silver buffalo over his bright white shirt. Silver threads highlighted his long black pony tail. This day, his fifty-something face looked especially like Jim Thorpe's — the day the white man stripped him of his medals. He looked ready to live up to his name. Mitch was ready to duck for cover.

"Did you get the message that someone named Cheer Cheer called for you this morning?" asked Wasaquom, vis-ibly trying to control his temper.

"Yeah. Thanks. So, how did it go?" Mitch asked, already seeing the answer.

"Cheer Cheer. Doesn't sound like an Indian name," said

Wasaquom, ignoring Mitch's question. The word "Indian" did not sound at all pejorative coming from the lips of this noble savage, who often came into the office after his morning jog wearing one of two red sweatshirts —United States Marine Corps or University of Wisconsin.

"No. He's kind of a displaced Irishman," said Mitch, feeling a bit awkward, wondering if Wasaquom knew that Cheer Cheer was the nickname of the senior HD&H associate working on the Desert Development project.

David Wasaquom obviously knew Mitch had just resigned from HD&H. They had discussed at length whether there was any conflict of interest with Mitch renting an office from Native American Legal Services, which had just joined a coalition of environmental groups to bring a legal challenge against the gambling-water referendum. "Did you ever do any work on the MDDC project?" Wasaquom had asked. "No," Mitch had explained, but he had briefly represented Reverend VanderHook's son in an auto case that was quickly settled. "You mean the boy who jumped off the church steeple on Thanksgiving Day?" Wasaquom had asked. "The same one," Mitch had nodded sadly.

Wasaquom had concluded there was no conflict as far as he could see, but declined Mitch's offer to do any *pro bono* work, which might create the appearance of impropriety. "Besides, you're going to be fighting for your own survival, white man." Wasaquom had been confident that the referendum would quickly be struck from the August ballot because it was improperly drafted, just like Mitch had supposed.

If not, Wasaquom was sure the federal court would uphold an environmental impact challenge, finding that diversion of any Great Lakes water was environmentally unsound. He did recall that some years ago, an Illinois Governor, Jim

Thompson, had briefly explored a major sell-off of Michigan water. The plan eventually had been dropped due to lack of support from the other Great Lakes states.

Recently there had been other plans floated. One Canadian-based plan involved shipping Lake Superior water by oil tanker all the way to Asia.

And for years, the Cree Indians in Canada had been fighting a multi-staged plan by Hydro-Quebec to divert entire rivers that now fed into the James Bay and Hudson Bay region. After large tracts of native hunting lands were flooded, the plug had been pulled on later phases of that grandiose plan with the help of environmentalists on both sides of the border. Still, the blueprints waited in Hydro-Quebec's filing cabinets for the right time to move forward.

Regarding the pipeline scheme by the Malone Desert Development Corporation to supply a flow of Great Lakes' precious freshwater to Las Vegas, Wasaquom had believed in his heart that good Indians and good white men would eventually win at the ballot box. To ensure that, Wasaquom had been in federal court today, seeking to have his faction of the Ottawa Indians sanctioned by the court as the official representative of the Ottawa tribe in the pending legal suits.

This was a matter of money and power. Money, as the steady revenue generated from the quarter-slots alone at the tribe's small-time Beaver Sands Casino could still pay for a major TV campaign against the referendum. Power, as the Ottawa held key water-rights that could be invoked to stop a foolish project to drain a Great Lake.

David Wasaquom picked up a wicked-looking tomahawk that was prominently displayed on his laminated bookshelf along with volumes of Michigan Compiled Laws. Mitch watched Wasaquom weighing the heft of it. It looked more formidable than the rubber one Mitch had owned as a kid.

"How did we do?" Wasaquom asked rhetorically, finally coming around to Mitch's question. Hatchet raised in his hand, almost touching the low ceiling of the low-rent storefront office, Wasaquom looked directly at Mitch. Did he know that Mitch had not yet found a hair stylist he was totally satisfied with since leaving Philadelphia? Maybe it was an ugly experience as a Marine in a Vietnam jungle or a Saigon alley, like Giovanni used to relate, which Mitch now saw seething in Wasaquom's deep, dark eyes. Or maybe what Mitch saw was the genetic remnant of an ancestor about to filet a deer carcass or an encroaching French fur-trapper.

Whatever the cause of the fire he saw in those eyes, Mitch was relieved when the tomahawk split the plaque on the wall at the other end of the office and not his skull.

"It was a bloodless massacre. The only screaming was my young staff yelling at their brothers and sisters out in the hall afterwards. I sent them all home for the day." Wasaquom walked over and slumped in his chair.

"As soon as I walked in, I knew which way the wind was blowing. Judge Alkema's first question from the bench was, 'Mr. Wasaquom, just so I'm clear here. You represent the renegade tribe?' I knew there wasn't a chance of our group getting control of anything.

"So I reversed field and argued to enjoin all factions of our tribe from using gambling money in any way, pro or con, for the referendum. But Alkema countered, saying that was a state issue. He had no jurisdiction there — though he went on to gratuitously comment that state election-finance law does not bar such spending. The son of a bitch is right."

Mitch had walked over and picked up the wooden plaque. "For Outstanding Service to His People — The Ottawa Tribe."

It had been splintered in two by the weapon, which remained partly buried in a stud behind the paneling.

Mitch tried to console him. "There's still the environmental impact hearing. My former colleague ..." Mitch started to say Cheer Cheer, but he stopped. "My former colleague, O'Leary, says the EPA issues will be heard by Judge Winslet. The MDDC people are afraid of him. Winslet was a Carter appointment and is an ardent environmentalist. He won the Miles Lord Award — named after that federal judge from Minnesota who enjoined a mining company from dumping taconite tailings into Lake Superior. That gives us all a big leg up," Mitch said confidently, hoping to reassure Wasaquom that this was just the first round.

David Wasaquom smiled. But it was not a nice smile. "A big leg up — on a fire hydrant that's opened full bore."

"Excuse me?"

"Don't ask me how," Wasaquom paused, and his jaw tightened, not wanting his lips to actually speak the news. "I don't know how it happened, but somehow the EPA suit was reassigned to Alkema. He's going to hear all federal environmental water-quality control challenges. Before our hearing today, all the parties were in there. The courtroom was packed. Your old boss Ken Calley spoke for the other side. Alkema set briefing schedules, a date for hearing and oral argument."

Like people do when a family heirloom or even their favorite coffee mug gets cracked, Mitch was holding David Wasaquom's plaque in his hands, trying to find the original angle or position that would make it whole again. Such things are never the same.

❖ ❖ ❖

Other than losing a steady paycheck and a sturdy three-hole punch, leaving Cheer Cheer was the only regret Mitch had about resigning from Holland, Dawson & Hager. Mitch, who found lots of free time at his new office to stare at a blank calendar, had called Cheer Cheer several times for lunch. But Molly, the secretary they used to share, would say, "He's gone with Mr. Calley to St. Paul" — or to Madison, or Springfield, or Columbus, or Albany. Mitch got the picture, having memorized his state capitols at an early age.

But Cheer Cheer did accept Mitch's invitation to the festive lunch at the Miller family residence on December 25th. Cheer Cheer showed up proudly wearing all his new Christmas presents. He must have received everything on his Santa wish list, because he looked like a mannequin from the Notre Dame college bookstore.

Since his Purdue Golden Girl had broken things off with him, Cheer Cheer had regressed. Mitch had seen him in a Notre Dame sweatshirt a few times before. He always wore one on Saturdays at the firm, when there was no dress code. But never to this extreme. In addition to the official jersey and sweatpants, Cheer Cheer wore Notre Dame socks, wrist sweatbands, a green-and-gold wool beanie, and his usual ND watch. After a couple of cups of eggnog and a good portion of a holiday six-pack, a tipsy Cheer Cheer also admitted to Mitch and Mitch's dad that he was adorned with ND underwear.

However, the crowning touch was actually on his feet: white and green sneakers with that outrageous, red-faced leprechaun on each toe. "Mitch said to be very casual," Cheer Cheer had apologized, when Mrs. Miller answered the door. She had momentarily wondered whether to let him in dressed like that, but she knew the poor guy had nowhere else to go.

Mitch sympathized. The recent break-up with Stacey had left Cheer Cheer high and dry for Christmas. In any other year that would have meant a trip home to Buffalo, but his parents had long-standing plans to take his two younger sisters to County Something in Ireland in search of the ancestral yule log.

Logic, custom, and Cheer Cheer's outlandish attire dictated that good American boys would toss a football — after a slice of pumpkin pie and a token offering to do the dishes. On the playground adjacent to Mitch's old elementary school, Cheer Cheer exhibited surprising aggression for such a well-fed primate.

"You be Purdue," Cheer Cheer shouted as he drilled a twenty-yard spiral. The pigskin bounced off of Mitch's chest before his cold hands had a chance to react.

"I don't want to be Purdue against you. I'll be Kent State." That was a poor choice. "No, make that the purple haze. I'll be Northwestern," Mitch said quickly, recovering. He had not wanted to appear threatening. He did not want to incite this borderline leprechaun. The temporary stinging in his sternum from the hard-pointed bullet was another reminder to Mitch that he should have tried to be a better friend, when Cheer Cheer really needed him.

Eventually Cheer Cheer had settled down, and Mitch had gotten his fingers moving. Between them they completed sixty-nine passes, a new record for a Notre Dame-Northwestern game. But on the walk back from the playground, they had both reverted to adults and worse — to lawyers. Cheer Cheer had gone on and on about how the MDDC deal guaranteed him a partnership in two years. And how it was a real win-win situation for the firm, for the Midwest, for the West, for America.

"I see it as a pipeline to the 21st century. Mitch, I'm sorry to say this, buddy, but you should have stayed. In fact, you know I'm pretty tight with Calley. Just say the word. I'll give it the old college try to get you back on the team."

Mitch was tempted by Cheer Cheer's magnanimous offer. At the end of that wondrous day of hope, joy and, anticipation, as blood sugars spiked and dipped, a deep melancholy crept up on Mitch. The two friends, intermittent boys and lawyers, had turned the corner towards Mitch's parent's house for their last slice of pie for the day. Mitch had temporarily struggled with a brief urge to assent, but did not waver.

"No thanks. I'm happy with my decision to leave," Mitch said firmly. Determined to anticipate Christmas future, he had resolved to make a new list for next year which had nothing to do with HD&H or any part of Christmas past. "Dear Santa, I only want this one special blue-eyed doll. Not the inflatable kind, the real thing. If you give me a chance, I promise to love and cherish her till death due us part. Earnestly, Mitchell Miller."

God's mail often gets addressed to Santa, thought Mitch, as Cheer Cheer waved him to run deep, past the house next door where Billy Koistra used to live. The ball had sailed into Mitch's outstretched hands as he ran on the dry pavement in the middle of the street. He had bobbled it for an instant and then tucked it in, running up the walk past the tall white-lighted spruce, which had been so tiny when Mitch was a little boy that his dad could completely decorate it with a single string of lights.

❖ ❖ ❖

Cheer Cheer was all adult and all business when Mitch returned his pre-holiday call. "Right, I almost forgot about that. I wanted to know if you would be interested. We have this death case," Cheer Cheer started.

Mitch's spirits instantly soared high like an eagle. In the law, death was always better than divorce — though never as good as lingering life with catastrophic injuries. "A wrongful death case." Mitch blurted excitedly. The careers of many starving young lawyers had been saved at the last second by such a case.

"No. Not that good. It's not exactly a death case. Just these senior citizens who died up in Manistee. Before they died, they made a claim on their homeowner's policy for damage to some kind of sea-wall, which has some holes in it. We represent the insurance carrier, Great Lakes Fire and Marine."

"Let me guess. Lattisaw?" Mitch interrupted.

"Yeah. Lattisaw denied the claim, which he should have, because the wall is neither a covered dwelling nor an appurtenance. Unfortunately he sent the wrong form letter to deny coverage. Before they died, the insureds wrote an angry letter saying that their daughter would have her revenge. It was weird, because the lawyer for the estate says they have no heirs. Left all their money to one of your favorite tree-hugging organizations. Anyway, I guess Lattisaw is a little spooked by what happened to VanderHook's kid. So he turned it over to us. Lattisaw will do whatever we say and pay anything you recommend as long as it doesn't cost too much."

"How come you don't handle it?" Mitch asked.

"Mitch, I'm phasing out of these low-profile matters," Cheer Cheer said with a cockiness that Mitch had never noticed before. His friend was exuberant and competitive, yes, but not what Mitch would call arrogant. Mitch wrote it off to any lingering insecurity Cheer Cheer felt over losing Stacey to the Chicago bean broker.

Cheer Cheer added, "We do have a small potential conflict, anyhow, because our firm represents the new owner who bought the old people's place. It's not a big case, but you can bill a few hours driving up there."

"I thought conflicts got spun off to Spector & Singleton? Does Calley know you're referring me a case?"

"Listen, I know you're on this power-to-the-people trip. Look at it this way, you'll be helping some crazy old dead people." Cheer Cheer paused, "It's up to you. If you don't want it, I'll refer it to someone else."

"No, I want it. I could use some business," Mitch said. Small as it is, he thought to himself.

There are lots of bands who sign with a label only to dry up and die like tumblin' tumbleweed. The key is getting real backing from the label. That includes money for a well-promoted tour, money to promote radio airplay, money for a video. In rock's early days, the means to that end was called "payola." But that word had long since fallen into disfavor.

Rick had flown back to L.A. to complain to Geltman about the lack of payola or whatever they called it these days. White Lies was only getting spotty regional airplay in Wisconsin and Michigan at a couple of independent stations, where Rick and his friend Austin knew the program directors. The band's video aired once on a local cable channel in Milwaukee.

"You said we would have a 'Hot-Shot Debut.' We haven't hit Billboard's basement yet," said Rick, pacing in Geltman's Sunset Boulevard office earlier that afternoon.

"This is my fault? Rick, you know this business is hurting right now. People upstairs in the boardroom are real nervous. Things are tight. Some heads may be rolling. It's all touchy right now. I'm doing what I can for you," said Geltman.

"I had to make the video with half the budget. And where is the tour deal? You said we'd open for a major act. You're in breach of your contract," said Rick. Rick was trying not to let Geltman see him sweat.

"Come on, Rick, we're trying to grow this thing together. You forget I'm out on the same limb you are," said Geltman. "The label is behind this project one hundred percent, and so am I. It's just going to take some time," Geltman assured Rick as they shook hands.

Rick closed his eyes. He lay back on the clean white starched pillow of the Le Parc Hotel bed and tried to count platinum records jumping over fences. Maybe he would buy a sheep ranch in New Zealand. The New Zealanders he met up on the roof on his last trip had described the most idyllic country. Still counting, he dozed off.

Dream, dream, dream. The phone on his bedside table rang.

"I got champagne, cocaine, and everything else you need. Can I come up?" the caller asked.

Rick mumbled, "Yea, or sure," or something, in a sleep-drenched voice.

The next thing he knew, she was at the door of that West Hollywood hotel with all the goodies she had promised. What a crazy night it was — not long after Rick had given Laura a three-carat zirconium on Christmas Eve.

❖ ❖ ❖

All Mitch had to do was drive up to Manistee to the Hanker property, look at the sea-wall, drive back, and write a "C.Y.A." opinion letter for Lattisaw's file that the wall was covered under the old folks' policy. And get an estimate about how much it would cost to repair the holes.

It started out easy enough. He crossed the Grand River on the Gerald R. Ford Freeway, turned north on 131, and was in Manistee in well under three hours. The route took him past fruit farms on gentle rolling hills. The roads were dry. For awhile the winter sun threatened to make a nice day of it.

Mitch had waited for Cheer Cheer to show up that night and finally left. One of Wasaquom's people must have let Cheer Cheer in the storefront office, because the Hanker file had been there on Mitch's desk the next morning. Mitch had quickly read the file before jumping into his Honda.

Mitch turned down the narrow county road and began looking for the mailbox on the right. It was early in the day for a deer crossing, but this was a densely wooded, sparsely populated stretch of road, with patches of ice remaining in the shelter of the trees. When the deer jumped out, Mitch nearly stood up on his brakes.

The deer was gone, its flashing white tail already a memory. But the car spun on the stretch of ice like a compass in a minefield. It then slammed into a bystanding tree, totalling both tree and car.

As Mitch got out on the passenger side, he could see the Hanker mailbox less than a hundred yards up the road. He looked at his small crushed Honda. The fees generated by this case would just about cover his deductible — instead of next month's office rent.

Mitch pulled up the collar on his jacket. Lake Michigan had to be close. He could feel her chilling dampness. He began walking towards the mailbox, somewhat dazed from the impact. Increasingly, he sensed his own isolation as he tried to steady his gait on the frosted gravel road. He vowed next time to buy American. He owed it to his state, if not his country. But he was resolved to complete his mission. As he marched down the road towards the Hankers' mailbox, he began whistling a tune that sounded a lot like the theme from *The Bridge on the River Kwai.*

He only whistled a couple rounds, when someone began firing. The Hanker mailbox exploded before his eyes. Mitch dove to the frozen ground, just like Giovanni had done one Saturday night on their way to the library when a car had backfired at the corner of State and University, and Giovanni had abruptly yanked him down to the ground, yelling "in-coming!"

On the other side of the road, a figure wearing camouflage fatigues emerged from the woods. A clean-cut, well-physiqued human specimen walked towards Mitch, a 30.06 rifle with scope gripped firmly with two hands. Mitch stood up. He wondered if he was expected to raise his hands. But what if his long fingers outstretched above his head were mistaken for antlers? Across Michigan, any number of people had been shot by hunters whose defense was that they thought they saw a ten-pointer. That was enough to convince a jury of a hunter's peers that excitement about a big trophy rack over-rode a reasonable expectation to look first and shoot second. Acquittal of reckless homicide was almost assured.

In the Upper Peninsula, Mitch wasn't sure they even bothered to prosecute a hunter in such cases, in season or out. The victim was likely just to end up on a wall in a crowded, smoky bar, stuffed next to Bambi's mother.

"This is private property," the hunter said.

❖ ❖ ❖

All her bags were packed and she was ready to go, when she first heard the song on the radio. Laura nearly drowned in the irony. "White lies telling me what you want to hear."

Laura had called Le Parc. A woman had answered. It wasn't the first time she had called a hotel room Rick was staying in and gotten a woman's voice. However, in the past Rick had always retrieved the phone and given her an explanation. It was never a very good explanation, but it was an attempt. "She's giving me a manicure." Or, "She's the seamstress for the band."

"White lies, it's your disguise," continued on the radio. This time he never came to the phone. "He's busy," the voice panted, suspiciously short of breath.

The next day Rick did call. Laura stood there next to the phone and let it ring, then picked it up and slammed it down, seven times, after Rick pleaded "Laura, Honey."

Her final housekeeping chore before she vacated their apartment was no doubt inspired by those seven curt "Honey, please ..." conversations. She got honey, a jar full. She laid a heavy bead of it along the eighty-eight keys of Rick's piano. She packed up her electric Yamaha in its long, black case, and she walked out the door.

She paused for a moment on the landing by Mitch's door. She was looking at his door, but it was not clear what she was thinking, other than that she was mad at men in general and furious at Rick in particular. She had given up her career for this?

Lake Michigan got annoyed that day, too, and so did her sisters. At first it looked like just a minor winter squall blowing in off the lake, the kind that your local television weatherman on the Noon News reports light-heartedly, "Well, we have a little flurry activity out there this morning, but it should clear up by evening. You might have to slow up a tiny bit on your way home from work."

How about: "You ain't gettin' home from work, unless you make a run for it now. I hope your old lady's stored up the beans, blankets, and candles."

The first flake touched down on the windshield of the concrete truck, just as Mitch hitched a ride. He had not had any luck trying to persuade the fatigue-clad security guard to let him inspect the Hankers' sea-wall. Mitch did try to explain that he didn't need to go inside the house. He only needed to take a look at the wall. But the guard was not persuaded.

"The Ottawas own this property now. No one is allowed on it without their permission."

About the third time that pre-recorded message was heard, a concrete truck rolled out of the woods in low gear like one of Patton's tanks, and drove up to the two of them. The driver stopped at what was left of the mailbox.

"You headed back into town?" Mitch yelled up.

"Hop in," the driver replied from his cab.

Real meteorologists, not the guy on the Noon News, would later explain how the five sisters had caucused and conspired to send humans running for cover. Miss Superior, the self-designated intellectual, communicated in a frigid torrent of wind something about hanging together or all hanging separately. Ontario, so distant and Eastern, howled to the heavens that this continent no longer brought forth honest lawyers. Sister Erie, a bit shallow and constantly afraid of what Cleveland might do to her, whined and splashed but contributed more than her share of moisture to the growing storm.

Sister Huron, not wanting to be outdone, and just as blessed by nature as the others, matched Erie flake for flake. And as usual, Michigan went far beyond the call of duty — pouring an endless deluge of heavy snow onto her designated target areas. For openers, Miss Michigan blew a man named Bert Parks off the pier at Muskegon.

What a show of nature it was! What pageantry!

The town of Manistee was less than ten miles from the old Hanker place. Mitch figured he would get a ride there and either find a tow truck or take a Greyhound back to Grand Rapids. It was good that the driver had grown up in these parts and had driven this route twice a day for five weeks, running concrete to the job site, because it was a white-out. A driving shower of white had already blanketed everything just a few miles inland. "Never seen snow fall this fast," said the driver as he turned onto the state highway, headed into town.

The driver told Mitch what little he knew about the job he was hauling for and about the security guard, whose name was Barstow. There wasn't much to tell. "He's not really the project manager, but them Indians treat him like he's in charge. Hey, all I do is dump and run. I don't ask questions. The pay is damn good for this county. We ain't no Charlevoix or Harbor Springs here. This has been good business. It's going to be the biggest casino in the U.S. of A. Bigger than anything in

Las Vegas. They're kicking butt to get it done by next summer. Fine with me. I can use the overtime."

Mitch's eyes were open wide as he stared into the mesmerizing, whirling snowstorm. They were not going to measure this storm just in inches.

"I wouldn't bet on your headin' back downstate today," said the driver, tightening his grip on the big black circle in his hands. The concrete truck would be the last vehicle to slide off the road, but he still had to concentrate to find the road. Starting to get a little nervous, the driver added, "I got to get this rig back to my yard on the other side of town. You might want to get out here at Koski's Diner."

Koski's Diner was just east of one of the drawbridges over the channel leading in from the big lake to Manistee Lake. The diner was one of those places that survive and sometimes flourish in small towns in spite of the fast-food joints down the street — because some people still liked to break bread together and eat off real plates. Normally it was packed this time of day, but the lunch crowd was thinned because of the weather.

Mitch took a seat at the counter. The waitress questioned him about coffee and spoke kindly about navy bean soup. Mitch ordered the soup and got a recommendation for a tow truck. He walked to the pay phone. The phone was in one of those add-on foyers tacked onto the entrance to the roadside restaurant. It was drafty and the windows were steamed up from the cold outside.

When he got back from making his call, Mitch reported to the waitress that all the tow trucks around had been called to a nasty pile-up on Highway M-22. "Call back in an hour" was what the dispatcher at the Marathon station had curtly relayed.

"Where 'bouts on 22?" asked a young man about Mitch's age, just finishing his coffee a few seats over at the counter.

"I don't know. She didn't say," Mitch replied, glancing over at the fellow. Not wanting the conversation to end quite yet, Mitch added, "I already had my accident today. Almost hit a deer. Instead I hit a tree."

"There's a lot of deer around here," said the man. He put a couple of quarters down for the waitress and got up off the stool. "Where 'bouts was this?" he asked, as he zipped up his coat and generally prepared himself for the elements.

"Over by some folks who just passed away. Did you know the Hankers?" Mitch asked.

The man paused. In a glance, he looked Mitch up and down. "You wouldn't be a lawyer by any chance would you?"

"I am." Mitch said without fear. He looked at the fellow quizzically. The man had what Mitch's mother would call "kind eyes," but they were keen too; Mitch didn't even have a tie on. "How did you know I was lawyer?"

"Mostly a hunch. Deer hunting season is over. Not that anyone would take you for a deer hunter," said the man. And then he added, "I also know there's still an unsettled legal matter over there." The man extended his hand. "I'm Ted Moore. I was the one who found Mr. and Mrs. Hanker," he said solemnly.

"Mitch Miller." Mitch gave him a firm grip back.

"I've been needing to talk to someone like you for a long time."

❖ ❖ ❖

"Wouldn't find any vacancies in this town even if there wasn't a blizzard. Town's all booked up with construction crews from as far away as Detroit. I've got a couple driveways to plow, but if you don't mind tagging along you can bunk with us tonight. Unless you want to sleep at the Greyhound depot 'cross the street." Ted Moore pointed to an old converted garage.

It was almost dark when Mitch saw the outline of Moore's dilapidated Victorian farmhouse. Ted and his wife were buying it on a land contract and slowly renovating the place. Moore had to plow their way up the drive.

Mitch had no complaints about the over-cooked vegetables that Ted Moore's wife served with her venison pot-roast, just minutes after they had stomped their feet at her kitchen door and Ted had kissed his baby boy hello. Ted Jr. sat in his high chair, all courses of his Gerber dinner still evident on various parts of his body and tray.

"Would you like some more venison, Mr. Miller?" asked Moore. "Sorry — Mitch."

Mitch had worked to break his host of the "Mr." habit on the long ride around town. Ted was actually a few years younger than Mitch, but Ted's wife said her husband had aged twenty years since the Hankers' deaths. "No, thank you. It's excellent," said Mitch, having just tasted his first venison.

Barbara Moore nodded with appreciation. She remained

silent. She was not dumb; she was intuitive. She knew her husband was getting ready to make his case. She had been listening to the man driving himself crazy, arguing for an explanation other than his own negligence as a cause of the deaths of Albert and Hazel Hanker.

Cautiously at first, and then with reckless disregard for what had to be the truth, Ted Moore had already outlined his Mafia-murder theory to Mitch as they plowed and drove their way through the snowstorm.

"I went to the Hanker lawyer and the Medical Examiner, and told them it was murder," Moore said.

Mitch listened patiently as he would in court to a deposition being read into the record. Politeness was in order. It was a small price to pay for genuine hospitality, whatever this desperate man's motivation. "What did the Medical Examiner say?"

"It was carbon monoxide, leaking from a cracked heat-exchanger. Case closed."

"And the lawyer?" Mitch tried to generate some enthusiasm.

"He says I'm lucky the County Prosecutor didn't bring charges against me for not properly servicing the furnace. He might as well have locked me up. No one will hire me for any new jobs, except snow-plowing. I wouldn't have done anything to hurt those people. I was good friends with Albert and Hazel. I was about the only person they would let hunt on that property. That venison you just ate was shot out there. And Hazel — she was Mrs. Hanker to us then — taught my sister and me in grade-school." Moore looked apologetically first at his wife and then at his son.

Mitch looked at his plate.

Ted pressed on. "We need a guy like you. A real big-city

lawyer. You say you're a federal prosecutor."

"Former," Mitch quickly qualified.

"It doesn't matter. Probably went after the Mafia, too. Didn't you?"

"Yeah. Well, I had one case. Once. Against this guy who might have had some loose affiliation with some Mafia-type people in Camden, New Jersey." Mitch bragged with much more modesty than he ever had exhibited during all his futile attempts to pick up girls at the singles bars in Philadelphia.

"What do you think, Mr. Miller?" Barbara Moore cut her husband off.

"I ..." Mitch didn't want to disappoint the man. "If this was Moscow and not Manistee, we might have Mafia to worry about."

"How do you explain that a project of this size is ready to break ground within a few weeks after the Indians buy the land? Damn Indians making all that gambling money and I'm close to losing this house if I can't make the payments. You can bet I'm not voting for that ballot thing in August. And I'll tell you something — if that thing doesn't pass they might just lose their ass on this deal. They paid almost four million dollars for the Hanker property. That's a hell of a lot of money for these parts. For white folks anyway." Moore was one angry white male.

"Just calm yourself," Barbara insisted to her husband. "You're scaring Teddy." She plucked the baby out of his high chair and handed him to her husband as she began clearing the dishes.

"It's no secret that the tribes are planning major casino expansions. I guess the Ottawa are just hoping to be first. If this thing goes through — but it won't win. It doesn't have a chance," said Mitch.

Ted walked to the cupboard and pulled out a bottle of Old Crow, while holding Teddy in the other arm. But his wife gave him a look that stopped him in his tracks, and he set the bottle back on the shelf.

"Well, if that's the way you want to be, then I say we go back there tonight! When I have my lawyer with me," said Ted Moore.

"In this weather?" Mitch asked.

"He means on his snowmobile," Barbara Moore explained for Mitch.

Other than the blizzard of '78 and snow angels with Maggie, Mitch had not accumulated many memorable snow stories. But Giovanni had been full of them. Making igloos. The ice pond his father used to make for him and his sister to skate on in their back yard. Giovanni loved to kick back, torque up Cream's "White Room" on his Sansui receiver, take a hit on a joint, and reminisce about winter in Michigan before Milli Vanilli. "Snowdrifts so high, so firm and high, that I could walk right over my old pa's fence. That's freedom, Mitch. That's as good as it gets. In March, our south-facing eaves would grow icicles thicker and longer than M-16s. Kill you just as quick, too, if one of 'em ever broke off and landed on your skull."

It had been Giovanni who first showed Mitch how to make a snow angel. "Chicks dig it," Giovanni had promised.

Mitch had been a receptive audience for all of Giovanni's winter wonderland stories. And Giovanni would have loved this snowmobile ride. Mitch hoped he was watching from heaven.

The snowflakes nipped Mitch's face about the same time

he spotted them in the single, careening headlight of the machine. The snowmobile intermittently paused, beating its way through unconsolidated drifts of snow like an over-worked hand-mixer stalling in a fresh bowl of sugar, flour, and eggs. Mostly it roared swiftly through the darkness.

Stuffed in a snowsuit, boots, and gloves like an Apollo astronaut, Mitch tightly hugged Ted Moore — and the shotgun on Ted's back. All Mitch could think about were those TV re-runs of Sergeant Preston of the Yukon, headed out to rescue whom? Or what?

And from whom?

❖ ❖ ❖

As soon as Moore spotted the maimed mailbox in his headlight, he killed the whining engine. There was a quick sputter
and then no more vibration. The two men remained motionless, straddling the snow ship. Both men looked and listened.
Moore was checking for enemies, Mitch was just waiting for
the ringing in his ears to fade.

The surroundings looked quite peaceful. The woods had
an innocent look, like the woods of a child's storybook or the
rhyme of a poet laureate. Gradually, as his hearing returned,
Mitch heard the sound. Something faint, fainter, all around
him ... it was the sound of snow falling. He knew, deep in his
soul, that this sound could be heard even if nobody was around
to listen, probably much better.

Ted handed Mitch a pair of improbably large, roughly
oblong contraptions: a set of snowshoes. Together they stepped
carefully, lifting their feet high and forward through the trees.
Mitch tripped and plunged face-first in the snow only once,
with the first step. Then he got the hang of it.

Storm clouds hid the moon. The sky offered only enough
light to tell up from down. It was very dark in the thickest
section of trees. Moore led the way with a squat heavy-duty
flashlight. Among other gear, Moore had outfitted Mitch with
a long-stemmed black flashlight, which looked like a night-
stick. No doubt their lights could be seen by anyone around,
as they bobbed through the woods. Moore was counting on

dumb luck and the cover of snow and darkness.

The wooded land rose and fell a couple times before they arrived at a flat open area that was half marsh and half pond in the summer. What would have been impassable terrain without freezing temperatures was now relatively easy going for the feet, if not the face. They had left the protection of the trees, where snow was falling mostly down. Now, horizontal gusts of snow once again tried to unmask their well-covered faces.

They mushed a hundred yards, when Ted Moore's flashlight caught the tip of it. They stopped. It was a concrete encasement at the other end of the white plain. An imposing gray bunker rose into a straight line, blocking their way. Ted was slowly massaging the edifice with his beam, back and forth. His light froze on a huge steel cylinder. Mitch squinted to see what Moore had uncovered. Visibility was poor. The scene was something out of *The Guns of Navarone*. He shivered as another gust obscured the concrete embankment.

Like the brave American rangers who scaled the heights of Pointe Du Hoc on the Normandy shore, Ted Moore with his newfound lawyer fearlessly closed the open ground between them and the bunker. They met no resistance before reaching the fortress, where once again there was respite. The high cinderblock wall stunted the prevailing westerly wind and the snow it was carrying.

They moved under the silent cannon. Both Ted and then Mitch stopped in turn to look up and survey it with their own light. Each discerned that this cylinder was nothing more than hollow pipe, albeit of enormous diameter. They followed the wall to its end and turned the corner.

On the new wall, an open doorway had been framed in the cinderblock. Its plastic cover had already been sliced open, to allow somebody entry. Into the building they shuffled, the first few strides on snow which had drifted through the plastic.

"What is this?" Mitch asked, trying to uncover as much as he could of the cavernous interior with the small strokes of his flashlight.

Moore stood in silence for a few minutes, painting with a broader brush, trying to make the big picture come into focus.

"I think it's a pumping station of some kind. See that big bolted space-saucer kind of thing over there. That's the main well-head."

Mitch and Ted's beams met at the well-head.

"What are they pumping?"

"Either water or oil. Got to be water," Moore answered. "That's a huge pipe. They could pull a lot of water with that."

"I thought you said this was going to be a casino?" Mitch questioned in a hushed tone. As he said that, the architectural rendition of VanderHook's Water Cathedral came to him.

"Aren't you glad you came?" Moore whispered back.

Mitch could see Moore's shadowed face as his flashlight caught the wall. Moore was getting excited. After being mocked in Manistee for months, he finally hoped tonight to be vindicated.

"The Hanker house is just over that hill. Is the big-city lawyer still with me on this?"

"Let's go," said Mitch. With a wry smile, he wondered if any of this would qualify as billable hours from Great Lakes Fire & Marine. He didn't care; this was more like the law practice he always wanted to have.

132

❖ ❖ ❖

Calley was also stranded by the blizzard that was blasting the Upper Midwest, closing the airports. That was not a problem for him, since he was stuck in Las Vegas. He knew his way around the town. Of course, it was not the same Vegas he knew back when he and Malone first bumped into each other at a craps table twenty years before. Back then, the things they fancied were everywhere and in your face. Nowadays you had to know who to call. Nowadays it was New York Stock Exchange certified legitimate business.

In fact, Las Vegas was fun for the whole family. Bring your son or daughter. Show them the treasures which bloomed in the neon desert. From the old days, only the cheap food remained. There would always be cheap food as long as all the Freds and Ethels from Kankakee never thought about how much their $2.99 breakfasts were actually costing them.

For authentic American entertainment, Vegas out-performed nearby Hollywood for real-life black comedy. No one ever yelled "cut" in Vegas. It just kept going and going, and growing and growing, twenty-four hours a day. Just as long as the water never ran out.

Calley looked across the crowded craps table at the cute redhead. Vegas sure had changed for the young folks. Her call service had their own website. It was a perfect match. This was Cheer Cheer's second trip to Vegas and his second "date" with the girl.

The girl gave Cheer Cheer a sweet and pouty look when he crapped out. "Oh, too bad, Cheer Cheer," she squeamed. "Let's play the don't-pass line on the next roll," she encouraged him as he took a sip from her strawberry-flavored straw.

"On red," the dealer said to a man leaning over the table next to Calley.

Calley slid five blue chips on red. He was feeling lucky. He never would have known that Cheer Cheer bet on football games, if the young lawyer hadn't confided in him at the firm's golf outing that "his habit" was why his engagement to his Purdue girlfriend was on the rocks. Otherwise Calley might have decided to groom Mitch Miller for the sensitive federal assignments coming up. But this was much better.

Everything was proceeding ahead of schedule. He knew better than anyone that the re-assignment of Alkema as the federal judge to handle the multi-district litigation sealed the fate of any environmental challenge to the pipeline. On the political front, Reverend VanderHook was going to deliver a substantial percentage of Michigan's powerful religious right. And in the Motor City and elsewhere around the Midwest, the "jobs versus environment" tune always played so sweetly.

He had it all scheduled to the last detail. By April 1, the Malone Desert Development Corporation would hold its first public press conference in Grand Rapids regarding the campaign for the referendum. In the meantime, the construction in Manistee was proceeding around the clock. Calley knew exactly what would happen and when. That was the way he liked it.

Initially, Calley had cautioned Malone that he had serious reservations as to whether all the governors from the Great Lakes states could be lined up to approve the pipeline. The gambling part was easy. With Congress bent on delegating more responsibilities and less money to the states, governors and state legislators were getting hooked on gambling revenues being pumped into local economies.

Every once in a while, a politician would stand up and wring his liberal hands about all those poor people out there who were becoming addicted to gambling. But they all knew quite well that they were the ones who were hooked. It was either that or raise people's taxes.

But when it came to the water-rights issues, Calley was pleasantly surprised with the lack of priority that the Great Lakes governors gave to the matter. This was in sharp contrast to water-poor governors of the Western states, who instinctively kept a jealous eye on every drop that their sovereign territories might drink, wash, flush, sprinkle, or otherwise use to make something in their state wet, clean, or green. The Great Lakes governors seemed to think their water came from faucets — either Standard or, especially in Wisconsin, Kohler.

One governor, new to his office, didn't even know that his state bordered on a Great Lake, until his crackerjack chief of staff showed him on a map. It was a great moment, to see the governor try to pull a fast "I knew that." But he kept sneaking a peek back at the map in disbelief.

One Great Lakes governor, in particular, was actually knowledgeable about water issues. At infrequent meetings of the Great Lakes Governors' Conference, he repeatedly had tried to discuss potential threats of extra-regional water diversions. He was always greeted with stifled yawns.

That governor was a tough nut to crack. Calley tried to point out that the MDDC pipeline was no different than drilling for oil or natural gas and piping it across the country. But the astute Governor replied, "Humans can waste oil and still survive. Not water." Finally, left with no choice, Calley made a dramatic appeal to the governor's green instincts. Given the governor's flagging popularity at home, it was really quite easy, once the size of the "campaign contribution" was established.

Calley sighed with satisfaction. His methods were so easy and free of chance. So unlike gambling.

After a half-dozen more rolls of the dice, Calley sidled up to Cheer Cheer and the redhead, "Don't forget you have a meeting tomorrow," he said to his associate. He discreetly squeezed a thousand-dollar chip into the hand of Cheer Cheer's website date and walked off to enjoy himself in the old part of Las Vegas.

❖ ❖ ❖

What an exciting law practice Mitch had developed in just one day! After exploring the pumping station built just inland from the shoreline bluffs, Mitch and Ted now moved on towards the big lake. Mitch recalled how he and little Billy Koistra used to stalk imaginary bad guys in Mitch's backyard.

Both Ted and Mitch used their flashlights sparingly, mostly to illuminate the ground immediately in front of their bulky snowshoes. Mitch was starting to wonder just how, this long after the Hankers' deaths, Ted thought that an illegal midnight search would turn up incriminating evidence. What would they find to disprove "accidental death by carbon monoxide poisoning," as the autopsy report had indicated?

Mitch knew about carbon monoxide, the old Detroit perfume. His first case for HD&H had been defending a doctor in a malpractice case. The doctor, who was more concerned about his golf handicap than his practice, had treated a family who had presented themselves in the doctor's office one morning with vague complaints of nausea and headaches. The doctor diagnosed the flu and told them all to take some aspirin and go home to bed. All of them did, except the teenage daughter who dragged herself to school because it was the last day of varsity soccer tryouts. The poor child was crushed when she didn't make the cut, but she came home that night to greater tragedy.

Mitch got the doctor dismissed before trial on summary judgment, because the girl's inexperienced attorney could not find any physician to testify that the family doctor should have diagnosed the symptoms of carbon monoxide poisoning, although this same doctor had two other failure-to-diagnose cases pending against him. Mitch felt sorry for the girl. It was just an accident. Just like the Hankers.

As soon as they climbed the hill past the pumping station, they could hear her roaring like Waimea Bay. Her surf was up. Moore directed his tiny searchlight down the bluff. A hundred feet below, waves crashed over the concrete barrier on the shore. Indeed, the sea-wall was in need of repair, overrun with white-foamed waves. Mitch tried to count how many holes it would take to fill in Albert's wall. But then he realized that the waves that lashed the wall were frozen, like so many tongues on a frigid flag-pole. A shroud of silver was covering Albert's wall.

Mitch could heard the crashing of real waves father out on the lake, somewhere beyond a shelf of shore-ice that extended out into the darkness. Out there, the lake was working itself into a midnight frenzy of passion, performed to a small, silent audience of two men on a bluff.

Moore switched off his light and turned his back to all the fury. Mitch tarried. Memories of Coppertone and half-naked female bodies broiling in the sun were far from his mind. The seething surf drew him closer to the edge, the tips of his snow-shoes extended slightly over the rim of the snowblown bluff. He looked down the steep slope, a dizzy black-diamond down-hill run on skis. At the bottom, he would tuck and curl into a white drift at the wet, endless edge of the world.

There was a sharp tug on his sleeve. "Hankers' house should be over there." Moore was screaming, but Mitch could barely hear him.

"Come on, Mitch," Moore screamed again as he pulled Mitch from the grasp of the lake.

Wham. Slam. Suddenly, there was sound and light. High intensity bright. Mitch was blinded by the spotlight that hit them. Simultaneously, Mitch thought he heard someone over by the house yell something, the words lost in the wind. "Damn," Mitch mumbled, as a bullet de-barked a tree over his head. At least with Billy Koistra, he had always been armed to the teeth and, if he got pinned down by bad guys, Billy would always return with the cavalry.

What happened next happened very quickly because, in spite of himself, Mitch was young and strong.

He ran, aided in gusts by the wind that blew off the lake, across the garden where Hazel had grown squash in the summers of her life. He didn't think at all. He was overwhelmed with a savage ferociousness.

Something primal had seized him, as if the lake's hydro-power had pumped his muscles into high gear. His mind was turning over an odd thought. As a place to die, this was great; most people expired in pathetic surroundings. An emergency room, or a coronary intensive-care unit with harsh fluorescent lighting. A two-lane highway with broken glass and a twisted torso mashed in sheet metal, the other driver drunk and unscratched. Or the penultimate worst, a nursing home smelling of urine, where zombies ambulated in slow, psychedelic madness.

As far as place goes, who could ask for anything more? "Go Blue!" Mitch screamed at the top of his lungs, running as fast as his snowshoes would let him; which actually was pretty fast, although he looked like a duck in heat.

Blast and shatter. Blast and shatter. The only thing that

probably saved Mitch were the screaming gusts of wind, suddenly doubled in intensity; they were throwing someone's aim awry. Something ripped through Mitch's borrowed snowsuit, but he kept on running. Behind him, Ted dropped, pumped, and fired with his shotgun, taking out the blinding floodlight. Mitch charged into the black spot where the light had been.

Mitch had never won his letter in high-school football. He quit after three days of practice. He liked wearing the helmet and shoulder pads which made him look like he had broad shoulders. He admired those varsity jackets with leather sleeves and big solitary letters. He loved the smell of wet grass in the fall. He loved everything about the game. Except the physical contact. Not exactly the kind of player the coach was looking for.

He was making up for it now. He was at the fifteen, the ten, the five-yard line, as the crowd screamed a mighty storm in his ear. Five, four, three, two, one. Mitch buried his shoulder into Barstow's stomach. "Ahug!" Mitch drove him down to the ground with the churning motion of his legs. It was a classic tackle.

The crowd went nuts. The waves of Lake Michigan went ballistic all along the shoreline. Proving once and for all that you don't have to be a football hero to impress a beautiful girl. From the Straits of Mackinac to Saugatuck and south, the lake waves crashed on the frozen sidelines with an even louder roar than before. Mitch grabbed Barstow by the throat and started choking him with a righteous anger that fumed from the pit of his soul.

There were no flags. No one called unnecessary roughness. No one called any personal fouls. There, in the frozen-water winter wonderland of his birth, Mitch Miller held the home-field advantage.

❖ ❖ ❖

In law school, Mitch had been taught with every other student: "Cross-examination is the single greatest tool ever created by man in search for the truth." Well, that sounded good in a classroom but was typical law school bullshit. Cross-examination buys a little justice once and awhile, but never gets to the truth, the whole truth, and nothing but the truth.

For instance, take the note which the doctor, whom Mitch had defended, had written in his patients' file: "Rule out CO poisoning next visit if complaints persist." Mitch saw that note his first week on the job, but the surviving daughter's lawyer never did. Because Calley had "sanitized" the doctor's medical records — right in front of Mitch and Cheer Cheer.

As he did it, Calley had gauged the distinctly different reactions of the two associates. "The note is the doctor's personal impressions and therefore a privileged document," said Calley, positing a novel legal theory, which Mitch had never heard Robbie Joe or any other legal scholar put forth. Thereafter, Calley assigned the file to Mitch. But it was Cheer Cheer who had passed Calley's little test.

When he resigned from HD&H, Mitch had left all that behind. He was now completely free to test his own novel legal theories. Such as: "Choking a man by the throat is more efficacious than cross-examination for the discovery of the truth." Mitch was following this approach to the letter. He suspected Robbie Joe would approve his decision to test a new method of self-help justice. He knew Giovanni definitely would approve. After all, Barstow had fired three bullets at him, in two separate encounters. Now Mitch's hands were around the witness's neck, squeezing firm enough to leave red finger marks that might disappear with good perfusion in a few hours, with marked ecchymosis in forty-eight.

Barstow could see Moore's shotgun trained on him. "Hey, it's just a casino they're building. That's all."

"I know that," Mitch snapped. "What's the well for?"

"Water. It's all about water," whined Barstow.

"What happened to the Hankers?" Moore yelled over Mitch's shoulder.

"They were in the way."

"Whose way?" Mitch screamed. Mitch was squeezing so hard on the guy's throat that the veins in Mitch's own neck were bulging. "Whose way?"

Ted Moore was starting to get nervous about Mitch's techniques. "Mitch. I think that's enough," he said. The only light on the scene was a solitary bulb at the Hankers' side door. Nevertheless Moore had the feeling the guy was turning blue. Barstow mumbled something that sounded like, "He's less vague ..."

"Who's less vague? Who, who, who?" yelled Mitch. Roger Tory Peterson would have been impressed with the call. Owls for a mile around perked up their tufted ears and rotated their heads.

"Mitch. Stop." Moore was now pleading for the guy's life.

"You wanted a big-city lawyer. You got one!" Mitch yelled at Moore. "You want to get the truth, don't you?" Mitch snapped his head back at Barstow. "You did kill the Hankers, didn't you. Didn't you?"

Barstow jerked upright. Then he fell limp out of Mitch's

clawed hands. He jerked again on the white snow. Mitch stared up at Moore. The deer they had had for supper earlier that night had died that same way in bow season. The shaft was sticking improbably out of Barstow's camouflage jacket, just an inch from Mitch's snowsuit-covered arm. The arrow had penetrated Barstow's lung.

Ted Moore grabbed Mitch's arm and rolled him away from Barstow in one motion. Coming out of the roll, he aimed his shotgun up and with one shot, blew out the Hankers' light. The darkness that followed was just as quickly interrupted by light coming up the Hankers' drive. First one light, then a string of them, blinking wildly through the maples that lined the narrow roadway.

"This might not be the cavalry," Mitch whispered into Ted's ear.

"His snowmobile," Moore nodded to Barstow's body with open eyes staring upwards only inches from their faces. "It's sitting behind the house, on the lake side," said Moore.

Moore grabbed his shotgun and started running. In the seconds Mitch delayed running for his life, he grabbed the shaft and yanked out the arrow from Barstow's chest. That delay saved Mitch's life, as another arrow sliced just over-head and thunked into one of the shutters on the Hanker cottage.

The lead snowmobile coming up the drive was almost to Albert's woodshed.

Mitch was up and running behind Moore who had mounted Barstow's Arctic Cat. It started right away, which spoke well for the product. An arrow pierced Moore's boot.

"Damn," Moore grimaced in pain. "Christ almighty. You drive." Moore dropped his registered firearm in the snow as Mitch leap-frogged over Ted and grabbed the handlebars.

In either direction there was less than three hundred feet of clearing on the rim of the bluff where the Hanker cottage sat. The rest was woods. Mitch headed south, following the line of the bluff. As he did, the first, second and third snowmobile crossed the driveway in front of the Hanker garage.

"Should I head for the woods?" Mitch yelled.

"No way! We'll get caught up on something!" Moore yelled back through his gritted teeth as the snowmobile lurched forward.

Mitch steered the Cat in a circle, and looked at the three snowmobiles. They paused a moment, on the edge of the Hankers' driveway. And then the three snowmobiles roared and charged in unison straight at Mitch and Ted, bearing down on them like a three-eyed monster. Mitch spun around again.

He didn't have a choice. Full throttle. He leaned and took a hard right, nearly losing Ted. The Cat charged straight over the edge of the bluff. Mitch leaned back hard into Ted, trying to keep the tips of the machine up.

The snowmobile was airborne. It flew. Hold it. Hold it. Hold it, Mitch thought, as his stomach rose and the machine dropped down onto the slope towards the bottom of the bluff. As it landed it stalled and sputtered, clawing in the snow. Then it took off again, charging onto another ramp that sloped up to a wall of ice that had formed along the shoreline. They hit the top of that barrier and again they were airborne, but only for a fraction of a second, as they shot out free and clear onto the smooth surface of a narrow shelf of lake ice.

Wonderful ice. Mitch spun the snowmobile around and paused. He and Ted gazed up at the escarpment. High above on the ridgeline, they could dimly make out the outline of the roof of Hankers' cottage.

On the edge of the bluff from which they had flown, three

headlights paused, contemplating a similar feat. With a roar, one of them cast itself over the edge. But unlike the flying Cat, this creature of the night did not soar at all. It missed the smooth slide. Instead, it caught a runner in an exposed tree-root halfway down the hundred-foot drop. It did a slow half-flip and landed with a thud on a patch of sand that held no snow, its ski runners in the air, its driver pinned underneath, motionless.

Mitch turned his machine south and gunned the engine. In the two headlights remaining on the bluff, Mitch saw three figures step forward to the edge to look down. One held an archery bow.

❖ ❖ ❖

Cheer Cheer was a little hung over for the strategy session with the head honcho of Malone Desert Development Corporation. The last thing he remembered was the cheerleader call-girl doing a handstand on the coffee table in his hotel suite, followed by incredible splits on his bed. Then he passed out.

"What do you think, Ken?" Malone often posed questions to which he didn't expect answers.

Malone was studying a map of the United States, which covered one entire wall of his office. There was something different about Malone's map. The odd feature was a collection of good-sized lakes that covered a portion of the once-arid territory of southern Nevada surrounding Las Vegas. Malone had hired the same graphic designer to design the Nevada Great Lakes who had designed the logo for his new casino. The artist had rendered a contemporary design using a pallet of bold blue.

The outlines of the five new lakes were abstract, yet strangely familiar. Given the lay of the land, the five lakes were not configured in exactly the same layout as the original five sisters of the Midwest, and they were obviously much smaller. But they were clearly playful caricatures of the originals. And there, on the southwestern shore of Nevada's Lake Michigan clone, was the city of Las Vegas, as if trying to be a desert version of Chicago.

"Wait until you see the T-shirts. I can pay for all the lawyers and half of the bribes — excuse me, 'political contributions' — just with the T-shirt sales." Malone was excited.

Calley managed a smile at that. Taking that as his cue, so did Cheer Cheer. Calley was sitting on an oversized Western polished rawhide sofa, watching Malone pace energetically.

"And I just acquired a map company. For the first time since Hawaii became a state, they're going to need new maps in every school in the country. In the entire world! Just think of the revenues," added Malone.

Thus far, politics had been the easy part of Malone's grand plan. What he didn't admit, and Calley didn't want to remind him of, was that the laws of nature might be harder to buy off. Malone's dream was very possibly just that, a rich man's fantasy. Transporting the water from MDDC's proposed main intake station near Chicago to western Nebraska would be expensive, sure, but not prohibitive. This wasn't the Aleyeska pipeline. There would be no risk of crude-oil leaks interfering with a caribou migration. Malone's pipeline would just run through a bunch of farmers' fields.

Uninsulated plastic pipe, relatively cheap, would do. Under constant pressure, only extreme low temperatures would cause the pipe to burst. And then some corn farmer in Grinnell, Iowa, would just get more water for awhile, until the pipeline could be patched. No real problem there.

It was the Rockies that seemed insurmountable. A series of fairly ordinary pumping stations would get the water through the heartland. But getting it over the Continental Divide would take a major expenditure of energy.

"It's prohibitive because of the cost," the engineers all told Malone. "If water was as valuable as oil, it might be worth it. But let's face it ..."

That news had sent Malone into a near state of depression. "But once again Tammy and the Lord were there for me," he would hope to someday tell a cheering convention of born-again capitalists. Tammy and Malone had gone together into the desert to pray, in scorching summer heat. They had picked a desolate place, brown and dusty, as yet untouched by irrigation.

Together, they had fallen to their knees — when the miracle occurred. It rained. Tammy was wearing jeans, her kangaroo-skin boots, bought by her husband on their honeymoon in Australia, and a designer T-shirt.

In the heavenly shower, the rocks and the stone-baked earth steamed. The water changed earth-tone colors to bright hues. The water transformed everything that was dry.

As they both felt the desert awaken around them, as they both began to feel quenched and full, Malone stared in wonder at his third wife. There, kneeling beside him was womanhood in a dripping wet T-shirt.

But there was no contest. Only Tammy spoke, moved by the spirit welling inside her, "Think big, my beloved. Think not of the cost, but what water will bring to the desert. Not just moisture. Not just pretty blooming cactus and all that."

Tammy continued, for she was a visionary who had minored in marketing in adult extension courses at UNLV. "Think of the merchandising and spin-offs, my love. Think condos on golf courses, filled by foreigners who want everything that Las Vegas promises. Think strip malls with fast-food restaurants and discount tire stores. Think T-shirts."

Malone smiled. He was thinking T-shirts. He was touched by her two marvelous preaching pulpits, peaking through virgin wet cotton. He knew the answer to the nay-saying engineers. Money.

With enough money, water could be made to run uphill.

❖ ❖ ❖

It was after midnight when they drove over the drawbridge and down Manistee's main drag. With a few Christmas lights, the Victorian Port City could have been Bedford Falls. There were a handful of snowmobilers and some cross-country skiers still out enjoying themselves. There were also heavily chained trucks from Michigan National Guard units, based in Grayling, which had been mobilized by the Governor's declaration of a state of emergency over a twelve-county area.

They stopped at the first tavern that was open, its neon Stroh's Beer sign lit by a Coleman lantern and a half dozen candles. Mitch pulled in front of the tavern next to a couple of cars that were drifted in. He and Moore dismounted the Arctic Cat and tried to stretch like one. Mitch realized the arrow was gone from Ted's boot. Moore had worked it out of the thick-soled heel and tossed it aside somewhere along the icy shore as the snowmobile had sped back to the safe harbor of Manistee.

"I'm doing better. Hey, I got that damn thing out," said Moore, noticing Mitch's displeasure at the missing arrow.

"You should have kept that for evidence," said Mitch, who was thankful that he had yanked out the bloody arrow which had killed Barstow, breaking off most of the shaft. He checked to make sure he still had it, then zipped the arrowhead carefully back into his pocket. "Let's call your wife and the Sheriff," said Mitch as he helped Moore limp into the bar. The bar was surprisingly full, with neighborhood regulars and dozens of stranded motorists. The fireplace needed a chimney sweep. It was smoking, but any warmth and light in a village temporarily gone primeval was welcome.

The power was out, but people had brought an odd assortment of lanterns, which now were spread randomly around the interior. The bartender was dispensing drinks with the aid of a helmet that had a strapped-on battery-powered light.

Moore ordered two shots and hobbled off to call his wife. The bartender gave Mitch the number for the sheriff. "It won't do you any good. Their line's down."

Moore had no success either. "I got to get home," said Moore after he downed his first shot.

"We've got to report this tonight," said Mitch.

"My neighbor is a Deputy Sheriff. As soon as I get home and check on Barbara and little Teddy, I'll tell him what happened."

"You need to see a doctor for a tetanus shot. Let's go to the hospital first."

"I'm okay, really," said Moore, tossing back the second shot.

"It's been a long day." Mitch laughed. "My car's smashed up, and instead I've got the keys to a dead man's snowmobile. I better get to the Sheriff's office, if you don't mind showing me where it is," said Mitch.

❖ ❖ ❖

Malone had scheduled a Sunday morning working breakfast for his inner circle. Calley was on his feet and going for seconds at the buffet. It was too early for Cheer Cheer, after yet another night with the redheaded call-girl. The only thing that looked tempting to him on the table was the crystal bowl of white, until he realized it was just powdered sugar for the extra-large irradiated strawberries. He retired to the big leather couch, clutching an unopened bottle of aspirin.

At least the subject matter of Malone's meetings was always cool, refreshing, and zero calories. Not that Cheer Cheer had to worry about calories anymore. His new frenetic lifestyle had taken care of that.

"Nevada is the fastest-growing state in the nation," said an exuberant Malone. "All that's holding us back is water. We need water to sustain that growth."

He turned to the map on the wall. "Sixty-five trillion gallons of water in the Great Lakes. Sixty-five trillion! That's a hockey-puckin' lot. If you emptied them, you'd have enough water to cover the entire continental United States ten feet deep." He began to pace back and forth.

"And all I need to drain from the Great Lakes is a measly two inches per year." Malone was pumped up. "An insignificant amount, really. And think of all the benefit to Nevada's citizens." And to MDDC investors, thought Cheer Cheer.

Malone looked at Calley and Cheer Cheer. "You know

what the biggest difference will be between my water and all those fountains, pools, and canals at the Venetian — and the Bellagio and the Luxor and the Mirage?" He pointed at the map on the wall.

"They'll be able to see my creation from the *Challenger*," he proclaimed triumphantly. "The Nevada Great Lakes will be the largest body of water ever created purely for amusement purposes."

Through bleary eyes, Cheer Cheer thought that Malone himself looked a little like a mirage. Cheer Cheer reached for his briefcase to pull out the MDDC projections of revenue flow from the pipeline and related investments, like the Ottawa casino on Lake Michigan. There was a knock at the door.

In walked Malone's chief of security, a man named Smith. He nodded to Calley and turned to Malone.

"Sir, we just grabbed a man with a card-counting device. We confiscated this." Smith laid two bundles of metal, plastic and leather on top of Malone's desk. "I didn't know if I should interrupt you, sir, but I thought you might want to see this one. It's an amazing little computer. Much more sophisticated than anything we've ever seen before."

Malone picked up the little keyboard and studied it carefully. "So it is," said Malone, obviously impressed. With the constant improvements in micro-processors, the casinos were always on the alert for players using the newest equipment.

"Doesn't this chump know that this is felony? Not to mention a violation of our own house rules. He's in a lot of trouble."

"Do you want me to fix him — I mean, fix the problem, sir?" inquired Smith, a little too eagerly.

"Excuse me sir," the voice on the intercom cut in.

"I'm in a conference," Malone snapped at the voice box. Just then the door swung open and in walked Tammy

Malone, well-dressed as always, like one of Donald Trump's ex-wives. She was clutching the King James version under her arm. "It's time for church, dear."

"There has been a security breach at the site," said the voice on the intercom. The scene in Malone's office suddenly became tense. Cheer Cheer sat up.

"What?" Malone blurted out. The voice on his desk had his attention.

"One fatality."

"There's been an accident?" Tammy gasped.

Calley got up. "A construction accident?" he insisted.

"A power line accident?" Cheer Cheer chimed in.

"A shooting accident," said the voice on the desk. "One of the Indians killed Barstow. With a bow and arrow. We've got a back-up crew on the scene, but ..."

"The good Indians or the bad Indians?" asked Tammy.

"Our good Indians," said the voice on the desk.

"I assume it has been reported to the Sheriff," Malone said.

"No sir. They got away," said the voice on the desk.

"The Indians?" Malone asked.

"No. The white men," said the voice on the intercom.

"The bad white men, I'm sure," said Tammy.

"Let me handle this," said Calley, who picked up the receiver and began a brief, obscure conversation with the voice on the other end of the line which ended with, "Trace the gun and the snowmobile. Do what you have to do to erase any signs of Indian involvement. We can't let this interfere."

Cheer Cheer sat on the couch, not sure he was following this. Everyone else was up and huddled around Malone's desk. Cheer Cheer unscrewed the top of the aspirin bottle and pulled out cotton.

❖ ❖ ❖

The morning sun was shining like a red rubber ball. But it was not going to get hot enough to melt anything. She surveyed the drifts of white madness from the apartment landing. She knew now that her decision to leave was foolhardy. She grabbed the shovel anyway. It would take her mind off of a lot of things and wipe out that Nat King Cole song.

Yesterday she had barely driven out of town, when she saw the red flares on the snowy shoulder of the road and the flashing lights of the police cruiser. About halfway between Grand Rapids and Holland, there was a roadblock. A single officer was routing cars across the median and back east to Grand Rapids. He didn't stop anyone in the line except her. He bent his head down to look in her car, made eye contact, and waved her out of the procession.

She knew enough about Rick's connections with police, who worked off-duty concert security for him, that she automatically assumed the roadblock was for her. Someone had radioed ahead about the honey on the keyboards. She was wanted for first-degree obstruction of a percussion instrument. She got nervous, as decent citizens usually do when pulled over.

"Ma'am, let me see your license and registration."

She was organized, but shaking a little as she quickly pulled the documents out of her purse.

"Where you headed, Laura?" The officer asked, handing

the documents back to her as quickly as he received them.

"California. Well, just to my sister's in Gary for tonight."

"California, hey. Haven't been there since the service. Not a bad place per se, but I don't understand all the rush," the officer said, while intermittently motioning cars to turn back across the median and yelling, "You can't get there from here."

"Officer. Please. I really need to get through."

"Everyone needs to get through, Laura. Make it through this life. The rest is easy," the Italian-looking officer said with sincerity. "If you head west tonight, you could end up just like the Donner party. Some of the surviving cannibals later became leading citizens of the Golden State. But why take that chance? This is a major storm." The man took off his police cap revealing his long hair. He looked up in the white sky and stuck his tongue out to catch snowflakes. Laura watched, as he seemed to satisfy his tongue with a couple.

"Makes you feel alive," he laughed. "If this keeps up, by tomorrow we will all be able to walk over fences." He looked back inside the car. "In fact, I ..." The sound of spinning tires screaming on ice interrupted his words. There was a Ford Falcon stuck on the shoulder. A little old lady with purple hair was behind the wheel. "Excuse me." The officer walked over to render assistance to the grounded Falcon. He turned and waved at Laura. "Watch out for icicles growing on eaves."

Other than tornadoes lifting farm houses off of Kansas sod, snow is the most inherently magical and mystical act of Mother Nature.

"Who will love you with a love true, Who can cling to a Ramblin' Rose, One more time ..." Last night on her way back into town, she had stopped at several motels on 28th Street which had been too busy to flip on their "No Vacancy" signs. Driving was becoming treacherous. She had decided to go back to Oakwood.

She knocked on Mitch's door. She hadn't been in there since the first day they met. She still had her master key from the management office. She assumed Mitch would be coming home anytime. She didn't know if Rick was, and didn't care.

More depressed than hungry, she looked in Mitch's refrigerator. Spartan. She looked in his freezer. Ice cream, but only a couple of spoonfuls left. So she got a spoon. She still had her coat on. She turned up the heat. She flipped through the blue milk-crate of albums.

She walked into his bedroom. Picture of mom and dad. A smiling picture of Mitch and a woman in front of a Christmas tree. She picked it up to look at it more closely. A deflated football on top of his dresser. She opened his closet. Suits and sport coats were neatly hung. She pulled a red tie off of a hook full of ties. She put it around her neck.

Then she walked over to the dresser and began opening drawers. There was a *Playboy* magazine in a sock drawer. She opened another drawer. She held up a pair of white traditional Jockeys. He hadn't worn any their first time together, to reveal a preference for briefs or boxers. She made a frowning face in the mirror on top of his dresser. She laid the underwear back in his drawer.

She saw the album lying out on the nightstand. Nat King Cole's *Ramblin' Rose*. She picked it up and examined it closely. Still wearing his tie, she carried the album to his turntable. She took off her coat and put on the record. "Ramblin' Rose, Ramblin' Rose, why I love you, heaven knows. Who will love you ..." She listened. She walked to the sliding-glass door. She looked out, but mostly saw in. It was dark outside.

Extra-Judicial Adjudication. It lay on the coffee table. She didn't remember the title. But she remembered picking up a book he had dropped the first day they met. The record was spinning. Nat was singing. She picked up the book, and a piece of paper slipped out from the front and fell to the floor. There some lines scrawled on it. Naturally she took a look.

I lived a life of statutes and limitations,
In libraries musty and old.
Some books get all the breaks,
This one you chose to hold.

It's not fair, 'cause books can't sing,
Songs to make your heart race.
Some books get all the breaks,
I'm down on second floor in second place.

She had gone back into Mitch's room; gotten undressed, except for the tie. She climbed into his bed and stared up. One man's floor. Another man's ceiling. Finally she had closed her eyes and slept peacefully.

Deep in her dreams, she heard Nat crooning. "Who will love you with a love true?"

❖ ❖ ❖

Malone, through Calley's good offices, continued to spin his webs. Of money. Of politics.

The press conference was only weeks away. By the time midsummer would roll around, everything would be tied up very neatly. The results of the gambling-water referendum would be anti-climatic, like any well-planned, well-financed, well-polled election should be.

If he so desired, he figured he could drain half the lake on the promise of jobs alone. Most blue-collar working stiffs were too busy getting downsized to have time to worry about the environment. And the official plans presented to the appropriate commissions called for only a two-inch reduction in water level.

Of course, that was two inches per year, but you had to read a lot of sub-clauses and obscure tables to figure that out.

And really, who could complain about Lake Michigan going down two inches? Certainly not the homeowners with prime lakefront property, who every twenty years or so fought losing battles with high cycles of the lake, which wreaked havoc on their cottage foundations, on their piers, on their sea walls.

The water would hardly be missed. Malone was confident.

Of course, there will be some flag-burning environmental nuts with nothing better to do than whine and scream against progress. But that's half the fun. When it comes right down to it, all we're doing is moving water from one place to another.

And on those grounds, Calley had assured him, they were on solid footing. The U.S. Supreme Court had long ago authorized the diversion of thousands of cubic feet per second from Lake Michigan for use by the State of Illinois alone. When Malone's project was finished, the farmers and ranchers along the pipeline route would have ready access to irrigation water — for a very reasonable price, he noted to himself. And Nevada would be swimming in it.

And what could be more politically correct than helping the poor Ottawa Indians enhance their gambling operations in exchange for some concessions on their long-standing Great Lakes' water rights, which no one had really taken seriously before this?

Malone leaned back in his leather chair and took another sip of his Perrier. He looked at the bottle. "What the heck. They already ship it from France to drink."

From Manistee to Muskegon, where the National Guard truck let Mitch off, the roads were walled in by snow, plowed and packed by ponderous orange trucks. Dozens and dozens of cars were engulfed in those halls of the white mountain king. Occasionally, you would see a chrome or plastic rear bumper, where an owner had started to shovel out and, waist deep in snow, realized it was hopeless. Many opted to wait and pray for a good thaw. Where driveways had been opened, they gave the illusion of tunnels, leading back to invisible houses.

When he stepped off the Greyhound, Mitch felt like he had spring fever. Already the sun was out, shrinking the white blanket. Concrete and blacktop were reclaiming the urban landscape.

After bobbing in the back of the National Guard truck, which had picked him up with some other stranded motorists at the Sheriff's office, and then sitting on the bus, Mitch was ready to run the few blocks to his office. He wanted to run to tell Wasaquom what had happened. Too hot for a zipped-up snowmobile suit. Mitch put his arms in the snowmobile jumper, but not his legs. It made for a funny-looking caped crusader running up Fulton towards Division.

The bells rang at the front door to the office. "Hi, Mitch," said one of David Wasaquom's secretaries, her mouth stuffed with a late-lunch sandwich. Her computer screen was filled with the text of a last-minute brief.

"Is he in?" Mitch asked anxiously.

She pointed to his office as she wiped her mouth and resumed typing.

Mitch walked in and pulled off his cape. He sat down in the chair in front of the desk and caught his breath.

Bifocals on, Wasaquom kept on reading. His desk was piled high with law books and journal articles. He was preparing for his next round with Judge Alkema.

"We were starting to worry about you, white man," said Wasaquom, still not looking up from his books.

"You do know what tribe is building the huge casino development north of Manistee, with help from the MDDC?" Mitch asked.

"It really doesn't matter which tribe it is. There's federal precedent for many tribes to control a share of Great Lakes water." Wasaquom continued, "The issue is not who controls the water, but whether it can be transported cross-country. I've pulled all the cases under the National Environmental Policy

Act. There are so many federal contacts involved. The pipeline will need easements over federal land. Wetlands issues. Even Alkema will be forced to require MDDC to file environmental impact statements."

Wasaquom still had his head down, reading and writing notes. "You know, Mitch, with your passion, I'm surprised you never went into environmental law. Working for the Environmental Defense Fund or one of those groups. They certainly need experienced trial lawyers."

"Way too much paperwork in those cases. Too much bullshit. I prefer to wait for someone to get murdered first," Mitch said. "It makes it much simpler."

This time Wasaquom looked up. He set his bifocals on top of a stack of "F. Supps."

Mitch laid the bloodied arrowhead with its broken shaft on Wasaquom's desk. It was in a plastic bag. Mitch and Moore had made the report to a dispatcher at the Sheriff's office. The dispatcher was alone, as all the Deputies were out on emergency calls. The dispatcher was no rookie, but he appeared to be overwhelmed by the havoc the blizzard had created. Mitch had decided that the chain of custody of this evidence was better left with him.

"Is this your tribe's arrow?" Mitch said.

David Wasaquom had spent most of his life fighting the Tonto stereotype that befell him at birth. He had been captain of his high-school swim team. Graduated with honors from college. Made the University of Wisconsin Law Review. Quickly rose to Colonel at the Judge Advocate General's Office after a combat tour with the U.S. Marine Corps. Such over-achievers had a right to have a chip on their shoulder. And to harbor a few demons deep in their souls to fuel their successes in life.

"Did you watch a lot of re-runs of old western movies when you were kid? I did too. Only they weren't re-runs for my generation," said Wasaquom. "I rooted for the white man. Not because I'm ashamed of who I am, but because the Indians were so fake." Wasaquom picked up the bag and examined the arrow. "This was made by the same company that makes hockey equipment for that Ojibwa guy who plays in the NHL."

"How do you know all that?" Mitch asked.

"My brother and I were champion archers, when we were kids."

Mitch thought about that. "Where's your brother?" Mitch asked.

"You know, Ted Nugent is an avid bow hunter. I saw him at a hunting expo once. I believe he hunts with this arrow." Wasaquom said. "Maybe he did it."

"Ted Nugent plays a mean guitar and drinks Vernor's ginger ale, too. But honorable hunters like him only shoot what they plan to eat. He wouldn't want to eat what I had laying next to me up in the woods in Manistee two days ago."

Wasaquom got up and closed his door. "Has the County Prosecutor charged anybody?"

"No. But I would expect to be hearing from them soon," said Mitch.

"You mean as the State's witness?" questioned Wasaquom.

"Well, of course. What else would I be?" said Mitch.

"I don't know. Tell me about it. I'm an environmental lawyer. I'm not used to simple cases."

"You can have a big-city lawyer if you want. But not him. He's a murder suspect, too," said the Sheriff.

"Murder! I didn't murder anyone. Anyhow, the killing was done with an arrow," Ted Moore pleaded.

"Medical Examiner says it was a shotgun blast at close range. From your .12-gauge Browning, Ted. There was no arrow. Just bird-shot chewing a hole to daylight through the poor bastard."

"The same Medical Examiner who says I killed the Hankers," Moore blurted.

"You did have some fish to fry up there at the Hankers. Didn't you? Barstow was probably the one who turned you down on the heating and air-conditioning bid for the casino. Am I warm or cold on that one, Teddy?" said the Sheriff. "Better not say any more, but between you and me, I'd cut a deal before the big-city lawyer does." The Sheriff often gave out free legal advice during custodial interrogations.

The Sheriff looked at his Deputy, Ted Moore's next-door neighbor who had been waiting for Ted when he got home that morning. "Deputy, do we have a more recent address for Mitchell Miller than ...let's see ... Oakwood Village, 2765 Oak Shadows Drive, Wyoming, Michigan?" The Sheriff was reading a print-out from the Department of Motor Vehicles.

"No sir."

"Then get this search and arrest warrant ready for the

County Prosecutor," said the Sheriff.

Moore looked like he was about to cry, thinking of his wife and little baby boy. So he did.

Mitch was beginning to feel the strain of the last three days as he climbed the wooden stairs to his apartment.

He unlocked his door. It had still been dark the morning he had left for his office to pick up the Hanker file. Maybe he had left the lights on in his kitchen and dining room. He heard someone in the kitchen rattling pots and pans. He grabbed the shovel that was leaning outside his door.

He walked into that apartment a different man than the one who left, the man who as a boy had gone hitless in Little League. The man standing there that night could kill with the shovel if he had to.

Laura saw it in his eyes as she turned the corner by the kitchen. She screamed. Mitch dropped the shovel in disbelief.

They looked at each other with knowledge. They both knew what the other one was thinking. She had read the inscription in his book and listened to his classic sound track. He had found her standing in front of him, uninvited to his home, but much wanted, hoped for, prayed for.

"Why don't you shut the door and come in?" It was as declarative as any question gets.

He walked towards her, shedding his cape on the carpet. She did not yet know the story of that cape. He would tell her about that later, but first he touched her.

With few exceptions, clothes-ripping embraces demonstrate the limitations of *Homo sapiens* in heat. This is not to say that such couplings are unexciting. They certainly are exciting, and fun too. Grabbing like kids at candy counters. Pawing clothes. Sucking lips. Tongues thrusting. Grabbing wildly at each other's appendages, hard and soft. Buttons pop. Inevitably — and before anyone knows it — a man, a purported Casanova, stands naked but for argyle socks, and a woman is tangled in panties rolled and twisted at her ankles.

More than anything else it is that awkward act of separating, however briefly, from clothing — relaxing the grip to step out of underwear and stockings — that detracts from otherwise passionate couplings initiated by fully-clothed upright mammals.

Well, it wasn't like that at all.

Mitch took his time. He made her tingle from the nape of her neck to the tip of her toes. He discovered her zones and then some, and he played them all, as softly and smoothly as Nat King Cole could milk a refrain.

As for Laura — slowly, quickly, slowly, quickly, like a child being told not to run at a slippery wet poolside — she caused him to melt harder and longer than ever before.

As for their clothes, each article was removed with reverence, slowly, by the other.

And in the end, Laura and Mitch were both reaching such a crescendo that Arthur Fiedler himself stepped down to man the cymbals. And John Philip Sousa arose at the bedroom door to conduct "Stars and Stripes Forever."

The first clue that something was wrong was his piano. When Rick walked into the apartment, he called out her name. No answer. He looked for a note on the kitchen counter. He didn't find one. Then he saw the sweet golden strings of a gluey substance laying on the keys of his treasured musical instrument. He walked over and touched an ivory key. It stuck to his finger. He put his finger to his tongue. He knew the number: it tasted much sweeter than wine.

Rick ran upstairs to their bedroom loft. He yanked the clumsy metal sliding door to their closet. It came off its runner and stuck, but he saw enough to know that she was already gone. He wasn't quite sure how to feel about that. Things were starting to happen for him out West with the woman from Geltman's party.

But Laura — she had always been there for him. He sat down on their bed. He jumped like a cat on a hot tin roof. Prongs and all; he had sat on the three-carat zirconium. He retrieved it from his backside. He walked over to the balcony where solar power was bouncing off melting snow and metal flashing through the sliding-glass window. For a moment, he held this diamond ring up to try and catch a gleam of that light. In his moment of reflection, he thought he heard voices from the apartment below.

Couldn't be. Could it? He heard the phone ring below. It was Mitch's voice, that was certain. He lay down on the kitchen floor and pressed his ear hard against the tile.

"For what? Murder? Should I turn myself in? How soon?"

"What is it, Mitch?"

It was Laura's voice. Then Rick heard the sliding-glass door shut directly below him.

Down on the second floor, there was a frantic dashing and darting by Mitch and Laura to grab essentials. Five minutes later, Mitch's door flew open, and Laura came out first. Rick was standing there leaning against the railing, one Hush Puppied foot comfortably crossed over the other. Laura gasped and stopped short, as Mitch ran into her from behind.

"Going somewhere in a hurry?" said Rick. And he added, "... with an outlaw?" Rick was smug as a cat.

The three of them stood on the landing for a second, with the faint sound of police sirens closing in the distance.

"You can take my truck," offered Rick.

Laura stared at him. "Go ahead, Mitch, load the truck. Rick's truck. Quick!" Laura ordered.

Mitch scurried down the stairs.

Laura flashed her blue eyes with a look that said, you still owe me big-time you philandering son of a bitch, but she spoke calmly, "He has a crate of albums in there that means a lot to him. Classic rock. You know, beautiful music like you promised me we were going to make together. Please see that the cops don't trash them."

Rick handed her the keys. Smugness retreated under the welcome mat he was standing on. "A credit card would be nice, too," she added.

Ted Moore's wife was not a well-educated woman, but she wanted to improve herself. So she bought the encyclopedia set on sale at Meijer's, even though she knew they could not afford it. That same day, their first notice for a delinquent land-contract payment came in the mail. But unlike most working-class encyclopedia victims, Barbara Moore actually began to read.

She had started from the beginning and had already finished the As. When she finished the volume, she decided to reward herself by skipping ahead to look at the pictures. It was the day of the blizzard. Little Teddy had been napping.

She'd been browsing through the Ls, looking at a picture of a small single-engine plane, the *Spirit of St. Louis*. The thought of flying solo over all that salt water intrigued her, and she had read all that went with that picture, from the mob at the airport outside Paris ... to the infamous ladder found at Lindbergh's New Jersey home, when his baby had been kidnapped.

Two days after the blizzard, when the voice on the phone asked, "How is little Teddy doing, now that his daddy is in jail?" it was almost more than she could bear. "But ma'am," the soft voice continued, "there is a way out. Just have him say that the lawyer from Grand Rapids was the trigger man. You just might find a land contract marked 'paid' in your mailbox. Sure beats something happening to a loved one, doesn't it?"

Little Teddy had been napping upstairs in his crib. She raced up the stairs and grabbed him in her arms.

An hour later at the jail, her husband pitifully nodded his consent to the proposal she relayed. "But only if it comes to that. My court-appointed lawyer says they haven't even found Mitch yet."

David Wasaquom was no Uncle Tonto, as he had been called at the last gathering of the Ottawa tribal council. He had vigorously challenged the premise that gambling was the panacea for Native Americans, that it was a pipeline of riches, what oil was to the Inuit or the endless herds of buffalo covering the plains had once been to the Lakota.

He had been forced to admit his late mother had benefitted from the health benefits, as she had a series of surgeries, all paid for by the coins that gamblers dropped in the slots. But he had drawn a sharp line in the golden sand of Lake Michigan's western shore against Malone's proposal put before the Council, to trade historic Ottawa water rights (and allow the sale of Great Lakes water to Nevada) in return for a promise of unlimited stakes gambling.

He supposed there was a certain logic to it. Once you started to gamble, where did you draw the line?

He was not surprised that certain business interests supported the plan. Malone's people had done their homework, dealing out large contracts for pipeline production, installation, and maintenance to suppliers in Michigan and other key states. All of the recipients happened to be major contributors to the incumbent governors' election campaign funds. And the governors were well informed of this by their favorite donors.

But to see a Great Lakes tribe selling pieces of Algonquin,

as his ancestors used to call Lake Michigan, was shameful.

That's when his small band of renegades, as Judge Alkema had referred to them, split off. They had challenged the right of the current tribal council to make the sale of water rights. In retaliation, the tribal council had ordered Wasaquom's supporters removed from the tribe's official rolls. Wasaquom had complained angrily to the Bureau of Indian Affairs. There was no legal precedent to excommunicate a tribal member under these circumstances. But the BIA typically declined to "interfere." They sent back the standard letter, saying it was an internal matter for the tribe to work out.

So David Wasaquom found himself fighting on two fronts.

For one thing, he had to work to re-establish his followers' tribal status. Currently they were banished from the tribal health clinic and other services. And they were not receiving monthly payments for their shares of the gambling profits from the small Beaver Sands Casino.

On another front, he had to fight in the federal court. Today was the last chance to save the lake following the rule of white-man's law. David Wasaquom knew the legal issues as well as anyone in the environmental defense coalition. In fact, he had been designated by the coalition to argue the case in front of Alkema. He was fully prepared as he walked with his staff to the federal courthouse, well-armed with his knowledge of the law, which he had upheld and defended all his life.

A group of anti-referendum protesters, led by none other than Sarah VanderHook, had formed outside the Federal Building. They cheered as Wasaquom passed through the cordoned walkway to the entrance to the building. Wasaquom acknowledged their encouragement with a modest wave.

Anticipating a much bigger demonstration, the federal

marshals and Grand Rapids police had Sarah's group outnumbered by four to one. The media had them all outnumbered. Few of their readers or listeners cared about the water issues, but the fugitive angle had everyone thirsty for news. From coast to coast the headlines blazed. "Outlaw Attorney at Large as Environmental Court Battle Looms." "Suspect May Implicate Former Federal Prosecutor as Michigan Trigger Man." And then there was *The Globe*'s take on it: "Little Old Lady From Pasadena Photos Elvis with Fugitive Lawyer."

"The Judge would like to see the two lead counsel in chambers," said the judge's law clerk.

Each side had assembled a half-dozen lawyers, although the Malone forces clearly outnumbered the environmental groups in the number of paralegals.

Wasaquom followed Calley into Alkema's chambers, which since the Oklahoma City bombing had been retrofitted to look like Fort Knox.

"Gentlemen, good morning," said the Judge, who was seated behind a large desk with closed-circuit monitors covering the courtroom and a hallway view of the Judge's offices, showing a second door to his chambers.

"Good morning, Your Honor." It may have been the only time Wasaquom and Calley were in harmony. They both remained standing, until the Judge encouraged them to sit.

"Is there any possibility of settlement? I've read the briefs. I note that the U.S. Supreme Court long ago authorized diversion of Great Lakes water. And then there's this line of cases involving the sale of aquifer water by that Arizona tribe. The Department of Environmental Quality and the Governor have issued permits to drill for oil under Lake Michigan, which is then transported around the country. There would appear to be precedent. After all, we use this water everyday. It's not just to look at."

"Your Honor, if I may," said Wasaquom.

"Certainly, Mr. Wasaquom. That's why we're here," said the Judge.

"In the hearing this week, we will make a *prima facie* case that the ecosystem which the Great Lakes supports would be irreparably harmed by the increased diversion. That the uses this water is being put to in the Nevada deserts would be an obscene waste of a precious natural resource. For one thing, MDDC will be using Great Lakes water to grow grass in the desert."

"You mean marijuana?" Judge Alkema looked shocked.

"No, your Honor. For lawns," said Wasaquom.

"Oh, thank God," said the Judge, looking at Calley, relieved.

Wasaquom resumed, "And finally this project has significant federal contacts requiring that environmental impact statements be filed."

"There's enough water in the Great Lakes to cover the entire continental United States in ten feet of water," said the Judge, coincidentally sounding one of Malone's favorite themes. "As for how the people who purchase that water use it — obscenity should be a local issue. That's their business. It's a free country, last time I looked at the Constitution," said the Judge.

The Judge didn't respond to Wasaquom's third point. He was going to need some help from Calley, or actually Fletcher Cratchett, to finagle that one — to write a comprehensible opinion that two thousand miles or more of interstate pipeline did not first require a federal environmental impact statement.

"I was hoping you two might split the difference. Throw part of the baby out with part of the bath water," the Judge laughed.

Calley laughed, because that's what lawyers are suppose to do when a judge cracks a joke. David Wasaquom couldn't muster a smile. He knew his case was in trouble.

Alkema looked at Wasaquom. "Seriously, though, Mr. Wasaquom. I believe that you people consider all parts of the earth to be sacred. At least, that's what some chief named after Seattle said once upon a time."

Wasaquom looked at the Judge trying to restrain his contempt. "Yes, basically that's a correct summary of indigenous philosophy. But ..."

"Well, if all parts of the earth are equally sacred, then I can't see how it matters if some water gets moved from one part of the earth to another."

David Wasaquom clenched his teeth. He knew they would go through the exercise for a couple weeks, but the case was already decided.

The Judge stood up and walked over to where his robe was hanging. The lawyers rose accordingly. "So, Mr. Wasaquom, where is Grand Rapids' infamous fugitive lawyer these days? The paper says he was last seen in your office," Alkema asked.

"I don't know. I wish I did. I could use his help right about now," said Wasaquom, as he walked out of the Judge's chambers.

Neither Calley nor the Judge smiled at that.

❖ ❖ ❖

"Canada via Interlochen. We'll cross the border at the Soo. I will become a professional hockey player to earn our daily bread. You can undress me as you do so reverently, only you'll have to start with my blood-stained jersey. And at night, by candlelight, I will write new songs, poems of blood and lust." Laura was excited.

"Canada?" Mitch asked.

"I'm not going to let them send you to Jackson State Prison. I'm not waiting for you. I'm not waiting for any man, anymore. I'll stay with you just long enough to write some new material. I'm not going to wait around for the happy ending," said Laura.

"That's a heck of a note to start on," said Mitch, looking out the window of the truck at the countryside running away from them.

"As honest as a high C," Laura smiled.

They drove onto the Interlochen campus under cover of darkness. A gray-haired woman met them at the back door of a building. Laura kissed her and gave her a long hug. "This is Edith," Laura introduced her to Mitch.

The woman laughed. "What have you gotten yourself into now, Laura Knight?" the woman said playfully. She looked at Mitch. "Come along with me," the woman ordered. She led them down a short flight of stairs. Mitch could see through some curtains that this was the backstage of an auditorium.

She escorted them to a make-up room. The woman turned on the lights surrounding the mirror. "You look better than your pictures in the newspaper. Let's try this wig. No. Maybe this color. And eye-shadow will lower his cheek bones. See how that changes his look. Okay, let me trim the wig," said the woman.

Laura left the room. She walked out onto the stage and looked out at the empty rows of seats. It was dark except for red exit signs. She had performed on this stage many times. No ticket sales tonight.

She sat down at the piano and, after a moment's hesitation, played a few bars. She stopped, and started again, faintly at first, then growing in volume. She began singing. It was a throwaway cabaret song, not one of the throbbing rockers that was on the demo she had slipped to Geltman on that disastrous trip to L.A.

> *Even teachers can be naughty boys,*
> *When the student brings out naughty toys.*
> *In Berlin beneath the rumbling streets,*
> *Marlena called from her satin sheets.*
> *In smokey caves that smelled from beer,*
> *They wanted more, they didn't care.*
> *The world was crumbling, you could feel the noise,*
> *But all she showed them was her naughty toys ....*

It was a song Mitch had never heard before. "Hold still," said the old woman as she re-directed Mitch's head, which had followed his ear to the strains of Laura's sultry voice. "She was a blue angel. One of the best to come through here in my book. But promise and delivery are two different beasts of burden," said the woman.

She turned him around. "There you go." They looked in the mirror together. "You're not as good-looking as some of the others she's brought around here. But I see the innocence in your eyes," said the woman as she brushed a few more strands of Mitch's new hair.

"Were the others 'wanted' men?" Mitch asked.

"Not for long," said Edith.

The next day, John Hiatt sang, "You must go and you must ramble through every briar and bramble," on Rick's CD player as the black Tahoe crossed the Mackinaw Bridge onto the Upper Peninsula. Their Canadian border crossing went without incident. Three hours out of Mackinaw City, they stopped for gas. The fill-up of the gas-guzzling truck was painful. It left less than three hundred dollars between them. They debated using Rick's credit card, but decided it was only for emergencies. Mitch's card was absolutely out of the question. "They'll trace us within seconds of the transaction," Mitch offered. At the gas station they splurged on a dozen day-old donuts, their first food since the pre-dawn breakfast Edith had prepared for them before they left.

Laura's old mentor had given them the key to her cabin. And had promised to mail the letter to Mitch's parents from Brownsville, Texas, when she visited her brother in a couple weeks for spring vacation. They all agreed the Texas postmark would be a nice touch. The FBI had obtained a warrant for him — unlawful flight to avoid prosecution. Mitch had sought dozens of UFAPs when he was with Justice.

The old teacher's cabin was on Manitoulin Island in the Georgian Bay. It was remote enough for privacy, but not so isolated they couldn't scare up some cash jobs in one of the nearby villages like Little Current or Manitowaning. Although Laura had visited Edith here three summers in a row, she still needed Edith's map to navigate Mitch off the Trans-Canada Highway, down winding Provincial roads, and then down the last narrowly-plowed logging lane which led to the cabin.

Mitch stood on the porch, surrounded by huge piles of snow, leaning on a garden shovel. Just to be able to open the front door, he had needed to excavate the implement from a pile of half-buried tools left on the porch, and then remove several feet of fresh snow. Laura was inside lighting a fire in the stove to supplement the petite propane-fueled furnace. In what light remained, Mitch straightened his aching back and took another look at the place that had been offered as a shelter from a storm that was building back on the State side of the Lakes.

Laura came outside. "Come on," Laura grabbed his hand. She was smiling now for the first time since they saw the sobering Toronto newspaper headline back at the BP gas station. Laura unlocked the door. They stared at each other for a moment.

"Aren't you going to honor the wishes of my dearest teacher. Our new landlord?" Laura questioned. "Carry me in."

"She said only if it is true love," said Mitch, still standing toe to toe with Laura at the threshold. The chill in the evening air was invigorating.

"Is that what she said?"

"She said this was hallowed ground for lovers. Lust could only be an accidental by-product. A mere afterthought," said Mitch. He kissed her lips.

She dragged him across the threshold.

There was absolutely nothing reverent about how he removed her clothes. Nor she his.

❖ ❖ ❖

A temple was rising on the shores of Lake Michigan. As spring came to the land, legions of construction workers swarmed over the job site. Reverend VanderHook stood on the bluff where Albert used to like to sneak a puff. Gil Bates, the renowned computer wizard who was designing the Cathedral's "Carrara" Ceiling Illustrator software program (named after the Tuscan town where Michelangelo got his granite), stood next to him. They were trying to read blueprints, which were being rendered unruly by a frisky breeze blowing off the lake.

Dodging hi-lows laden with sandstone, a half-dozen men in gray suits and gray hair walked towards the edge of the bluff where VanderHook stood. The contingency of gray men was the equivalent in their popeless denomination to the College of Cardinals.

"My dear friends. Welcome to our Water Cathedral & Casino," boasted VanderHook.

"It's not our casino, Peter. That is why we came up here to talk to you," said the leader of the gray contingency. Two of these men had attended parochial grade school with Peter VanderHook in Zeeland. One of them had officiated at little Peter's funeral. They had all gone to Calvin together. They could still recall the time that Peter Sr. had come off the bench to score the winning basket against their arch-rivals, the Flying Dutchmen of Hope College.

It was not easy, what they had come to do. Most of them believed that Jerusalem should be the capital of Israel; that the Apocalypse would come before fresh clean water was depleted from the face of the earth; and all of them voted Republican. However, the recent publication of the Reverend's pamphlet, "Wholly Material Redemption," was more than they could accept.

Another among them spoke, "We know you have been under a lot of stress lately with the death of little Peter and your estrangement from Sarah, but ..."

"Gentlemen, if you have a point to make, make it quickly," the Reverend interrupted, "for I am a man on a mission."

"Peter, this thing about spiritual salvation through blackjack, it's not ..."

"What did you do to your hair?" One of the men who had gone to grade school with VanderHook interrupted his colleague. "None of us were that blond in college." All the gray men nodded in agreement.

"If this is about excommunication, let me save you all some time. I accept your pronouncement. But consider this," said VanderHook, offering each of them a silver token for the WC&C. "Truly, I say to you, it will be hard for a rich man to enter the kingdom of heaven." VanderHook paused. He gazed up at the ever-rising structure. The six gray men followed his gaze.

"The odds are that most men who enter this temple will leave less rich. But purer of heart." With that, VanderHook turned and resumed his conversation with the esteemed software architect.

Native Americans are not supposed to drink. Christian Reformers are not supposed to drink or dance.

Sarah was standing at the Sebring jukebox drinking a beer. Three plays for a buck. Her CR cohorts were crowded into a couple of booths ordering food and more pitchers. They had just come from a Paul Schrader film festival. The screenwriter, whose credits included *American Gigolo, Raging Bull, Taxi Driver,* and *The Last Temptation of Christ*, was an ex-CR from Grand Rapids and a Calvin alumnus. His films had a certain appeal to the "Right-to-Lake" anti-referendum group, which Sarah had organized. Needless to say, Sarah's favorite Schrader film was *Hardcore*: the one where George C. Scott played the rigid minister in search of a missing daughter doing whips, chains, and Great Danes in L.A. porno flicks. Sarah was scanning the jukebox selections, while eyeing the man in the ponytail sitting on the barstool.

"Sarah, you want anything?" Verbrugge called from the booth. A fellow student at Calvin and a co-founder of the Right-to-Lake movement, Sarah had met Verbrugge at a campus bible study group run by a closet liberal on the faculty. Sarah would smuggle in Thoreau in a plain brown wrapper, while Verbrugge fomented the heresy that Christ was a card-carrying Minnesota Farm Labor Democrat, not an Indiana Republican. A victim of tainted water in his youth, specifically Hepatitis A, it was Verbrugge who had wanted to print "Have You Hugged Your Septic Tank Today?" bumper stickers to raise money for the anti-referendum cause.

"No thanks," she said as she punched in the codes for some dance tunes on the jukebox. The first was a Van Halen cut, a favorite among the young Dutch infidels who had crowded into the place.

Sarah walked up to the bar. She leaned on the top of the bar a couple of stools down from the man with a ponytail.

"You're the lawyer for the Lakes, aren't you?" she said.

David Wasaquom didn't even look up at her. He was busy nursing hard liquor.

"I've seen you outside of the courthouse. I'm with the pro-Lakes group. I was there today when the Judge made the decision. Sorry about what happened," Sarah said apologetically. "But this is only the beginning. You can appeal all the way to the U.S. Supreme Court. Right?"

"They opened the floodgates today," said Wasaquom, who looked up at Sarah for the first time. He was jolted by the rush of her fresh pretty face in the dimly lit bar, which was now being accompanied by A-3 on the jukebox. It was a jolt that felt like the liquid running down the back of his throat, his first taste of firewater since he and his Marine buddies completed boot camp. "Are you old enough to drink?"

"I'm free, white, and twenty-one," Sarah blurted without a thought to the skin color of the man she had approached. It was her mantra, whenever her mother called to urge some kind of reconciliation with her father, whom she hadn't spoken to since little Peter's funeral.

Wasaquom started laughing. This had been such an absurd day. The twisted opinion by the Judge wasn't the final judicial word, but it gave so much political capital to the pro-referendum people. And then there had been the media leeches sticking to him outside the courthouse after Alkema's ruling came down — with questions, not about the environmental coalition's next legal move, but about the rumor that he was the last person to have seen the fugitive lawyer.

"I'm sorry. I didn't mean to offend you," Sarah offered.

"Do you want to dance?" Wasaquom said, without giving

the apology a thought.

"I'm Sarah VanderHook." Sarah extended her hand.

Wasaquom was on the charming side of alcohol's bell curve. He took Sarah's hand. "You say I'm the Lakes lawyer?" Wasaquom questioned the moniker which Sarah had just bestowed upon him. He led her to an open space illuminated by the yellow glow of the jukebox. He felt her back tighten as he pulled her to his strong chest. Her pelvis remained purposely unengaged, like a teenage boy awkwardly bending to avoid too much contact when kissing his grandmother.

"I'm just one of the Lakes lawyers. Their real lawyer is missing in action."

"You mean Mitch Miller. Don't you? Do you know where he is?"

"Your father is the famous minister. The darling of the west Michigan media and political point man for the referendum. Are you his secret agent?"

"I hate my father," said Sarah.

"That would be the perfect cover, wouldn't it?" said Wasaquom, as he pulled her tighter with less grace than when he first took her hand.

"Test me," Sarah challenged him, as she engaged her pelvis.

❖ ❖ ❖

On April 1, Malone announced the campaign for the referendum before a private group of supporters and select members of the press, like Mike Kopicubb from the *Manistee New
Advocate*. It was raining cats and dogs. It was no fault of Lake
Michigan; it was from a southern system that had little to do
with the lake effect. Low pressure from the Ohio Valley had
curled and stalled over most of the upper Midwest for days
and days and days. Where basements weren't damp, they were
soaked. Where rivers and streams weren't swollen, they were
flooded. Now the proponents of the referendum had the
weather as well as the federal judge behind them.

Malone pointed to a bucket that had been placed near the
podium in front of a gaggle of reporters. It was catching water
from a leak in the ceiling. "Silence, please," Malone waved to
quiet everyone.

"Drip, drip, drip." The water dove from the Peninsula Club
ceiling and splatted in the bucket. It was a wonderful touch.
Little did they know that Calley had directed this drip, with a
little plastic tubing run up into the dropped ceiling.

"I guess you folks in the Midwest can spare us Western-
ers a little water," Malone quipped. The tables of well-dressed
men, with their well-dressed wives, laughed. A radiant Tammy
beamed with delight. Cheer Cheer clapped with the others in
the audience. Even the usually dour Calley managed a broad
smile. Malone's western brand of humor was playing well.

Malone again directed silence from the audience. "The Reverend Peter VanderHook, Sr.," Malone said solemnly.

VanderHook came forward to the podium. "Let us bow our heads in prayer. We thank thee, oh Lord, for the limitless bounty of your gifts. For the endless resources of your Great Lakes ..."

Sarah was running late for class, but she and David were in the middle of something. Actually, well past the middle. They had both lost track of time. Wasaquom rolled over onto his back, his two hands firmly keeping Sarah joined to him. He to her.

She kissed him hard. Then drew her knees up along his sides to where most men his age usually had love handles. She began to rock back. And forth. Her eyes were open. Fixed on a place that she had always wanted to visit, but had never been able to book. Her eyelids were heavy, suggesting she was almost there. She tickled her own lips with her own tongue, as he cupped her breasts in one long fingered hand. His other hand was guiding her pelvic thrust, redundantly. Fast. Faster. Fastest.

She began to pray herself. "Oh God," she said quietly, almost sweetly. Thankful for her lover's endless resources. "Oh God," she said a little less quietly, a little less sweetly. "Oh my God," she screamed in rapture.

When Sarah dismounted her lover, she sank down in the sheets. She kissed Wasaquom and cuddled next to him. She could skip her first class of the day. Verbrugge would let her borrow his lecture notes.

She propped herself up on one elbow and studied his faraway look. Now it was he who was booking a trip.

For a long while she lay beside him. "My father's people are not going to win. Are they?" she finally broke the silence. "You're going to stop them with the law."

Wasaquom threw the sheets back. He put on his pants *sans* underwear.

"Don't leave. I'm not going to class," Sarah said. She followed him out of bed. She hugged him fiercely. "What's wrong?" Sarah questioned as she fondled the amulet which hung around his neck, a gull carved out of Petoskey stone. "What's got into you? In case you didn't notice, I just had an orgasm."

"If you're going to run the risk of unprotected sex, you should always have an orgasm," said Wasaquom. "That's what they taught us in the Marine Corps."

Sarah tried to brush off her lover's uncharacteristic coldness. "Is this about my father?" she asked.

"We can't blame him for everything. At least I can't. Not until I get my own lodge in order," said Wasaquom as he slipped on his shirt. He grunted and thumped his chest. "You. Yellow hair. Need to stay in school. Find nice Dutch boy to marry," he said in a self-mocking tone.

"Thanks for the public service announcement. I suppose now you're going to shed a tear for the environment?" said Sarah angrily, no longer trying to cover her hurt. "Where are you going in such a hurry?"

"Back to my people. To make war, not love. There's no in-between in this thing anymore." He finally paused to look her in the eyes. He was trying to be as mean as he could, in case he never saw her again. He did not want to leave a sweet taste in her mouth. He did not want to leave her like all those Marine wives and sweethearts had been left, who thereafter spent the rest of their youth getting over a picture of a man in dress blues resting on top of a TV console.

Maybe that was presumptuous. Maybe she didn't care as much as he did. After all, she was almost thirty years his junior, a member of a different tribe, and the daughter of a powerful chief.

"Thanks for the memories," said Sarah.

Wasaquom was already out the door.

❖ ❖ ❖

The CNN broadcast was playing in the lunchroom of the Sudbury, Ontario, Detachment of the Royal Canadian Mounted Police. This was the everyday, plainclothes version of the RCMP. There was not a brilliant-red serge jacket in sight. Two corporals were seated at the round table watching the tube. A constable, Dan Jennroyd, was standing at the counter examining a day-old Bismarck through the plastic top of the white pastry box, much like he had been recently trained to examine crime-scene evidence at the Depot Division in Regina, Saskatchewan. Jennroyd decided it had been dead for 48 hours. He put the box back down on the counter and went to pour some coffee.

"That's stale, too," said the portly corporal at the table.

Malone was on the tube, speaking outside his casino in Las Vegas, with the name clearly positioned to be visible to all viewers. Tammy was at his side. "Over two months ago, a trusted employee working at one of our projects in Michigan, a fine family man and a good Christian, was murdered in cold blood by an environmental-law terrorist — with known ties to an anti-referendum group. We are personally offering one million dollars, and an all-expenses paid vacation for two to Las Vegas, to anyone offering information leading to the arrest and conviction of Mitchell Miller for the murder of Walter Barstow."

"Constable Jennroyd," said the skinny corporal, while

keeping his eyes, like the cameraman on CNN, trained on gorgeous Tammy. "Rich Big Daddy's got quite the looker." He waved a recent fax at the young constable. "This is from Interpol. Says nothing new. But hey, this is a chance for you and your betrothed to get a free honeymoon in Las Vegas."

He handed Jennroyd the paper. "And you'd get promoted. Not that you would care with a million dollars in the bank." He paused. "American dollars," he added. "Not Canadian."

Constable Jennroyd studied the fax. "Do you think this man could be here in the province?"

The heavyset constable sighed. "Jennroyd, if you ever watched American westerns, you'd know this Miller guy is not about the province. Any decent American criminal always high-tails it to Mexico. It's a tradition with them."

"So how will I ever capture my first real criminal?" asked Jennroyd.

"Paperwork, Jennroyd. Paperwork," both corporals said in unison, as they got up from the table. All three Mounties headed out of the lunch room.

The little portable TV sat all alone in the lunchroom, talking to itself.

Mitch stepped back to the water's edge and looked at his new mistress. "She has suffered from neglect in the last few years," Laura's teacher Edith had said, with a brief choke in her throat. "Maybe you could help her."

"Thanks," Mitch had responded at the time, "but I only went sailing once in my life and nearly drowned."

That winter's day when they had fled to Canada seemed like ages ago. Little had Mitch suspected that the cottage's old sailboat would slowly capture his fancy, as he sat snowbound in the cabin and read the how-to books on sailing, and looked out the window at the shed where it was kept.

He smiled at the fruits of his labor. She was looking better every day. He had gone over every foot of her with a loving hand. He looked at his fingertips. He had no fingerprints. They had been worn down by hours of intensive sanding from bow to stern. The perfect pastime for a fugitive. The twenty-five footer was almost ready for varnish, which Laura would pick up at the hardware store in Sudbury before her first gig.

"What do you think, Hudson?" Mitch said to the bird. Hudson was a scrawny little waif when Mitch and Laura found him half-dead, entangled in some plastic six-pack wrap on one of their first explorations of the deserted beach. He was either a Herring gull, *Larus argentatus*, or a Caspian tern, *Hydroprogne caspia*. They decided to classify him as "Hudson, *Gullus Manitoulinus*," as soon as they began nursing him back to health.

"You wouldn't poop on my deck would you?" Mitch asked the gull, who was perched on the bow waiting for a piece of cracker. "It won't be long. Yeah, you're going to help me rig this schooner. We will register her under a Liberian flag like every modern-day pirate ship. Next winter we'll sail to the Caribbean. Grab us some of that change in latitude, change in attitude thing. What do you say, Hudson?" Mitch broke off a piece of cracker and fed it to the white bird with gray shoulders.

"He's never going to fly if you don't stop treating him like a pet," said Laura. She put a hot huckleberry muffin to Mitch's lips and he bit.

"Mmmmm," Mitch mumbled with a mouthful.

"So you really think you can sail that thing once you get it in the water?" Laura looked unconvinced.

❖ ❖ ❖

The incessant promotion of the Water Cathedral & Casino in the pro-referendum ads on TV and radio was having a negative effect on the last days of the dingy Beaver Sands Casino. Obviously people were saving their money for the big coming attraction. Other than a bus load of retirees and a few regulars, it was a light day. Consequently, when David Wasaquom walked in, it had an immediate chilling effect. Dealers stopped dealing. The waitresses stopped serving. All Ottawa eyes were on the brother of the boss. They all knew the Tonto of the renegades, who had splintered from the tribe because of conflicts over gambling.

A dealer here. A bouncer there. A young waitress. Wasaquom tried to engage them in direct eye contact. None of them accepted the challenge. It was one thing to call him Tonto from the anonymous safety of a crowd — and another thing to engage him one on one. Without a single challenge, he walked over to an empty blackjack table, which was roped off by thick red cords strung from heavy metal stands. Gracefully he surmounted the low hurdles. He walked to the half-moon shaped table.

The white gamblers paused, taking in the tall, dark and handsome Indian who looked ready to play his last hand. For a moment the room quieted, but for the chang and clang coming from the adjoining room filled with slots. "Who's got the cards?" David Wasaquom's voice boomed.

Jonah Wasaquom exited the counting room from where he had caught his brother's imposing entrance through the one-way mirror. At the site of their boss, a couple bouncers began to make their move towards the renegade. Jonah waved them off. He gestured to the rest of his employees to go back to work. With that the volume in the room returned to normal.

Jonah Wasaquom walked around the green crescent moon to where the dealer stands. He laid a deck of cards on the faded green felt. He sat down opposite his brother.

Brother glared at brother with looks that could kill. And after all, these were men who had killed for their respective nations.

"Do you want to play by white man's rules or red man's? Which is it today, lawyer brother? Are you fighting people of color in the jungle or in the courts? It does not matter to me. It seems that I have already won. Why don't you go home to your white squaw?" said Jonah with more than a modicum of deep-seated anger and resentment.

David let the last comment pass. Barely. "Why did you have to sell Algonquin waters to gamblers from the desert? If it had to be sold, why not to drink or grow food? Not just to make a brown place green."

"Why? You've grown addled in the brain, older brother." Jonah laughed so loud that the Ottawas, who had gone back to harvest what few buffalo grazed in the tired old casino, thought that the brothers might be reconciling. "Why do we sell to Malone? Because this is America. White man's America. Where money talks and you know what walks. Or do you think we should still live off the land like our ancestors?"

The anger grew in Jonah's voice. His copper face flushed. "Perhaps we should feast on the fish from Algonquin? Fish which pregnant women cannot eat and others must ration, because the white man has infected them with mercury, PCBs, and so many other chemicals I cannot name because I did not go to college. The reason, lawyer brother, that we are selling water to the gamblers in the desert is because they offered more than money. With our desert partners, we will raise a herd of Super Buffalo."

David Wasaquom picked up the deck of cards. He pulled the cards out of the box. "I suppose the seal has been broken on all your decks. Is that how you and Malone plan to grow your Super Buffalo?"

"If you want to play for keeps, I can get a fresh deck," said Jonah calmly.

"I am prepared to play for keeps," David replied coldly. "But will you hold my chips? First I must return to the court one more time to talk to the great white judge. Only this time I will go as a *Jessakid*, not as a lawyer."

They stared at each other, neither blinking for a long time. They both knew of the power of the Jessakid. A Jessakid was an Ottawa endowed with supernatural powers, able to summon spirits to a special lodge. There, he would hold a supernatural court of inquiry, to investigate troubles that may have befallen a village. A Jessakid sought to restore proper balance to the Ottawa world.

Both David and Jonah held sacred the powers of a Jessakid. Since childhood, they had been schooled in tales of evils cured and wrongs righted by the Jessakid's magical ceremonies.

David Wasaquom got up from the table. He reached in his pocket. "Here's my stake." Onto the green felt he tossed the broken arrow which Mitch had given him.

Jonah's cocky composure was suddenly shaken. "You do not have the power of a Jessakid."

"I will pray to Nanabozho that I do," said the older brother. David Wasaquom turned and walked past a grazing herd of old buffalo, who were headed towards the slots for slaughter.

❖ ❖ ❖

Mitch had vowed to stay awake with one of the hundreds of books that served as decoration and insulation on the walls of Edith's cottage. He picked a dog-eared paperback thriller, Elmore Leonard's *City Primeval*. Mitch lay wide-eyed in bed, reading, when he thankfully heard the Tahoe's tires crunching on the gravel in the clearing on the woods' side of the cottage.

Yellow candlelight was at its greatest power. The cottage was lit up like a shrine to fight the lonely darkness as Mitch waited for Laura to return.

All day he had been anxious, like a little boy whose parents are about to leave him with a new babysitter. "I can wait in the truck. No one will see me," Mitch had fretted as Laura loaded the truck with her Yamaha keyboard to play her first gig at a bar in Sudbury. "I'll be home before you know it. Put a candle in the window," Laura had said as she drove off.

"So you gonna be a rock 'n' roll star?" Mitch asked as Laura walked in the door.

"The crowd was more country and western than rock 'n' roll, but with a little bit of soul I brought them around. The manager only wants me to play covers, which was kind of a drag," said Laura as she took off her coat.

"You can teach them the classics," Mitch said, as Laura walked into the bathroom.

"Yeah, we worked our way through 1967 tonight." She

sounded tired, but optimistic.

"All You Need Is Love," said Mitch. That had to be the high point of 1967. As an afterthought, he rattled off another. "Happy Together, She'd Rather Be With Me." And a favorite of Giovanni's, "I Was Made To Love Her."

"Come back when you grow up," Laura's voice came from the bathroom.

Was she referring to the Stevie Wonder tune or to him? "Gimme a little sign," said Mitch, suddenly unsure of himself. Was he making it or just faking it in his new role as a non-breadwinning homebody? "There's apples, peaches, pumpkin pie in the fridge," said Mitch. "I suppose there were a lot of men lusting after you tonight?"

"Never my love. The other man's grass is always greener," said Laura, her mouth full of toothpaste. It had been a great night for her. She hadn't felt this good about herself since before she met Rick. The crowd had loved her.

"I think we're alone now. I'll pay you back with interest," came Mitch's plaintive voice from the bed. He didn't get a response. He waited. "I've been lonely too long," Mitch desperately offered, yet another classic from a year when rock was great and the seasons were four.

"Did you ever have to make up your mind?" Laura finally responded. She was brushing her hair smiling at herself, thinking, baby, you're a rich man, when she paused and added somberly, "You know Mitch, I've passed this way before."

She had too. He'd heard it through the grapevine from Edith about the earlier wanted men in her life. How can I be sure? Mitch obsessed. Finally he said what he had been thinking since he went out fishing in the bay after she left for her gig, "Your love keeps lifting me higher."

Laura now stood at the door of the bathroom. Her naked

body was backlit by the bare bulb over the sink, the only artificial light on in the cottage. She turned to give him a silhouetted side view. He could see for miles and miles and miles and miles. "Words of love won't win a girl's heart anymore," she announced. It was her best Lauren Bacall voice ever.

"Gimme, gimme some lovin'," said Mitch. He couldn't take his eyes off of her.

"Light my fire," said Laura, walking towards him.

"Don't you want somebody to love?" asked Mitch, pulling back the quilted comforter to let Laura into the warm bed.

"Sock it to me baby," said Laura.

"I'm a man," said Mitch as he went up, up, and away.

"Ain't no mountain high enough," said Laura pushing hard on Mitch.

"I second that emotion," said Mitch trying to conceal the feelings of inadequacy stirred by that comment.

"You got what it takes," said Laura with loving reassurance.

"Strawberry fields," said Mitch. "Strawberry fields forever."

David Wasaquom was dressed like an *ogema*, a respected Ottawa leader. He wore a brightly-decorated beaded robe and buckskin leggings as he walked into the main entrance of the Federal Building. He carried two jugs of water, one under each arm. Two semi-translucent containers. One looked clear blue, the other a murky brown. The blue jug contained three hundred and twenty ounces of potable drinking water. At eight ounces a day, the bare minimum for survival, that was forty days and forty nights.

Wasaquom did not anticipate his wilderness journey taking nearly that long. During the Gulf War, he had been assigned to assist naval intelligence with interrogating some Iraqi soldiers, who had been captured after one day in the desert without water. They were ready to sing "God Bless America" for a drop of water even faster than Americans at home were ready to sing that song for a drop of cheap oil.

The well-muscled ex-Marine hefted the blue jug onto the black conveyor belt that slowly took it into the security x-ray machine. It passed with flying colors. The guard screwed open the top and sniffed it.

"Exhibits for the court," said Wasaquom, thinking an explanation was owed the man in uniform.

A second amiable guard was standing behind the x-ray machine. He wore a blue blazer with a badge that read "U.S. Marshalls Service," but he worked for a private agency under contract to provide security to the federal courthouse. He was dazzled by the lawyer's native costume.

"With all that buckskin, Mr. Wasaquom, I barely recognized you." The guard had gotten familiar with Wasaquom from all the lawyer's recent court appearances. "You look like that lawyer from Wyoming, what's his name? I saw him on Larry King last week. He got that lady from the Philippines off a couple years ago. You know, the one with all those shoes they found in her closet. But I don't think he brings his own water to court."

"You're thinking of Gerry Spence," said David Wasaquom. He watched the guard stare into the monitor screen as the brown jug rode along the black conveyor belt. "He might bring his own water. He's a cowboy at heart. I'm sure he knows the value of water on the open range."

The brown jug also got by the federal inspector, after a cursory sniff. Now it was Wasaquom's turn. He managed a smile to the second guard standing behind the metal detector. He had no idea whether the machine would detect the weapon under his native garments, as the deadly weapon was fashioned from stone instead of steel. He was prepared to do what was necessary to have an *ex parte* communication with the judge. He took a deep breath and walked through the metal detector. It didn't make a peep.

"I hope Judge Alkema is thirsty," Wasaquom said to the guards as he lifted the two jugs under his powerful arms. He walked to the elevator bank.

❖ ❖ ❖

There are many prescient people in America and around the world who assume that terrorism will be the true art form of the 21st century, albeit a tragic replacement for the 19th-century French Impressionists or a 20th-century film directed by Preston Sturges. Judge Alkema certainly never thought of terrorism as an art form. However, he did think about it. After all, he was a duly appointed representative to the commission charged with improving security at federal installations in the wake of Oklahoma City. While the venerable Judge had not gotten around to the weakest link in security, the front door, he had transformed his courtroom and personal chambers into a fortress.

The door to the Judge's courtroom was already locked for the day. Wasaquom walked down the hall to the door that said "Judicial Staff & Lawyers Only." Alkema's chambers were along this hallway. Wasaquom nodded to a couple of secretaries, who were leaving for the day. They smiled in return, impressed by his handsome face and his stunning buckskin. He walked to the foyer of Alkema's chambers, and took another deep breath. As he went to ring the buzzer, the door opened. It was one of Alkema's law clerks.

"Mr. Calley?" the clerk said innocently. "Oh, excuse me. I thought it was Mr. Calley coming to see the Judge." The clerk looked him up and down, not sure what to make of his native dress or the water jugs. "Anyway, can I help you?"

"Me Jessakid. Me need pow-wow with Judge," said Wasaquom in a humorous self-deprecating manner, like a true TV Tonto. It worked.

The clerk laughed and looked at his watch. He was obviously running late for something. "Let me ask him."

Close on his heels, Wasaquom followed the clerk into the office just off the Judges's chambers. "Your Honor, David Wasaquom is here to see you," the clerk spoke into the intercom.

The Judge looked at the monitor screen in his office. He too was intrigued by what he saw. He buzzed open the steeldoor to his inner chambers.

"Sir, do you want me to stay?" the young law clerk asked.

Alkema waived him off and the clerk quickly disappeared. Like the guards and secretaries, Alkema was both fascinated by Wasaquom's outfit and curious about the water jugs under his arms. "Are you going to a tribal pow-wow? What have you got there? Nitroglycerin?" The judge laughed at his own joke.

Wasaquom heard the heavy outer door close shut. The clerk was gone. "Water," Wasaquom said. He sat down the heavy jugs. His arms and shoulders thanked him. "Water for the Jessakid." He pointed to the blue jug.

"And water for you," He pointed to the brown jug. "Plenty of water for both of us," he said as he reached under his buckskin garment and pulled out a pre-Columbian weapon.

❖ ❖ ❖

By the time summer came to the Canadian north woods, word had gotten out about the American girl who played classic rock 'n' roll and more recently, her own original material. Performing under the name Laura White, Laura and her musically challenged but good-hearted sidemen, three brothers and a cousin from a family wheat farm in Alberta, were fast becoming an event in Sudbury and much of Georgian Bay country.

A prominent Toronto businessman had already offered Laura a well-paid gig at one of his hotels. But as she told Mitch, "I think he just wants to get in my pants."

If the full parking lot — and the cars and trucks parked for blocks along Kingsway — was any indication, Laura was being modest. At least Mitch thought so, as he stood at the bar which ran the length of one wall. On any other night, this was just another two-stepping country-and-western joint. But not when Laura played.

During their walks and more recently, their daytime skinny dips, as the late spring sun began to warm the shallow waters just beyond the cottage's front porch, Laura had described every detail of her life, on the "outside," as Mitch called it. As Mitch took a swig of Molsons, he now saw one of those details. It was a white plastic jock cup and garter belt, up on the wall in back of the bar. Standard-issue hockey undergarments, these treasures were supposedly autographed by Wayne

Gretzky. No one could tell for sure because the items were fixed to a large lacquered wooden plaque, hung high over the top shelf of liquor bottles, which in turn was centered between two moose heads.

"The Great One, eh?" commented the young man standing next to Mitch.

"Yeah, Gordie Howe," said Mitch, trying to brush it off, wanting Laura to come on right now. When they debated the risks of Mitch, a fugitive, making a trip into Sudbury to see her perform, he had promised that he wouldn't talk to anyone. "Don't worry, I've never been picked up in a singles bar in my life."

"Gordie Howe?" said the young man, incredulous. "Gordie Howe is Mr. Hockey. Gretzky's The Great One. Every Canadian knows that." Mitch could see the fellow had the potential to be an aggressive forechecker. "Where are you from, anyhow?" the nosey man asked.

The crowd erupted as Laura and the boys from Alberta came up on the platform that served as a stage. "Where are you from?" the man persisted. The band launched right into a gender-changed version of "Already Gone." It was a raucous cover that suited the crowd and Mitch, who finally yelled "Philadelphia" at the man whose gaze was fixed on him. Unlike everyone else in the house, who was stuck on Laura.

Laura and the band were finishing the next to last song of their final set. Next was the number Mitch had really come for, the song which he had risked his freedom for. Mitch knew the words by heart. He should. He had written the lyrics, while Laura wrote the melody. Rogers & Hammerstein, Lennon & McCartney, Knight & Miller.

It came about the third week after they had fled to Canada, the first day that promised spring. They had opened all the windows and aired out the musty cabin. As a matter of fact, it was the same day he had started sanding the sailboat.

He had heard Laura inside, windows open, churning out a seductive melody on the little upright Steinway. The song's hook came to Mitch like a breeze off the Georgian Bay. Then they worked together on the bridge — after Laura explained what a bridge was in the structure of a song, illustrating with a few classics.

Apparently the regulars in the crowd knew the number, too. There were enthusiastic whistles and hoots, and then a chant: "Go Blue! Go Blue! Go Blue!" Mitch was impressed. These Canadians were committed fans. Inside the confines of the tavern, it was as deafening as any chant at a Michigan home game. Laura hadn't told Mitch about this, when he had made her describe the scene at the bar the first time she played their song. Maybe the crowd was just starting to get into the words and melody.

"This next song ..." Laura was seated behind her keyboards. She smiled that ship-sinking smile of hers. "This next song ..." Laura raised her hand to quiet the house, "is dedicated to the one I love."

Mitch glanced around the crowd for signs of the forechecking stranger. He was gone.

"This song is about a special feeling in our hearts about every lake any of us has ever loved. Especially if she's a great one. Certain money-grubbing gamblers in that country down there," Laura pointed with a middle finger in the theoretical direction of the States, "should leave their greasy hands off her." There were more hoots and cheers from the audience as Laura gave her back-up band a nod and they started to rock.

The song was so wondrous. A siren's summons, but it was not like the songs of Young or Lightfoot. Giovanni probably would have described it as Laura Nyro meets Elton John. To the Canadians, it apparently sounded like "Oh, Canada" with a rock 'n' roll beat, because they were all standing on their feet.

❖ ❖ ❖

As Ottawa legend goes, Nanabozho was born on Mackinac Island, just off the straits between Lakes Huron and Michigan. He was both rascal and noble hero, a prankster like Mother Nature herself. He could make rivers flow backwards — or he could be a life-giving force, as when he created the earth and all its living creatures. Nanabozho was the ultimate Jessakid.

As Wasaquom had anticipated, the FBI shut off the water and air-conditioning to the federal building. This happened within an hour of the fax that he sent out from the Judge's office to the major media. The fax explained that "a Jessakid had entered the lodge to determine what ceremony should be performed, to heal the sickness that plagues the great white Judge."

In the flickering candlelight, with half his face painted a dark indigo-blue, the Jessakid tried to work his magic — dancing, singing, chanting. The Judge sat passively. He had no choice, as he was snugly secured to his chair by the rawhide straps that Wasaquom had smuggled in along with the bow and the stone hatchet. As he danced, the medicine man waved the stone hatchet menacingly. The bow and arrow had been secured to the podium from which lawyers speaking in Alkema's courtroom made their arguments.

It was the same podium from which Wasaquom had cogently presented the white-man's environmental laws: F.Supp this and F.3rd that. From that podium, Wasaquom had made his case for saving the five great sisters, which had sustained the white man for only a few hundred years, but which had sustained the ancestors of the Ottawa, Iroquois, Huron, Potawatomi, and Ojibwa since sometime not long after the lake-gouging glaciers first retreated north more than ten thousand years before. Now, Wasaquom's argument was more pointed.

"I'm thirsty," said the Judge, staring at the silver-tipped arrowhead, which Wasaquom had fashioned from a file clip. He had removed the clip from one of the dozens of volumes of pleadings in the case of *Great Lakes Environmental Coalition v. The Malone Desert Development Corporation et al.* It was more than a symbolic gesture. The bow and arrow were spring-loaded. It wouldn't take much vibration to send the arrow through the Judge's heart, like the arrow through Barstow's. A tear-gas canister sent through a window in the Judge's chambers or his clerks' office could easily set it off.

Of course, if agents from the Bureau of Alcohol, Tobacco, and Firearms got the green light from Justice or Treasury or whichever department claimed jurisdiction, they might just blow off the lead-lined door to the courtroom or set the whole courthouse on fire. Then Wasaquom and the Judge would both be toast.

"I told you days ago. Drink your water first. Then you can have mine. I filled yours from the Grand River, just west of town," said Wasaquom. He pointed to the brown-hued jug sitting up on the bench. It wasn't really the Judge's water. But Judge Alkema had denied the injunction brought by Grand Haven (downstream) and other affected towns, to enjoin the citizens of Grand Rapids (upstream) from polluting the Grand River. Grand Rapids had refused to approve a bond issue for a new sewage and water-treatment facility, figuring it wasn't their problem what washed downriver.

"Is it because you know what's in it that you won't drink it? How many parts per million of biological waste are acceptable for human health now, Your Honor?" the Jessakid queried, as he plunged his hand into a half-eaten bag of salty snack food he had found in the drawer of one of Alkema's desks. "Want some Cheetos?" he offered the Judge.

"Savage," sneered Alkema.

The Judge had not cracked, but if he didn't drink water soon, he would be jerky. Human jerky.

❖ ❖ ❖

Rick rolled over and looked at the clock next to the bed. He had a powerful headache from last night's carousing. It was almost two in the morning. Unmoved by the ring of the phone, a woman next to him was sound asleep. "Me," Rick answered the phone.

"Ricky, Ricky, what's the good word?" said the effervescent voice on the other end of the phone.

Geltman? Couldn't be. The record executive had not returned one of Rick's calls about White Lies in the last five months. Rick had tried to see Geltman at his Hollywood office, but had been escorted out the door by security after Geltman refused to see him.

"Hey Rick, my man," said Geltman, trying to sound like a home-boy calling from the safety of his walled-in Bel-Aire estate. "Hope I didn't interrupt your getting any knock-knock," said Geltman, using the current Hollywood slang for the old in and out.

"If this is about White Lies, I'm in negotiations with Azoff's Revolution label over at Warner Brothers. We're very tight these days," said Rick, lying through his sleepy teeth. Rick had heard the legendary music-man speak at a conference in Aspen and had almost gotten to shake his hand afterwards. "After the way you dropped promotion of the album, it would take more money than you've got to sign them to another deal."

That was bullshit and Rick knew it. After his last conversation with Austin, he wasn't sure that there was a White Lies. The lead guitarist had left to manage a Little Caesar's Pizza in Madison.

"Let's not talk about ancient history. You know I wasn't calling the shots on that, the head office was," complained Geltman. "But if you read the recent *Records & Radio*, not to mention the *Journal*, you'd know I've got my own label now. I want to sign her as my first act."

"Get in line. Everyone wants her," said Rick. His card-shark Nana would be so very proud of her favorite grandson right now. He wasn't letting it show that he didn't have a clue who in the world Geltman was talking about.

"Look, Rick, paybacks are hell. You got a right to be yanked off at me. But this won't be a replay of White Lies. She's no one-hit wonder. My A&R guy thinks she's got international appeal. Name your price."

The rave review had actually come from a female, one of Geltman's domestic servants. An illegal worker from Ensenada, she had found Laura's demo tape in Geltman's holiday cocktail jacket, before she took it to the dry cleaners. Ever since the new year, she had been playing Laura's songs everyday on the home sound system as she went about her housekeeping. Only tonight had it dawned on Geltman that there was something special about the sound. He had promptly questioned her in halting Spanish, "*Quien es ... la mujer?*" or something like that. Maybe one day that conversation would be documented for posterity, like the picture of Jim Morrison in his cub-scout uniform at the Rock 'n' Roll Hall of Fame on the shores of Lake Erie.

"Geltman, you're looking at a seven-figure signing bonus. And you have to escrow money to cover the videos and promotion," said Rick. He was wide awake now. He was curious who he was negotiating this contract for, other than himself, of course.

"*Mi checkbook es su checkbook*," said Geltman. Then as a pure afterthought, he asked, "You do manage Laura. Don't you?"

Laura! My God! The name had crossed his mind more than once since he first reported his Tahoe stolen. Many times in fact. He had hoped to hear from her. He missed her. He was regressing. He did not even know the last name of this woman who was sleeping next to him in the bed right now.

"You do manage her," Geltman anxiously asked again.

"Exclusively," Rick said.

"Why don't you come out here next week? Better yet, I'll fly and pick the two of you up. Bring your own lawyer if you want. It'll be fun," said Geltman.

"Give me some more time to present it to her. She's got a lot of options." Rick could not believe what he was saying. Now he really, really missed Laura.

"Just promise me that you won't sign her to any other label until I present our package. Deal?"

"Deal," said Rick.

"We'll be in touch," said Geltman.

❖ ❖ ❖

"Shoo, Hudson. Off. I don't need another one of your commentaries on my artistic talents." Mitch was holding a wet paintbrush in one hand and an open can of polyurethane varnish in the other. He carefully flapped his forearms and elbows at the bird, who was perched directly above him on the stern.

As if imitating his master, Hudson flapped a short angle to the water's edge, a long flight for him. He strutted around, acting like he had just been insulted. "Don't take it so personal," said Mitch, as he stepped back and inspected the final polyurethane coat over the moniker on her transom. The boat was named the *Folk*.

"Hudson, you'll have to help me step the mast," said Mitch as he closed the can of sealant, which was sitting on a brown stained copy of the *Sudbury Times*.

Hudson flew up to the top of the cockpit as Mitch walked around the side of the boat towards the refinished mast, which spanned two saw-horses. The Scandinavian sailboat had a jib and a main, no spinnaker, the perfect boat for the beginning Great Lakes sailor, just what all the how-to books in Edith's library advised. Of course, Mitch should have started with a little Sunfish on a safe, flat inland lake, before setting sail on a big lake. But there had been no Sunfish in the boathouse.

Walking out of the shadows cast by the boat which sat high on its trailer, Mitch felt the hot summer sun on his face.

It felt good. He paused for a moment holding the mast with two hands. He closed his eyes, and lifted his face to its most exposed angle. "Hudson, the difference between your average fugitive and an international environmental terrorist like myself is that I still worry about the long-term harmful effects of UV rays."

The sound of a vehicle coming towards the clearing interrupted him. It couldn't be Laura. She hadn't been gone that long on her trip to town.

But it was Laura and she was in a hurry. "Mitch! Mitch!" she started yelling as soon as she opened the door. "Quick. Get inside. Someone's following me," she yelled as she ran towards him.

Mitch put the mast back on the saw-horses. Damn, he dinged the perfect refinishing sheen. He ran towards the cabin.

"Your hair. Don't forget your hair," Laura yelled just before Mitch shut the door behind him.

Jennroyd pulled up behind the black Tahoe, blocking any chance for escape. The Mountie was working alone, like his noble predecessors riding horses or mushing sled dogs a hundred years before. "Goodday, ma'am," Jennroyd asked. "Constable Jennroyd, RCMP." He flashed a badge as he walked towards her and the sailboat.

"Hi," said Laura trying to regain her composure. She didn't need the introduction. The unmarked car had cop written all over it.

"What a classic. They sure don't build them like this anymore. Did you refinish it?" said Jennroyd, as he walked over towards the boat and then circled it. He stopped at the transom. He touched the recent polyurethane finish. It was sticky. He looked up at the cottage. "I take it you don't live alone."

"With a friend," said Laura, looking up at the cottage. It

was no use lying. Laura felt butterflies in her stomach.

"Look, I'm not going to beat around the bush. There's not much time. I know who you are."

Laura felt her knees buckle.

"We understand in Ottawa tradition that a Jessakid is a kind of healer or medicine man? Does that mollify any of your tactical options?" asked the correspondent from the BBC.

The FBI spokesman frowned. The media had latched onto the Jessakid idea as soon as Wasaquom's first press release hit the major news desks and the Internet. The Indian was a kidnapper and extortionist, plain and simple. The Bureau had wanted to shut off the power with the water, when the hostage situation first developed. But they needed a phone line to negotiate with the Indian. And their line in to him was his line out to the nation and the world. "He is armed and extremely dangerous," said the Bureau's top spokesman.

"He claims to be armed with only a bow and one arrow? If that is the case, it would seem to be easy to take him out," asked a salty reporter from an arid Western state.

How stupid, thought the Bureau spokesman, who was showing the strain of the last few days. They weren't looking to replay the incident at Wounded Knee. Besides, there was a United States District Court Judge in there, not some pregnant woman and her kid being held hostage. If a federal judge got killed, it could mean years of retribution by federal judges against FBI agents, who had to beg for search warrants and wire taps.

Mike Kopicubb also thought the question was stupid. The aspiring reporter from Manistee had seen his stock rise when he filed the first "Murder in Manistee" story. Now, he was

214

looking for a fresh angle to distinguish himself from the rest of the pack. The Indian's bribery accusations against MDDC and Calley were being run down by the guys and gals with the bigger budgets in the national media. So far there was nothing to suggest a pay-off to the Judge.

With typical brazen confidence, Calley had appeared in person behind the barricades set up around the federal courthouse on the second day of the stand-off. Striking a photogenic posture, just out of bow and arrow range, he had made a public statement emphatically denying any improprieties. Calley said this was simply a case of a "poor loser, who could not live by the rules of a civilized society." He likened the Indian to the Unabomber, and offered to open the accounting books of HD&H to any audit.

Kopicubb shouldered his way out of the crowd of reporters and photographers surrounding the FBI spokesman. How about a story on former U.S. Senator Vandenberg after whom they named the plaza where the SWAT teams were bivouacked? Kopicubb took a gulp of bottled water and wiped his brow. He could try to make some sort of link between the far-sighted legislator, who had led his isolationist Republican colleagues kicking and screaming to ratify the Marshall Plan after WWII, and the Indian medicine man now holding the federal judge hostage, claiming "he sold the Great Lakes for a few pieces of silver." But that was kind of a stretch. And it also wasn't sexy.

Kopicubb needed sexy, like that young blond-haired woman over there. The one who had been standing vigil, night and day, since the hostage crisis began. Why not do a "person on the street" piece? Who knows? Maybe he would get lucky.

Stepping over the television cables strewn all over Michigan Street, leading to a cluster of trailers and satellite dishes,

Kopicubb drifted away from the FBI briefing and headed towards the corner of Michigan and Ottawa, the closest vantage point for civilian non-combatants.

"I know who you are." Jennroyd repeated, as Laura felt her knees grow weak. Jennroyd looked like he wasn't enjoying this any more than she was. But like the Mountie that he was, he plunged ahead bravely.

"By now, everyone in Ontario knows who you are," Jennroyd looked squarely into her big blue eyes. "I'm getting married this Saturday. The maid of honor was suppose to sing at our wedding. But she's got a terrible case of laryngitis. I was wondering ..." Jennroyd looked down, kicking the stony dirt.

"Look, my fiance is freaking out. There's a hundred and twenty people coming. All her French relatives from Quebec City. It's not an easy situation under the best of circumstances. I know it's a lot to ask of a big star like you."

Laura smiled, not at the accolade, but in relief. The Mountie was not going to haul Mitch off in leg-irons. "I'd be honored to sing at your wedding."

"Great. Fantastic," Jennroyd bubbled. "We're having a rehearsal tomorrow night at the Sacred Heart of the Holy Immaculate Virgin in Sudbury. I'm sure you're expensive. I'll pay whatever it takes." Jennroyd started writing on one of his investigative pocket-size spiral notebooks.

"Ma'am, I can't tell you what this means to me. I'll pick you up myself. About five-thirty, if that's okay. Here's the details." He tore off the page and handed it to her. "We'll see you tomorrow evening. Thanks." He backed away to his car bowing, as if leaving the court of some queen who once ruled his vast country.

Squinting through the slats of one of the cottage's wooden window shudders, Mitch had a good view of all this. There was grave concern on his face as the Mountie drove away.

❖ ❖ ❖

"Laura, he's the same guy who questioned me at the bar. Don't you see? This is a set-up. He came in here to scope it out. To see how many of us there are. To find out if we're armed." Mitch was fuming. It was their first fight and it was not about a trivial matter.

"And then there's this." Mitch waved the page which Jennroyd had ripped out of his notebook. "Come on. 'We've Only Just Begun'? Nobody sings that sappy song at weddings anymore. It's a set-up, I tell you."

"You've got a lot of nerve for someone who had a 1910 Fruitgum Company album in that crate of yours," snapped Laura.

"It was Giovanni's. His sister sent it to him in Vietnam," said Mitch.

"Giovanni this. Giovanni that. Giovanni's just some sort of excuse for your lack of taste." Laura's eyes were getting bluer. "I found that *Playboy* in your drawer. You know it's men like you who killed Karen Carpenter. It's all about food and silicone."

"Food and silicone? Laura, please. This is no time for radical feminist politics. We got to get out of this place. Sooner or later there'll be a regiment of Royal Canadians coming back down that road."

"Maybe the Mounties won't turn you back over to the States. You've read the editorials up here. The Canadians are pissed off about selling Great Lakes water to the West," said Laura.

"There's a big difference between being pissed off and being up in arms. We blow polluted smoke and acid rain in their face all the time. They never do anything about it. Other than on an ice rink, the last time the Canadians beat us physically was the Aroostook War in 1800 and something. The Canadians in Ottawa will argue among themselves in French or English for awhile. Then they'll cut a deal with the States for a share of the money. That will be the end of it."

Laura knew that Mitch was probably right. But she hated to leave the verdant woods and the land of sky-blue waters, which had renewed her energy and her music. "There's nowhere to run."

"We'll sail away." Mitch looked at the boat. "To ... to ..." He was questioning the *Jeopardy* answer: "What country harbors pro-environmental terrorists?" Not Libya. And probably not Cuba, if Fidel was at all like his former patrons, who had created all that toxic tundra in Russia.

"We'll figure it out when we get to Nova Scotia."

"Do you really believe you can sail that thing?" Laura was softening.

"I read all of the books about sailing in the cottage," said Mitch.

Laura scrunched up her pretty nose. "Okay. But I've got to record something before we go."

The time and temperature sign on the Old Kent Bank in Grand Rapids read a sticky 86 degrees.

Inside the courthouse, the temperature was well into the triple digits. The FBI had turned up the heat, literally. In control of the environmental controls, they had shut off the air-conditioning and cranked up the thermostat. Alkema was sweating like a pig, which was a good sign for him. Humans don't sweat in terminal stages of dehydration.

In contrast, the Jessakid was freezing. He had chills from the fever that had overcome his body. At times, it caused him to shake uncontrollably.

Alkema had finally confessed to accepting a small cash payment in return for his ruling in favor of the pipeline plan. But it all seemed forced. For one thing, Wasaquom knew he was lying about the amount. No federal judge would risk a distinguished career for ten thousand dollars. Malone could afford to pay a hundred times that, and it would still be a bargain.

Wasaquom also knew that any confession by Alkema would be legally void by reason of extortion and whatever else the FBI charged him with. If he lived to be charged for this kidnapping. Wasaquom needed to get some corroborating details of the pay-off scheme, so that somebody could uncover and prove the whole truth.

"Your Honor, may I have permission to address you from

counsel table?" The Indian's teeth were chattering.

"Feel free," said Alkema with great relief. His Honor had reluctantly resumed the bench after their customary noon recess to allow the Judge to use the private toilet in his chambers. Alkema was no longer wearing his robe. He had been permitted to strip to his waist, which was quite gross, but then there was no reason to keep up appearances.

Wasaquom walked to the counsel table nearest the jury box, where the party with the burden of proof always sits. He was dizzy. He sat down. The courtroom was starting to spin, much like it had when Judge Alkema had handed down his opinion that an environmental impact statement was not required for the sale and transportation of Great Lakes water to Nevada.

Wasaquom grabbed for the wastebasket and vomited. That brought him some temporary relief. At least the room stopped spinning. "That's what I get for drinking your water," said the Native American. "Speaking of desecration and destruction of downriver water flow, did you know that the Gulf of California used to be inhabited by wonderful game birds and jaguars as recently as the 1920s? I came across that when I was researching the law for the injunction." He added, "Back when I still thought the white-man's law mattered."

Alkema ignored the comments. He did not feel well himself. However, it was more from hunger than anything else. Three nights ago, the Cheetos had been his dinner. The Judge was living off the rolls of fat around his ample waist. He had never actually been forced to drink from the brown jug. When he had gotten so parched, when his mouth felt like dried muslin cloth, when his lips were cracked and bleeding, when he had begged for his first sip from the brown water — Wasaquom had mercifully held a glass of the cool clear water to his lips.

It was the Indian and only the Indian who had drunk from the dirty brown jug. It was a generous act of penance by the Jessakid for the environmental sins of the judge. That was about forty-eight hours ago. Enough time for Wasaquom to develop an elevated white-blood-cell count and a lot of exotic stuff festering inside him.

"So much for the Colorado River and the Gulf of California. That was fornicated a long time ago. Let's stick with the Great Lakes," said Wasaquom. He was obviously drunk with fever and holding on by a thread. "Who was the enemy? Who betrayed our sister Lakes? Who was the traitor who laid before your greedy hands the luscious fox and beaver pelts?"

Alkema wondered how the wily Indian knew it was not merely money, but sex, which had turned the tide in favor of Malone's cause.

Wasaquom walked to the podium where the cocked arrow was mounted. He tried to steady himself by holding onto the podium, which made the bow and arrow tremble menacingly. Even in his delirium, Wasaquom did not want to kill Alkema, especially not now. He was so close to exorcising the truth out of the forked tongue. He reached for the bow and arrow. His hand shook terribly. Alkema started to sweat now, from fear, not fever.

"Stop. Away from that podium. Please," the Judge begged and then blurted, "It was one of Calley's lawyers."

"Which one?"

"The one who used to carry his briefcase to court," said the Judge. "O'Leary. At least, he made the introductions."

"Where?" asked Wasaquom. The shakes were coming on again. He was not listening closely as a good cross-examiner should, or he would have followed up on the word "introductions" instead of adhering so rigidly to his prepared cross. A thorough lawyer should always follow up on such answers.

"At the Hilton," said the Judge.

"The Hilton on 28th Street," said Wasaquom.

"No. At O'Hare," said the Judge.

"O'Hare? That was a long way to go for it," remarked Wasaquom, who still assumed they were talking money.

"I didn't want my wife to find out," said the Judge with bowed head.

Oblivious in his fever, Wasaquom nevertheless managed to muster the perfect follow-up question. "Did you stash it all under a mattress, Your Honor?" His voice reeking with contempt of court, he added, "Or wouldn't it fit?"

The Judge could no longer tolerate the humiliation and sarcasm. "I stashed it on top of the mattress," Alkema screamed at the lawyer. "Twelve times in twelve trips." He paused. His confessional rage subsided. He turned pensive.

"There was this nubile redhead. The girl's from New York City. She calls herself a human trampoline. She wants to be a cheerleader for the Dallas Cowboys. But she has a record of drug arrests. I told her I could help her. As a judge on senior status, I get to visit the Northern District of Texas often, to handle an overflow of criminal drug cases. I told her I could fix everything for her."

The Judge was starting to cry big salty tears. "Please just let me go. I'll sign whatever you want. Please, please, I can't take anymore of this," Alkema begged. He grabbed for the Cheetos bag. It was empty.

❖ ❖ ❖

"We'll take the Northwest Passage." Mitch had charted a roundabout course, first west along the northern shore of Manitoulin Island and then out to Huron via Cockburn Island. It appeared to offer an easier route for a beginner than sailing east around Cape Smith and then south past Fitzwilliam Island through the Main Channel to Lake Huron.

For one thing, there was more open water. The rocky islands and coves around Little Current were more than he thought he wanted to navigate with the *Folk*, which was a fully ballasted boat. More importantly, if the Mounties were coming they would expect him to sail or drive out that way, because it was the shorter route to Lake Erie, the Atlantic and freedom, by at least a day.

As they sailed towards the sunset, Hudson was at the bow with his wings extended and lifted by the wind. It appeared to be an exhilarating simulation of flight for the physically challenged bird.

"Hush, listen very carefully," Laura whispered into Mitch's ear as the brilliant orange-red circle of a sun made a tangent with the western horizon of the Georgian Bay waters. She was cuddled next to him in the cockpit. "Do you hear it sizzle?" she asked.

"I'm trying not to," said Mitch dutifully. His right hand was on the tiller. His eyes were on the "road" ahead.

Laura had slipped her hand down under his poplin pants.

"Up North, it's the only way to celebrate the summer solstice," she assured him. Laura was kissing the helmsman's neck and grabbing his tiller. Mitch could feel the swell. The blue-eyed beauty was obviously bent on steering her own course. He kissed her mouth full and hard. Laura's lips naturally parted and their tongues tangled. Mitch let his firm grip on reality slip away. The boat lurched to the leeward. Hudson protested loudly.

Mitch quickly retrieved the tiller, which was wagging like the tail of a very happy hound. "It would probably be better if I lashed it to the stanchions," Mitch offered as he grabbed some rope on deck.

"Anyway you want it, as long as it's now," said Laura as she kicked her shorts and panties down the hatch.

"Should I go below?" Mitch questioned as soon as he had re-secured their current course.

"It's not necessary. If you want to. You know I always like it, when you do," said Laura as she smiled seductively and tugged at Mitch's stubborn belt buckle.

The afterglow of the summer sunset lingered until almost eleven. The afterglow of their boat-rocking love-making lingered into the star-filled night. After midnight, Laura served tuna fish sandwiches, pickles, chips, and a peach cobbler that Mitch had made for what turned out to be their last supper at the cottage. The wind and water had worked up the sailors' appetites more than any white wine ever could, though they happened to have that, too, a half-full bottle of Pinot Grigio, which the First Mate had salvaged when she cleaned out the cottage refrigerator in their hurried departure.

They passed the green bottle between themselves. It was

fine seafood dining, like dinner at the old Joe Muir's Restaurant in downtown Detroit, only without the oyster crackers and the starched white tablecloth. Hudson got a bellyful, too, of everything but the pickles and wine.

Her windbreaker zipped against the wind, Laura laid down in the cockpit across from Mitch. It was cramped, but cozy. Cozy felt good. They were the only night-time travelers in the North Channel. "Why don't you get one of the sleeping bags and get comfortable," Mitch suggested. "You should get some sleep. You're going to be the duty officer at three bells," Mitch looked at his watch on his free hand and yawned.

Laura was staring upwards at a thousand stars in the sky, working on a calculation. "If it's infinite or close to it, there has to be intelligent life out there. And if Jesus is Lord, like the billboards say, does he travel from planet to planet doing his passion play?"

Mitch followed her heavenly gaze. So far away from any city of size, there was no distortion from any artificial light. The stars were not bashful. Some were downright brazen.

"One time Rick and I saw a guy at a comedy club. His routine was about the silliness of all the competing religions in the world. How it proves God has a sense of humor. His entertainment is watching all of us argue over whose God is true. It was pretty hysterical. We laughed until we cried. Like that time with you and me at Steketee's."

Laura laughed at her memory of Mitch with floppy silky apparel dangling over his ears. "God is love and laughter. And cool, clear water," Laura said, sitting up and reaching over the side of the boat. Her hand was carving a wake in the water. "No matter what happens to us, remember that, Mitch."

"We'll always have Sudbury, sweetheart," Mitch replied gallantly.

❖ ❖ ❖

Jennroyd had found it odd that the Tahoe was parked in the drive, until he saw that the vintage sailboat was gone. When he pushed open the unlocked door, the first thing he spotted in the cottage was the cassette tape. It was on the oval oaken kitchen table with a note that read, "Best wishes for a long and happy life together."

He could see that there had been two people living in the cottage and that they had left in a hurry. But it was not until he found the newspaper clippings stuffed in the bookshelf in the sailing section that it dawned on him.

"It's her voice," said Jennroyd, smiling broadly as the wedding party listened to "We've Only Just Begun" at the rehearsal.

"I know it's her voice. Everyone about these parts knows her voice. But who wants a tape recording for their wedding? I wanted her live," the future Mrs. Jennroyd started crying. "I wanted it to be special."

"It will be special, darling," said the bride's mother, in Quebecois French.

And so it was special, beyond belief. On Saturday morning, the sun was out and the sky was blue. The humid heat that was choking the Upper Midwest translated sunny and dry in the Georgian Bay region. It was a great day for a white wedding.

Strains of the "Wedding March" announced the opening

of the front doors to the church. Mr. and Mrs. Dan Jennroyd emerged to a snowstorm of rice and the rest of the world. The bride looked beautiful, as do all brides. As for the young Constable, he looked dashing in the red serge of the Royal Canadian Mounted Police, now worn only for special occasions. The bride and groom stopped at the top of the church steps to waive at the cheering throng of well-wishers.

"We can't collect the reward if they catch that Miller guy?" the new wife whispered to her husband.

"The men joke about it, but in fact, members of law enforcement can not collect rewards. Besides, I didn't have a clue she was his girlfriend," Jennroyd whispered back, while proudly waving to his comrades in bright red.

"That's fine, dear. I was just curious," said the new Mrs. Jennroyd as she smiled and waved with renewed vigor to her friends and family.

After the cake cutting, bouquet and garter tossing, and shortly before leaving on his honeymoon, Constable Daniel Jennroyd promptly reported his suspicions about the wedding singer and her companion to the Staff Sergeant, who was the NCO in charge of the Sudbury Detachment.

The wedding reception was still in full swing and the Staff Sergeant was in the midst of debating the virtue of Irish Catholic whiskey over Irish Protestant whiskey with other colleagues and guests. Upon receiving the report from Jennroyd, the sergeant, an avid salmon fisherman, spontaneously proposed a toast, "To the Great Lakes! May they always separate us from the Yankee Hun."

After helping with clean-up duties, as they had promised, the Sudbury Detachment of the RCMP fully intended to begin their hot pursuit of Mitch Miller.

Thunder and lightning at the same time. That's the name the Ottawa would have given her. Rick stepped back and admired her fine lines. She was wrapped in silver and turquoise finery, covering a rich, creamy-white body. She was of soft-tail heritage. There was a long wait for these limited edition Harley Davidson's, but his had finally been delivered.

It was Harley weather. Rick exited off U.S. 131 at Market. He headed up Grandville towards the old brick Anheuser-Busch warehouse where they used to bring in the beer on ice-and-sawdust refrigerated railroad cars. It was a short cut to downtown. He wanted to avoid the worst of the traffic jams caused by that Indian hostage thing.

He had drained his bank account to make the payment, but now he would have a big contract with Geltman. It was practically a done deal. He felt flush.

All he had to do was to find Laura.

There was a red sky in the morning. As magnificent as it was foreboding, Laura barely caught a glimpse of it. How could she? She was too busy sailing west. Of course, that was not their plan. Their plan was margaritas in the Caribbean. But the stubborn Scandinavian boat just wouldn't go that way.

"Close reach," "broad reach," "long fetch," "short fetch," were just a few of the nautical terms Mitch had shared with Laura as he poured over the sailing books in Edith's cottage during the last few months. However, "getting into irons" or simply "in irons" was something he'd purposely failed to mention. It was understandable. For Mitch the term, which every sailor knows and the novice sailor experiences often, had dire connotations on land as well as sea.

Yet when Laura slipped the sailboat into Lake Huron on the course set by Mitch and tried to steer to the south-south-east, "in irons" was precisely what she got. She was headed into the wind, unable to come about or tack either way.

Mitch probably hadn't been down sleeping in the cabin for more than half an hour. As the mainsail flogged in the beating headwind, Laura had debated whether to yell for him. She knew he needed sleep. Besides, she was determined to sail the boat.

For sometime the sailboat bobbed in the heavy Huron water, until degree by imperceptible degree, it was turned about by a force of nature beyond Laura's control.

And Laura, other than the fact she was bearing due west, was having a ripping good time. The *Folk* was doing four knots, a fine clip for such a craft. Under the sail and boom, Laura could see the thick tree-green of Drummond Island to the north off the starboard side.

What she didn't see until it was too late was the freighter bound for Duluth coming up from her port side. The freighter was headed towards De Tour Village on the eastern tip of the U.P., then north along the eastern shore of Neebish Island, the up-bound channel to the Soo Locks. It was a dangerous un-marked crossing.

The sound of the freighter's fog horn was a violent intru-sion into Laura's contemplation of the great lake and her un-certain future. Down in his bunk, it startled Mitch from troubled sleep, a nagging dream in which he was desperately trying to get away from bad guys, but kept ending up in the same place. Mitch ran up on deck in time to read the name, the *Mighty Quinn*, on the starboard bow of the rust-red ship bearing down on them. There wasn't anything Mitch could do but hope that wind prevailed over fossil fuel.

It was a near miss — by a slip knot. As the big ship passed to the sailboat's stern, it temporarily stole the *Folk*'s wind. The sailboat rocked in the freighter's wake. The fetchless *Folk* stalled and listed. A wash of waves rushed over the deck.

"Where's Hudson?" Laura screamed, fearing "bird over-board." Sure enough, Hudson was thrashing in the waves about ten yards off the port side. Without a thought, Mitch dove into the water and swam to Hudson, and swam back to the *Folk* just in the nick of time as the mainsail billowed again.

Later that morning, Laura squinted and aimed. "Hold it. Smile, Hudson. Perfect," said Laura from the cockpit, hold-ing the tiller in one hand and the camera in the other. She snapped a picture of Mitch, standing above her on deck, with Hudson perched on his shoulder.

Somehow, between last night and this morning, they had charted a new course. The old boat had won them over.

❖ ❖ ❖

"All the News That's Fit to Print" and "All the News That Fits." Never knowing when the government might cut off his lines of communication, Wasaquom routinely faxed his communiques to those two major dailies. This would be his final, but triumphant message to the world. He fed the Judge's signed confession into the fax machine. His hands were shaking from the chills of his fever.

As he heard the bird-like tweet inside the fax machine, he pushed the send button and collapsed on the floor of the Judge's office.

The authorities in the makeshift command post outside the federal building had finally decided it was time to cut off the Indian terrorist. They were preparing to storm the Judge's office. Right at the moment, however, they had their hands full. With water hoses, the police were preparing to put down a full-scale riot that was being led by a young blond-haired woman.

Actually, it was Sarah's mother who had fomented the riot. Not until the Associated Press picked up Mike Kopicubb's story about "The Minister's Daughter and the Jessakid" did Mrs. VanderHook have any idea that Sarah had been carried off and ravaged by a savage.

That struck a responsive chord deep in her soul. For it had come to pass that as a teenager, in spite of the historic Christian Reformed prohibition against going to "shows," Ruth had crept out to see a movie, *The Searchers*, which she still vividly recalled. Consequently, Ruth VanderHook demanded, yes demanded, that her husband make like The Duke and bring their daughter back to the fold.

The pushing and posturing was getting extreme as fire trucks began to move in. Out-numbered, but not out-spirited, Verbrugge was yelling at anti-Lakers that, "Jesus was a Green, for Christ sake!" And he was citing scripture to support his position, which infuriated the anti-Lakers. "In the meadows of green grass, He lets me lie. To the waters of repose, He leads me. There He revives my soul ...." Verbrugge was arguing that the "meadows" and the "there" in the original Hebrew version of the 23rd Psalm clearly referred to the Great Lakes region.

The confrontation between the pro-Lakers and the anti-Lakers was most heated at the corner of Michigan and Ottawa, where Reverend VanderHook confronted his youngest daughter. "You're acting like a teeny-bopper runaway child. What are these, Indian braids?" Reverend VanderHook contemptuously tugged at Sarah's braided blond hair, which fell below the brilliant beaded headband she was wearing.

"Don't ever touch me again. You baby killer," said Sarah simultaneously slapping his hand away from her hair. Neither one of them paid any attention to the U.S. Marshalls' warning for the crowd to "clear the streets," nor the fact that the Reverend's assault on his daughter had sparked a swinging free-for-all around them.

The Rev was stunned by her words. Sarah gave him no chance to recover. "You killed my baby brother with hypocrisy and fear. When your money-changing friends get done draining our Lakes so you can have your holy tabernacle, there'll be a lot more dying around here."

Sarah was just warming up, when a twenty-foot wall of water hit them like a ton of lead. The Reverend got knocked to the ground. Sarah got wet, but her father's body had shielded her from a direct hit. A phalanx of a hundred helmeted police officers led by German Shepherds charged east down Michigan towards the crowd.

Emergency rescue vehicles followed the police with sirens blaring. Some of the crowd ran north up the interstate exit, which quickly caused a multi-car pile-up as motorists tried to avoid them. The core of the crowd, most of whom were still on the fence and neither pro- nor anti-anything, tried to escape through the battery of media trailers to the south towards Caulder Plaza, but people began tripping on cables and were trampled.

A police officer fired his tear-gas. The canister landed near Sarah. The bitter smoky gas made her sick to her stomach, like she had been feeling every morning for the last month.

In the chaos and confusion, Sarah hopped on the back of a rescue vehicle as it temporarily slowed, while guards inside the besieged cordoned area around the courthouse temporarily moved aside one of the barricades. Sarah held onto a long stainless steel handle. The acrid smoke which was burning her eyes was also providing her cover.

She peered around the corner of the boxy vehicle. Further down the hill, she could see uniformed personnel carrying out bodies on two canvas combat stretchers from the courthouse. Sarah's eyes filled with another kind of tears. She jumped off the vehicle and ran. She was at the side of the dying U.S. Marine before anyone could stop her.

"Ogema," she cried, as a couple of Marshalls restrained her, but respectfully let her say goodbye. She kissed his forehead. Wasaquom did not open his eyes. He was paddling a canoe to some place along a golden coast where music was playing.

"I love you, Ogema. I will always love you," she said, as the EMTs closed the door to the back of the wagon and headed back up their short, but riotous route to Mercy Hospital at the top of Old Michigan Street hill.

Only a few feet away, paramedics were transferring Judge Alkema to a stretcher from the rescue unit. Sarah was overcome by grief. However, she did hear the honorable judge say to his wife in a weak, but earnest voice, "He tortured me, dear. He was a wild animal."

It appeared that all the Judge needed was a good spin doctor and he would be just fine.

The *Folk* continued to sail west towards a configuration of water and land which the first Americans called Michilimackinac, "Land of the Great Turtle." It was the only place where any of the great sisters went head to head. It is here that undercurrents of sibling rivalry between Huron and Michigan, dating back to the dawn of the post-glacial age when they both were barely potty trained, frequently erupted into violent acts of nature.

Mitch and Laura could see Fort Mackinac, high atop Mackinac Island, built a couple centuries before to protect the vital trade routes first developed in this region by the French and Indians. Almost three hundred years later, there was still trade to protect. The specialties of the region now were domestic fudge, sweet enough to finally cure anyone's diabetes, and Indian-looking trinkets made by authentic Asians from the Pacific Rim, whose pre-historic ancestors may well have contributed to the Native American gene pool.

As they passed under full sail, the guns of the island fortress boomed and recoiled. The fugitive sailors saw the puffs of white smoke. Less than a mile off the southern side of the island, their boat was easily within range, but no cannonball hit their deck. It was only a mock salute to the Fudgies, as the tourists, the Chamber of Commerce's most important dignitaries, were affectionately known. Yet another of the stocky white boats, which continually ferried tourists from Mackinaw City to the carless island in summer and early fall, headed out from the island's harbor.

"Did they get all the building material over there by boat?" asked Laura, feeling a little bit like a tourist herself as the Grand Hotel came clearly into view.

"Boat, barge, and the easy way. By horse," said Mitch, who would never forget the stories told as the horse-drawn carriage clopped around the island the first time his parents brought him to this mystical place. "Before the globe got hot, these lakes used to freeze over every winter. They brought a lot of building supplies over on the ice.

Mitch pointed ahead to the tip of the lower peninsula, about five miles away to the south/southwest. "I don't know if you can see the other fort, Fort Michilimackinac, over there under the Bridge. A group of Ottawas took that over in 1763 by cheating at a ball game. The Indians were playing a lacrosse match outside the fort, when one of them 'accidentally' threw the ball over the wall into the fort. When the guards opened the gates to let them retrieve their ball, the Indians grabbed their weapons — hidden under the robes of their women — and stormed the fort. The natives held the place for almost a year, until Chief Pontiac's alliance of eastern tribes was defeated." The thought of David Wasaquom's ancestors made Mitch wonder what his former landlord was up to.

"That wooden fort on the mainland was torn down when the British moved the post out to the island for better security. The timbers that were salvaged were hauled across by horse and sled on the ice."

"Look!" Laura interrupted her favorite mariner's ancient history lesson. Bearing down on them from the east from neighboring Bois Blanc Island was a freshwater albatross with a big orange stripe. It was a U.S. Coast Guard Cutter out of Cheboygan. Probably tipped off by the crew of the *Mighty Quinn* after the near-miss.

Mitch looked at the radar reflector, which he had hoisted up the halyard after his frustrating fight with Laura about why the boat was sailing towards the Port of Gary, Indiana, instead of the harbor of Gustavia, St. Barts, or any other Caribbean refuge. The aluminum sphere was supposed to somehow deflect radar.

Mitch had stumbled across the silvery ball along with a lot of other dusty sailing gear the first day he opened the cobweb-laced boathouse and found the *Folk*. For a long time, until he saw a sketch in the yellowed pages of the sailing log, Mitch had assumed it was some kind of giant tree ornament for a Canadian Christmas. The *Folk* did not have much of a "free board" profile for radar to pick up anyway, and the bigger waves they were sailing through would present a confusing image. That could give them a decent chance to avoid radar detection. But now they were in binocular range.

"We would never have made it through the St. Lawrence anyway," said Laura, as both of them desperately labored to grab a little more wind for their losing race with the steely cutter.

❖ ❖ ❖

They had left the parsonage. Verbrugge was driving his old Volkswagen bug. Sarah was sitting on the passenger side. Verbrugge finally broke the respectful silence with a profound question.

"Well?"

"I told my parents that I'm going to have an abortion, because at the rate we're going, there won't be enough clean water tomorrow for babies born today," said Sarah. For a change she was not defiant, but somber.

"What did he say?" Verbrugge asked warily.

"He preached his usual. Apocalypse now," answered Sarah.

"Damn the sperm! Xeriscape now! I have not yet begun to fight for clean water," said Verbrugge in his best John Paul Jones voice. "We'll waste those water suckers so you don't have to make that choice."

"Thanks," Sarah managed a smile at her loyal friend.

The Bug pulled up in front of the Oplendyke Funeral Home. It was directly across the street from the Klemtowski Mortuary. Other than the occasional case of intermarriage, as evidenced by a "Van This" or a "Dyke That" sprinkled among the city's westside Catholic parishes, the Dutch and the Eastern Europeans didn't desire to mingle in the next world either. The hospital administrator, dealing with dozens of bloodied and battered patients sent by the police riot to his hospital, had been relieved by Sarah's willingness to be take care of the funeral arrangements.

Her "husband's" body had been sent to the funeral home owned by one of the prominent families in her father's congregation. The Oplendyke's had mixed emotions about the circumstances. But a call to the Reverend had assured them that it was best to handle it all as quickly and quietly as possible.

John Oplendyke, grandson of the founder of this very staid establishment, and his son John Jr. somberly greeted Sarah and Verbrugge at the door.

"Sarah," John Sr. spoke with a pinch of sincerity. "We are so grieved by your loss. Our Lord truly works in mysterious ways ...."

"Cool it with the Lord stuff. I want his body," said Sarah. "We're going to take him with us. He deserves a proper Ottawa burial."

Verbrugge looked almost as startled as the starchy Oplendykes. Verbrugge had not realized exactly what Sarah had in mind, when she adamantly insisted that she needed to go to the funeral home to make other arrangements.

"It's going to be kind of tight in the Volkswagen, Sarah, unless we can flex him like Gumby," said Verbrugge, who was thinking *rigor mortis*.

"That's not legal," said John Jr. with righteous indignation. "You can't walk out with a body. Besides, we're getting ready to embalm."

John Sr. frowned at his indelicate son, who was more skilled working in the back room with the dead than with the living in the front. "Dear Sarah, I know this is terribly upsetting for ..."

At the sound of the blood-curdling scream, all four of

them looked in the direction of one of the unmarked doors towards the back of the old Victorian funeral parlor. At first they thought it was just one screamer. Then they distinguished the sound of a second screamer, this one male. The screamers were going at it like dueling banjos.

The door to the back room burst open. There was a temporary jam of shoulders as the two plucky embalmers lodged like stooges in the doorway. Once freed, they ran directly to John Sr. to give witness. Each one wanted so desperately to be the first to report the resurrection — especially John Sr.'s daughter, Carol, who was a summer intern majoring in premortuary science at Ferris State. It would be her first and last stiff. Already she was planning her transfer to another field of study, any other field.

Understandably, the best vocals that her equally young assistant, a young man, could muster under these circumstances was a lyricless croak from an extremely dry throat. They both failed completely in their attempts to expressly describe how the Indian in the cupboard had just opened his eyes and raised his head.

However, Carol could have won a nomination in the new Grammy category for "Best Young Female Vocalist Impression of Madeleine Kahn doing Beverly Sills in a Mel Brooks' Horror Flick."

❖ ❖ ❖

"Tammy here is modeling a lovely little outfit she had specially made in Milan just for the opening festivities on Saturday," Malone jubilantly proclaimed into the speaker phone from his Las Vegas office. Tammy pirouetted her behind to the smiling approval of her husband. "And how're things doin' on your end?" asked Malone.

"Among those registered voters most likely to vote, our latest polling data says we're ahead two to one. Looks like the Reverend will deliver the voters for the referendum. Although we need to watch him. He's been a little distracted lately," said Calley on his speakerphone in his Grand Rapids law office. The chief of MDDC security, Smith, stood at attention next to Calley's desk.

"How's that?" asked Malone, curious, for he had read the Reverend's pamphlet on "Wholly Material Redemption" and found it totally to his liking.

"The architect called to ask me about some change orders VanderHook was insisting on. Of course, I told him no. We are barely going to get it finished as is. But we are going to make it."

"And the fugitive lawyer?" Malone asked.

"Our men lost him in the fog. But don't worry, sir. We will intercept and debrief him before the Coast Guard," Smith confidently volunteered.

"I got your e-mail this morning about Ted Moore. I'm

glad the young fellow has decided to do the right thing," said Malone.

"I'm going up to attend his plea hearing. Afterwards, I'll plan to meet you and Tammy at the airport. Look surprised when you see the local high-school bands playing when you get off the plane," said Calley.

"How delightful," Tammy squealed. Her glee was suddenly interrupted by a loud bang over the intercom. Cheer Cheer had barged into Calley's office, causing the door to slam against the wall and rattling a cabinet containing Calley's valuable collection of stuff.

"I heard the news today. Oh, boy!" Cheer Cheer was wide-eyed and out of breath.

"What news?" they all asked in unison, including Malone and Tammy on the line in Las Vegas.

"The resurrection," exclaimed Cheer Cheer. "Oh, boy! Can you believe it? Oh, boy," Cheer Cheer kept repeating.

Tammy chimed in cross-country. "I believe. Praise Jesus. I believe."

"What resurrection?" asked Calley, always the skeptic.

Rick was home in his apartment watching the evening news, when the cable news channel showed a stock photo of a U.S. Coast Guard Cutter behind an attractive newscaster. "The sailing boat, named the *Folk*, vanished into heavy fog just as it sailed under the Mackinaw Bridge into the waters of Lake Michigan. It was believed to be carrying alleged murderer Mitchell Miller and his girlfriend, who had been reportedly hiding out in Ontario. Coast Guard craft in pursuit have been unable to detect the craft. For a live report, we go now to Ripley Reed in Harbor Springs, Michigan."

"Alexis, the pea-soup thick fog behind me has blanketed the entire west coast of Michigan. The U.S. Weather Service tells us this fog was precipitated when a rapid-moving Canadian cold front clashed with unseasonably hot weather, which has been suffocating the Great Lakes region for weeks. Coast Guard officials will resume their search for the craft as soon as this weather system breaks."

The news anchor continued: "In another story from Michigan, we have Kimberly Comstock at an impromptu press conference which has been called at the site of the so-called Indian Resurrection. Kimberly, do we know any more about Sister Mary Pulaski?"

"Alexis, the big question here seems to be 'Where's the body?'"

The television screen showed a concrete and brick alley strewn with colorful mementos and memorials. The alley was filled with more flowers than a Rose Bowl Parade float, all sorts of stuffed animals, including Barbie and Ken dressed up like Pocahontas and an Indian brave respectively, crucifixes, totem poles, miniature plastic Indians from Fort Apache sets made in the 1960s, hundreds of "We Love You, Jessakid" personal notes, a life-size cardboard cut out of the Lone Ranger and Tonto, and a black-velvet painting of the King with a cartoon loop drawn out of his mouth, which said "Viva the Great Lakes."

The news anchor was incredulous, as the correspondent in the field continued excitedly. "Alexis, as you know, the Oplendykes have refused to comment other than to say that the so-called Indian Jessakid was taken after his alleged resurrection to an undisclosed site for burial. Cynics are beginning to point to facts which they say suggest that the eighty-year-old nun has Alzheimer's. I spoke with a number of her former students at Mount Mercy Academy. They all said Sister Mary taught the Palmer Cursive Handwriting Method with a hard yardstick, but her credibility was beyond question. Here she is now."

On the television screen, Rick saw the wrinkled, but bright and friendly face of the nun as she began to answer questions from an uncharacteristically respectful media:

"I was pushing my grocery cart down the alley. That's how I supplement my meager church pension. The boys in the Vatican don't let their treasures trickle down to working-class women," said the nun, not looking for reward but merely for recognition of her Order.

"They were helping him out the back door of the mortuary over there." She pointed. "I recognized the Native American lawyer from all his pictures in the press. He looked pale and sick. He was walking with assistance from an Indian princess with golden hair and a white man. They did not speak.

"Yes, well I don't agree with his tactics, but I do agree with what he stands for. You know, we need clean holy water, if we're going to continue to baptize babies," proclaimed the only independent eyewitness to the Indian Resurrection.

"Of course I believe in miracles or I would not have chosen to live my life as I have," the nun said out of habit.

"Yes." Sister Mary looked directly into the camera. "And I did have a crush on Daniel Berrigan. It was about twenty-five years ago during the change of life. I still keep a picture of him in my boudoir." Her shocking admission was the moral equivalent of having admitted that she once inhaled.

Rick's phone rang. It was Geltman, wanting to know what that was on the news. He made it clear he still wanted to book Laura before the FBI did. Rick put him off.

❖ ❖ ❖

The Ottawa Council had sponsored an annual summer gathering for years on the shores of Lake Michigan. Some years, it had been overwhelmed with political speeches and squabbling. The year of the Wounded Knee stand-off, a fit and trim Jonah Wasaquom had declared it an "Un-celebration of Independence Day," in sympathy with their Plains brothers and sisters in South Dakota.

But as other blood brothers like David Wasaquom went off to universities or war, many at home like Jonah had turned to other issues, like keeping the grant money coming into the tribal headquarters. Eventually, slot machines captured the attention of the tribal council. And the summer pow-wow became just another American picnic on the lake, with fry bread and potato salad for all, elders watching the playing children from their places at picnic tables.

This year, the Ottawas made camp a few miles south of the State Park which bears their name. The news had spread quickly on the moccasin telegraph about the Indian Resurrection. Nearly five hundred people were in attendance.

A personal call from Sarah to one of the tribal council members, one who often tried to play the role of peacemaker in the blood feud between David Wasaquom and the rest of the council chiefs, had started calls throughout the region. Less than twenty-four hours notice had brought out a throng of dark-skinned, bowling-jacketed Indians, wearing cowboy hats and baseball caps. They swarmed over a few acres of sandy dunes along this western shore, a small piece of tribal land recently purchased with proceeds from the slot machines and blackjack tables of the Beaver Sands Casino.

While the aroma of Indian cooking rose on the breeze, everyone was talking about the Ogema, the Jessakid who had risen from the dead. Theories were rampant as to why Nanabozho had made him a chosen one.

Verbrugge made a couple wrong turns down private drives of exclusive properties on the shore south of the channel which runs between Lake Macatawa and Michigan. "This can't be it," he said, as they came to a barred iron gate, probably the home of a rich land baron from Chicago. Finally, they found the right road, lined with cars and lots of pickup trucks. In past years, the vehicles would have been virtual wrecks, junkers reclaimed for their second coming as reservation cars. Now, with the distribution of gambling money, there were a good number of late-model sports-utility vehicles and well-equipped pick-up trucks. Many of the vehicles had canoes strapped on top or resting in the truck beds.

Verbrugge found a parking spot off the heavily wooded drive. When the egg-beater motor of the Volkswagen ceased, David Wasaquom opened his eyes. It was the first time he'd opened them since they left the home of one of Verbrugge's professors that afternoon.

Wasaquom was slowly returning from a far-away place. It had been a trip full of fevered dreams. He sipped slowly on a bottle of pure water.

He could vaguely remember having taken a sip during his long interrogation of Alkema from the little brown jug he had brought for the Judge. What had cause him to do so, he could not remember. In one gulp, Wasaquom had ingested a veritable smorgasbord of exotic bacterial strains, which the planet is producing in great numbers in its toxic polluted rivers, faster than the shrinking Amazon can deliver up cures. As he had sat there watching the Judge watching him, a fulminate microbe had divided and divided into a million little organisms. Gradually, the bacteria had driven his fever to a spike, and had sent his heart into a beatless arrhythmia. Then, his system went into a state of suspended animation.

The paramedics in the Emergency Rescue vehicle, working frantically on Wasaquom between the courthouse and the hospital, had mistakenly assumed that he had gone to the happy hunting grounds. Mercy Hospital had been a madhouse in the hours after the downtown riot, filled with battered, bleeding, and angry patients. An exhausted second-year resident, who had already been on call for thirty hours, had pronounced him dead, then rushed off to close a bloody head wound on a pro-lake demonstrator.

In a trance, Wasaquom's greatest journey had begun.

"I've brought you back to your people, Ogema," Sarah whispered. She felt the smooth Petoskey stone amulet hanging on the thin cord around his neck. The stone gull had survived cardiac massage and first-degree attempted embalming. Sarah made a prayer for his life, and promised to cherish whatever time they had left. "Are you sure this is what you want to do? Please let me take you to a hospital," Sarah gently urged.

"A hospital means going to prison. I don't want our child to visit me in a prison. I'd rather die out there," Wasaquom whispered, with dignity and grace. He was very sick, and his journey was still underway.

Verbrugge tugged and Sarah strained to push Wasaquom out of the Volkswagen's tiny back seat. Verbrugge steadied

Wasaquom's limp body against the car. The sun dropped below the soft hills, which rose before them and the beach. Standing in the shadows, they looked up and could see a yellow glow through the pine trees, which meant the promise of a sunset. It would be the first sunset this shore had seen in almost a week.

Some young Ottawa boys and girls were playing tag, as a border collie tried in vain to herd them back to order. The children's giddy frolic ended at the sight of the cachectic ghost and his two companions. They darted back with word to the rest of the tribe that the risen Jessakid had arrived. The collie remained behind and barked at the odd trio.

❖ ❖ ❖

So far, neither the Coast Guard nor Calley's clandestine search had pinpointed the ghostly pirate ship. Through the fog and troubled waters east of the Beaver Island archipelago, the *Folk* had managed to sail undetected. Continuing south along Michigan's western shore, the boat made by Viking descendants had glided into the Manitou Passage, where the annual Chicago-Mac racers get their mettle tested. About the time Mitch saw what he correctly assumed to be the lights of Leland, the currents completely overcame what was left of the lazy wind.

They drifted into Good Harbor Bay. It was almost three o'clock in the morning. Mitch dropped anchor so as not to run ashore. Silently they surveyed what little they could see of the land which was locked in the night.

"That was our last can of tuna and this is all the bread," said Laura, holding up a plastic bag containing one dried-up piece of curled crust. Hudson was perched on the cowling begging for his daily rations. "You're such a pig. You know that," Laura said to the bird. "If you eat now, then there won't be any later."

"I'm going ashore," Mitch announced.

Laura didn't plead with him not to go. She was starving too. It had been six days and six nights since they'd left Canada. Better sailors might have made better time. Then again, maybe not, for the same pockets of fog that shrouded them with a protective cover brought vast stretches of glassy flat water. She watched as Mitch stripped naked in the half moonless night.

Mitch put on swim trunks and stuffed a shirt into a baggy waterproof bag. Like a brave Navy Seal, he slipped into the cold water. He swam until the toes of his canvas shoes dug into the stony sand of the underwater ground, which dropped off sharply from shore. Laura could barely see the outline of a dim profile as Mitch walked up a boat-launch ramp at the end of a street. Soon he was out of site. She heard the faint sound of squeaky wet Keds running up the deserted street, hopefully running towards food.

Mitch paused at the middle of an intersection and looked around. He did not see any all-night fast food or stop-and-go joints. They wouldn't be eating Twinkies tonight. Maybe they wouldn't be eating anything. He heard a screen door slam. He followed the sound to the back of a building on the corner he had just run past. It was a bakery. His nostrils flared and his mouth watered at the sweet aromas. For a moment, Mitch stared through the screen door at the cheerful woman making her daily bread.

"Excuse me. Can I buy some?" Mitch asked in a soft voice through the screen, causing the woman to temporarily leaven higher than her bread.

"Jesus Mother Mary of God," she gasped clutching a flour-covered hand to her chest. "You scared me," said the woman, who didn't get any visitors this time of the morning, unless it was one of her children coming to help. She caught her breath. "Sorry, they cleaned me out yesterday."

She surveyed the young man in need of a shave and a haircut. He looked so familiar, like a friend of her oldest son, who used to work for her during the summers. "What I have in the oven will be ready in ..." she looked at the timer on top of the well-used oven, "five minutes."

"Do you know where I could find a newspaper or a phone?"

"Newspapers don't get delivered out here until after eight. But help yourself to the phone," said the personable baker, pointing to an old red rotary on the wall.

"Thanks, but I'm all wet and it's long distance," said Mitch, preferring to stand in the shadows, still unsure whether his long hair and beard made a better disguise than Edith's wig.

"Across the street there's a pay phone," she directed as she rolled a Danish.

"I'll be back for the bread," said Mitch.

Mitch ran across the street to the phone. He picked up the receiver and began to dial his parents' number. He stopped. He knew that would be tapped. As far as Mitch was concerned, the lines of every one of his potential allies would be tapped. Well, what about the lines of his adversaries? Last he knew, Cheer Cheer didn't have caller ID, and there would be no reason for anyone to put a trace on his phone. Calley's associate was not his first choice, but then Mitch put some trust in his lingering friendship with Cheer Cheer. Maybe Mitch could at least get some headline news out of him.

Mitch dialed the number and listened as it started to ring.

❖ ❖ ❖

There were traces everywhere. Mostly under Cheer Cheer's nose. The redheaded seductress had showed up to party with him in Grand Rapids, unannounced, only a few hours before. She had been called out by Calley to check on the morale of the partner-to-be, after the hostage crisis at the federal courthouse had apparently ended, and then suddenly reappeared as a bizarre resurrection story. She found the fighting Irishman in a manic mood. Even her pre-game cartwheels, performed with stunning exuberance — in the outlandish green and gold outfit which she had had custom-made to please him after they were first introduced by Calley — not even that could lift him from the major guilt trip he was on. Not until she brought out the nose candy did Cheer start to get back in the groove. Then came the surprise call from his old friend Mitch. That, combined with the paranoid effect of cocaine, completely undid him.

"Mitch Miller. You were right, man. You were right about this godless desert water scheme. Jesus wears Irish green, not because he's a Touchdown Jesus, like they made him appear on the mural next to the stadium. But because he's an environmentalist. That's why we won so many games when Father Hesburgh was President. Civil rights, clean environment, all that knee-jerk liberal stuff. Hesburgh had connections to the Big Guy upstairs. It's all plain as rain. Back then the Badgers, the Wolverines, a whole lot of schools went to artificial surface. Sure, some of them recognized the error of their ways and came back to grass. But we Irish remained true green all the way. Get 'em on grass and beat their ass —that's what we used to say. It's the natural green of Ireland that Jesus loves," said the hopped-up leprechaun with staccato speed.

"Right, Cheer Cheer," said Mitch, almost as blown away by Cheer Cheer as Cheer Cheer was blown away. "So, man, *como está?*" Mitch queried. It was a lame attempt to pretend that Mitch's call was being made from some dark, dingy bar in Mexico.

Cheer Cheer ignored the question. "And now the Indian Resurrection." Cheer Cheer began to weep in quantum sobs. He had never wept like this before in his life. Not after his Purdue honey left him. Not even after a bowl loss. "I believe, Mitch. I believe that nun. I know that nun. I mean, I don't know her, but I do know her. Do you know what I mean, Mitch?"

Mitch couldn't get a reply in edgewise, which was okay, because it wasn't a question. Cheer Cheer continued without losing a beat.

"Mitch, you gotta meet me in Manistee. Can't trust anyone but you, Mitch. Moore is scheduled to cop a plea tomorrow in exchange for testifying against you. The poor bastard was pretty noble, Mitch. He tried to hold out for you, but he's got a family to feed." Cheer Cheer took a deep breath and a sniff-sniff. "And I got a confession to make. Do you know where the drawbridge is? Meet me under there at noon. I promise I won't be high."

"I'm not sure I can make it there in time," said Mitch. It sounded like Cheer Cheer knew he was a lot closer than Matamoros.

"Mitch, you got to meet me. I've got something major.

Something important to give you. Like man, you're the Gipper and this one's for you."

Mitch thought a lot about that phrase as he swam back to the boat, pushing a floating double-wrapped plastic bag packed with fresh bread.

❖ ❖ ❖

Two strong young Indian men, one with a bare chest and one wearing a Red Wings T-shirt, slowly trudged up the sandy dune carrying Wasaquom. Verbrugge and Sarah walked to the side. They knew they had been expected, but they were amazed at the magnitude of the reception. At the crest of the dune, hundreds of Ottawas, who had been waiting all afternoon for the arrival of the Jessakid, stood before a spectacular scarlet and lavender sky.

As the two men carried the half-conscious man down to the lake, the crowd parted in reverence. In places where the Native Americans stood four or five deep, fathers hoisted young children on their shoulders to catch a glimpse of the man, the Marine, the lawyer, the Ogema, who only days before had been considered a renegade and a disgrace, even to many of the tribe.

The strange sickness which plagued Wasaquom was once again at high tide. His eyes were open but his eyes were like glass. He could not muster even a grimace to his people's tear-stained faces, as they watched him being slowly carried down the sandy slope. At the end of this human channel of respect, a semi-circle of elders, who once had been sworn enemies of Wasaquom, waited by the water's edge. They stood next to a large birchbark canoe.

The canoe was more than twenty feet long. In the middle of the large canoe was a bed of soft, tender cedar boughs laid over a deerskin. There were stocks of provisions for those who would paddle. For those who were not destined to die. The elders bowed in silence as the young men laid Wasaquom on his makeshift bed. One of them took off a brilliant blue and green robe. He handed it to Sarah. She accepted with bowed head, saying only, "Love and forgiveness is the essence of any faith worth keeping."

Verbrugge looked around awkwardly, feeling out of place. Sarah motioned him into the canoe with her. The two young men were joined by half a dozen others. They pushed the large canoe into the slapping waves. Once underway, they handed Verbrugge a paddle.

Wasaquom's temperature had spiked again. Sarah dipped a rag into the water and placed it on his fevered brow. He did not appear to be in any great pain. She assumed that he was slipping away. She looked at the sunset and waited in peace, resigned to let it be. This was where he wanted to die.

The canoe traveled with steady surges out onto the lake. The powerful shoulders of the paddlers became a hypnotic motion, pulling the canoe ahead. Verbrugge's paddle flailed in shallow water. After some time, one of the young men turned around and said to Verbrugge, "Learn to be still." Verbrugge took a deep breath and exhaled. He began to enter the stillness of the paddling, following and being drawn into the native rhythm. He began to stop worrying about where or when out there the Jessakid would die, and just entered the world of the long-distance water traveler.

As Sarah cradled the Jessakid's burning head, a dozen canoes slipped into the water behind them. Another dozen followed, and another, and another.

When Mitch climbed back on board the *Folk*, there was a slight but steady breeze which greeted him along with his two hungry sailors. There was not going to be any fog this day. After a quick breakfast of bread and water, they hoisted the mainsail. Slowly but surely, they made their way west out of Good Harbor Bay, then south past Sleeping Bear Dunes, where native legend has it that Mama Bear still waits with forlorn hope for her drowned cubs to return to her side.

Completely unaware of history below, they sailed over an old shipwreck at Empire. By sunrise they had attained a respectable clip, which Mitch estimated would get them to Manistee by noon. Mitch was far from convinced it was a good idea, though.

"It's stupid. I know he's one of Malone's hired guns. He sold out a long time ago," Mitch yelled from the helm. Laura was trying to secure a batten. "And what's he got to give me? Why does he need to see me? It's either a trick or he's crazy. And what's this nonsense about an Indian insurrection?"

"Resurrection is what you said," said Laura, returning to the cockpit.

"That's even crazier," said Mitch.

"Mitch, I think this is the thing to do. I think this is why the wind carried us into Lake Michigan. We can't run and hide forever. Are you going to be afraid every time we hear a car coming up a lane, or see a stranger look at us sideways in a bar somewhere?"

"Maybe we can steal a car in Manistee," said Mitch.

"Sure, I always thought you looked like the kind of guy who could hot-wire a car in a second," Laura snipped.

"Maybe we could just sail around these lakes forever," said Mitch.

"Mitch, you know what we've got to do." Laura told him the answer with her eyes as much as her lips. "Either that or we left Ontario for nothing." She was scared, but mostly she was speaking from her heart. "Mitch, I told you Christmas Eve when we met in Steketee's that the time would come for you. These lakes need you. And a lot of good people need these lakes."

She looked out at the water. Maybe they had been out on the lake too long. Reality seemed different out here, floating on a sea of ancient legend, past a coastline that from this distance looked as it must have looked to the first peoples to push their birch canoes onto its jewel-like surface.

"Mitch, you have to walk in, tell 'em the truth. Once in a while the law must recognize the truth. Doesn't it?"

"It's not impossible," said Mitch without bitterness.

❖ ❖ ❖

Without all the white frosting, the shoreline north of Manistee looked very different to Mitch than it had the past winter. Nevertheless he could see where the old Hanker cottage had stood. The bluff had been clear-cut like a mountain in Oregon. And there was a towering broad structure rising out of the sand. They sailed past the lighthouse at the end of the pier and up the Manistee channel towards the first drawbridge, which Mitch and Ted Moore had crossed last winter in the blizzard.

The tourists were out in full force and rightly so. There were only so many bowling alleys and movie theaters. Five days of cold wet fog had put a real damper on a week's vacation "Up North," huddled in a tent at a state park.

But today dawned with liberating sunshine. Boats of all shapes and sizes were venturing out to the Big Lake in spite of the same steady westerly wind, which had brought the *Folk* south in record time. The town's riverwalk, which ran most of the length of the channel to Manistee Lake, was shoulder to shoulder with Fudgies lapping ice cream and strolling in sunshine.

Mitch steered up the channel. Before she dropped the buoy-like plastic bumper to protect the side of the boat, Laura hung a wet sweatshirt over the back of the bow with some other laundry, to cover up the name of the boat. After trimming the sail, Laura hailed some Manistee home-boys in frayed, low-riding bell-bottoms carrying skateboards. She tossed them a line. Glad for something to do, the teenage townies secured the boat rear and aft to crimson-colored steel moorings.

Laura and Hudson stayed on board as Mitch jumped ship. He walked into the crowd heading towards the drawbridge. He didn't notice the two men standing on top of the draw-bridge wearing dark sunglasses looking in his direction. Everyone was wearing sunglasses today.

Mitch walked into the cool shade under the bridge. He stopped and watched the crowd go by. He glanced at his watch. He was beginning to wonder if there was a second drawbridge farther into town, when he spotted a gaunt and anxious Cheer Cheer walking briskly down the riverwalk from the opposite direction. Mitch moved to greet him.

A couple pushing a baby stroller came between them. Cheer Cheer walked on by without a second look at Mitch. Mitch was pleasantly surprised. It meant he didn't need to pack a hair-piece anymore. Trying to catch up to him, Mitch narrowly avoided minor collisions with distracted sight-seers watching a freighter coming up the channel.

Mitch grabbed Cheer Cheer by the arm. Cheer Cheer spun around. Fist clenched. Prepared to throw a punch at his assailant. He stopped and stared a decent interval into the sunglasses of the long-haired, unshaven man who had dared lay hands on him.

"Mitch," Cheer Cheer gasped, giving him an unconditional embrace.

"Not so loud," replied Mitch, who couldn't help but smile at the outpouring of Irish affection.

"You look like a goddamn hippie," said Cheer Cheer. Mitch noticed the bloodshot eyes behind the smile. The strain of something was written all over his face.

"I'm letting my freak flag fly," Mitch proudly quipped.

No one close by was watching them. The drawbridge was being raised for an approaching freighter. The two halves of the metal bridge saluted skyward. The Fudgies were enthralled. Cheer Cheer leaned towards Mitch as if to give him another hug. He slipped something into Mitch's hand.

Cheer Cheer's eye caught the sun's reflection off a broad stainless steel blade. One of Smith's goons was only a second away from transecting Mitch's back.

❖ ❖ ❖

Ever since he was big enough to fumble a football, Cheer Cheer had dreamed of playing for Notre Dame. Back in the days when smaller men with terrific hearts still had a chance, he might have made it onto the field for a couple of downs in the last game of the season. He had gone so far as to make honorable mention in a suburban Buffalo league his senior year. However, no Division I schools expressed any interest, and when the biggest college to tender him a letter of intent was Slippery Rock, he became as stoic as anyone nicknamed Cheer Cheer ever could be. He resigned himself to be all that he could be: an undying ND fan.

Perhaps deep down, he had always harbored resentment for anyone who looked like a poster boy for ND linebackers. Whatever the reason, Cheer Cheer shoved Mitch aside and lunged towards the gargantuan goon with the kind of intensity which would have impressed the likes of Rockne and Parsegian.

Cheer Cheer's quick lateral move caused the goon to stumble forward. Cheer Cheer hit him with his best forearm shiver. The goon responded with a crude attempt at sidewalk surgery. Blood trickled from under Cheer Cheer's arm. Undaunted, Cheer Cheer charged the goon, driving the man with the knife crashing into the back-up man, who was standing on the edge of the concrete channel walkway. The three went plunging like falling dominoes into the murky water, which was being churned up by the passing freighter.

The Fudgies almost trampled Mitch as they ran to the edge of the riverwalk. They licked their ice cream in a state of morbid and frantic pre-occupation. The black channel water was thrashed white as if a school of piranhas was feeding on a lame water-buffalo. The water turned blood red. And then the water was still.

Jake was a pretty mature eight-year-old, who had learned how to spell "custody battle" before he finished kindergarten. He wasn't afraid to travel alone. He was excited about his first trip for summer visitation with his daddy in Green Bay. He'd been promised a Brewers game and go-cart rides in the Dells, "near where grandma lives." When he needed assistance, he knew enough to stretch up to reach the orange call button, which the flight attendant had told him to push if he needed anything.

"Is that an island? It's not on the map," asked Jake, looking at the foldout map from the airline magazine, with bold red lines arching out of black dotted cities like NYC, ORD, LAX.

"There are no islands in this part of Lake Michigan," said the flight attendant as she leaned across the empty seats next to Jake and peered out the window at the clouds. "I don't see anything," she said sweetly.

"There. Look," Jake urged, pointing to big fluffy white clouds through which the wings of the 737 were flying.

The flight attendant caught a glimpse of what Jake was describing. "It's ..." Whatever it was, it was gone again, obstructed by clouds.

Then there was another break in the white puffs. She saw

the giant island floating in white-capped blue. "It's boats!" exclaimed the flight attendant with as much excitement in her voice as Jake's.

Sixteen thousand feet below there was a fleet of canoes. What Jake and the flight attendant could not see were the scattered points, up and down the coastline, from which other canoes were setting forth to join the floating armada.

❖ ❖ ❖

Summoned off the drawbridge by the Manistee harbor master immediately before it was raised, Smith reluctantly had to relinquish his dark perspective of the planned hit. Consequently, he did not see whether the fugitive lawyer had locked into the bloody little scrum, which had staggered off the edge of the riverwalk and into the channel.

But Smith had seen the dissident lawyer hand off something to Mitch. "Find the bastard," he snapped at his men, even before the first body was retrieved from the water. It was not until the scuba divers from the Sheriff's Department fished out the third and final body that Smith concluded that Mitch had once more alluded the posse, which had been pursuing him since Canada. By the time Smith and his men had thundered out of the channel in their obnoxious sounding muscleboats, the *Folk* was once again seeking temporary asylum on the Big Lake.

A powerful wind was whipping the wooden sailboat farther and farther from the sandy shoreline. They both had put on life jackets. The summer sun was still shining hot, but to the west there were onyx and purple-hued clouds, one tumbling under the other like unreal time-lapse photography. Mitch was staring down at the cassette tape in the palm of his left hand. A leprechaun's last gift in this life.

"I should have gone in after him," Mitch said sadly. "He took both those goons on." Still in a state of disbelief, he was filled with respect and admiration for his former colleague.

"There was nothing you could do," said Laura. She was yelling to be heard above the wind which was blowing harder and harder. "From what I could see, it was all over before it started. We got out of there just in time. They would have killed you, too."

"Something held me back. I guess I just got gutless," said Mitch.

"Hey, you saved Hudson, didn't you?" Laura nodded to the second mate, who had resumed his favorite perch on the bow.

"Sure," Mitch scoffed at this commendation of bravery.

"He's part of the plan, too. Or accident. Or whatever gets us all here, living and breathing on the same planet at the same time."

At first Hudson seemed to applaud Laura's Rachel Carson commentary by squawking wildly. But the applause quickly faded into an announcement, as Mitch and Laura saw the two speedboats heading off their starboard bow. The Riva cigarette boats, the choice of Caribbean drug smugglers, could do forty knots in a heartbeat. The *Folk* was doing only a fraction of that. The approaching weather front was building too much chop for its crew.

Mitch stood up, completely shaken out of any semblance of regret. In one motion, he lifted Laura off the cockpit bench and held her as close as anatomy would allow. "Do you know how empty my world was before I met you?" She started to attempt an answer that would have only sounded mundane. He gently hushed her lips with his fingertips.

"I love you, blue-eyed girl. I will always love you." He

kissed her with passion as the tiller stayed hard pressed to his side, like a well-heeled dog. The *Folk* was beginning to rock.

"Laura, they want me. Not you. Keep sailing. There will be boats trying to beat this front into port. Maybe the Coast Guard is out there."

"Mitch." Laura trembled. A part of her brain had sent up an unthinkable message. "Mitch. No."

He handed her Cheer Cheer's tape. "This could be the B-side of one of your greatest hits." He squeezed her arms tight. "If not, try 'Beyond the Sea.' It will keep me going wherever I may be."

"I don't know that song. I'm not singing covers anymore. I'm only performing my own material. No more collaboration with anyone," Laura screamed.

But Mitch had dived off the back of the *Folk*.

"'Beyond the Sea.' That damn Giovanni!" she yelled. She knew the Bobby Darin tune. Her mother used to play it all the time after Laura's daddy left.

❖ ❖ ❖

"Ottawa" derives from an Algonquin word meaning "to trade." Historically, the Ottawas were peaceable traders and fishermen, who saved their war paint for run-ins with more militant tribes like the Iroquois. But Malone's promise of endless green pelts inscribed with graven images of Grant, Franklin, and others permitted MDDC operatives to dictate the art direction and costuming for the grand lodge on the great lake. Consequently, the Ottawa doormen looked unusually colorful and fierce in their war paint and headdress.

"Holy shit," said Rick as he stepped out of the limousine and looked up at the grand entrance: "The Water Cathedral & Casino — Where your dreams answer your prayers." The architecture was beyond extraordinary. Teetering high on the sandy bluff, overlooking that seemingly limitless watery horizon to the west, Native American, Great White Religion, and Vegas had been concatenated into one broad-shouldered form.

Had Malone, with the aide of VanderHook's connections, commissioned Frank Lloyd Wright from beyond his grave at Taliesin? After all, the arrogant architect of the Johnson's Wax lily-pad building in Wisconsin and the Falling Waters house in Pennsylvania had boasted shortly before he died — to a Michigan graduate named Mike Wallace — that not only his works, including church and synagogue, but he himself would be immortal.

Even the usually jaded Geltman, who had spent a lot of time and money in Nevada's gaudy palatial casinos, was impressed. "Not bad. Not bad at all," he pronounced as he exited the limo.

White men dressed like poor 19th-century settlers served as bellhops. "It's a politically correct touch," Malone had guffawed to his entourage, when they checked in earlier that day. "So clever," a bubbling Tammy had added.

Geltman stopped. He craned his neck to catch a glimpse of the marquee cantilevered out from the grand sandstone portico, which formed the main entrance to the casino.

"How come Laura's name isn't up on the marquee?" he demanded. "Who the hell is Brother Peter? I don't understand what religion has to do with gambling? If you ask me, it's all a lot of Michigosh." Geltman had never visited America's hinterland before, but he had seen a picture of it on that quintessential *New Yorker* cover. He was so genuinely perplexed by what he saw that he had reverted to Yiddish to best describe all the crazy nonsense going on at the grand opening celebration.

Rick also stared up at the marquee, as if waiting for a sign. Hoping the letters would miraculously roll over like a *Wheel of Fortune* game to reveal: "Live & In Person, Laura Knight — Rick Loan, Mgmt." Or simply "Laura" would do. Come on, Vanna baby, turn em! No luck. The grand marquee still showed only: "Pearls! Pearls! Pearls! — Wholly Material Wisdom — Brother Peter's Salvation Show."

"Peter VanderHook is the political point man for the gambling-water referendum here in Michigan. They got to get through the political stuff before they get to the main attraction," Rick tried to placate the impulsive music exec.

Geltman did not look completely convinced, like when

he had showed up unannounced at Rick's door the night before with a recording contract and a sweet seven-figure signing bonus in hand. Rick's ragged impromptu response was to tell Geltman that, "Laura is gone. Ah, ah, ah ... Up North." Rick had uncharacteristically stuttered. "Yeah. Way far up North. She's headlining the opening of that big new Indian casino." Rick's Nana would have been disappointed with her favorite grandson. The not-so-white lie didn't even buy Rick twenty-four hours, because Geltman had quickly retorted, "So, how far is way far?"

"Well, the boys from Vegas sure better get their little referendum passed next month or they'll be sucking sand," said Geltman, temporarily taking Rick off the hook. "They're not going to carry the debt on this fancy joint with nickel-dime action."

Limo after limo continued to stream up and around the broad circular drive to the hotel. A warrior doorman ushered Geltman and Rick into the lobby, which was already packed with guests and dignitaries.

"I'm gonna go get a drink," Rick announced before the two of them reached the reception desk across the expansive lobby. Rick did not have a reservation. Rick did not have anything, not even his 9-mm. Glock, which he used to pack when he was carrying cash late at night after some shed gig.

The bartender poured Rick a tall Stolys, which he promptly put down. He ordered a second and walked out to the veranda.

Outside, people were crowded along a long row of whirring and chinking one-armed bandits. Rick stopped a hostess in a buckskin halter top, buckskin mini-skirt, and suede high heels. He pulled out his bankroll from his front pants pocket.

It was getting quite thin, inflated by ones. The heavily-fringed hostess gave him a shiny silvery house coin for his dollar. He nudged ahead of a beady-eyed middle-aged woman carrying a 16-ounce paper cup bearing the snazzy Water Cathedral & Casino logo and brimming with coins. The woman was drooling to get to a slot machine before hitting the casino's all-night all-you-can-eat buffet.

Rick fed the machine his solitary coin. Its hidden gears and wheels went round and round. The mischievous pre-ordained metal spirit inside the mechanism let fly a tomahawk and another tomahawk, then ... a canoe. Too bad. "It's all yours, ma'am," Rick said to the woman as he stepped away from the slot machine.

"Problem with you young people. Always trying to get rich quick," the woman chastised him.

Rick ignored the woman's insult as he made his way across the fieldstone veranda. He stepped up to one of the outdoor bars under a canvas awning, which was beginning to billow with gusts of wind coming off the lake. He finished his second drink like it was water, too. The high-octane liquid was beginning to numb his gut-wrenching regrets about the blue-eyed girl who got away. He called for another drink, as he surveyed the strange sandstone and chrome structure which rose above the adjacent main lodge.

Bells and alarms went off by the slots from where he had just departed. The beady-eyed woman had hit a jackpot. "Gambling is better than religion. You don't have to wait until the next life for the pay-off," Rick gratuitously volunteered to a couple of attractive women who were standing next to him at the crowded bar. The women ignored him. Something women never used to do, thought Rick. "You just got to be in the right place at the right time," he laughed out loud as the haughty pair walked away.

The crowd of gamblers and revelers were beginning to retreat indoors. Rick found an empty barstool and sat down. He looked out at Lake Michigan. She was not a happy camper. A couple of hundred feet below, heavy white-laced waves were beating what was left of Albert's wall.

A storm was coming in.

When Mitch dove off the bow of the *Folk*, the two cigarette boats veered to their port sides. Malone's men soon lost
sight of Mitch in the rolling whitecaps. The two boats slowed
to a little more than a crawl, like charters armed with radar
trolling for whitefish, waiting and watching for a strike on a
shiny silver spoon.

Laura could not see him either. She had her hands full
trying to stay the course on the lake that had suddenly gone
berserk, chopping here, there, and everywhere like Lizzy
Borden. Laura glanced back to where Mitch had jumped over-
board. In a cresting of waves she spotted a flash of red. It was
a life jacket. Mitch's jacket.

But the life jacket was not floating. It was being waved.
Treading water like a cyclist heading for the finish of the Tour
de France, Mitch was waving his red life jacket. Not as a sig-
nal of surrender or S.O.S., but like some suicidal swimmer
taunting sharks with red ribbons of his own blood.

One of the Riva power boats took the bait. It climbed to a
horizontal plane as it accelerated to a break-neck speed over
the unruly water. Mitch disappeared. The boat knifed over his
head.

Hungry like a shark on a scent of blood, but lacking its
slithering grace, the attacking boat came about in a swirling
spin. A backwash of water temporarily threatened to swamp
it, but the boat muscled its way out of the grasp of its own

wake.

The second boat was idling and powering, trying to anchor without an anchor in the high seas. Smith was one of the men on the deck of that bobbing boat. He was looking through binoculars surveying for his primary target. The waves blocked his starboard view. He had lost sight of the fugitive lawyer. So had Laura, who was sailing south and out of sight.

For some time there was no sign of Mitch in the troubled waters. Then, like the "Black Azalea" from one of those fireworks warehouses whose billboards define the landscape along the interstates of Northern Indiana, Mitch's life jacket fizzled into the air like a short red flare. It was there and gone, but not without notice.

Smith spotted the flagging patch of red before it hit the water. Simultaneously, he barked into his boat's radio and summoned the attacking boat towards Mitch, whom he could now see intermittently between the chopping and rolling waves.

The attacking boat circled, until it drew a bead on Mitch.

Strangely, Mitch felt relief as he saw the sleek hull being aimed in his direction. His leg and arm muscles burned in the cool water. His lungs felt like they were about to explode. But it was a good tired. Swimming was a good tired. He should have done more of it. Maybe he could have relieved himself of his little phobia about drowning in the Big Lake a long time ago. Maybe even gotten some kind of Red Cross certification.

Maybe he should have retired from the practice of law. Become a lifeguard at Ottawa Beach, grow old on the shore like that dude on *Baywatch*. That was not an odd last regret for a drowning man. Certainly it was better than any last regrets about never having loved, thought Mitch. He had no regrets about love. Only about the end of time.

For weeks now, the crew of the attacking boat, like the rest of Smith's men, had had orders to "engage Mitch. And the girl, if she's a witness." Over the years, Malone's operatives had all had easier assignments back home in the desert. First it had been the vastness of the open water. False sightings of men and women in sailboats. Then it had been fog. Repeatedly frustrated in their search for the fugitive lawyer, their refrain to the daily chiding and upbraiding from Vegas had been, "Sir, I'm sorry, but it's a big hockey puckin' lake."

Primed for the kill, one last time the attacking Riva planed to the horizontal. Faster and faster. Full throttle.

But Miss Michigan hadn't earned her number-one ranking in Great Lakes shipping disasters just on good looks alone. In fact, liter per liter, she was as rough and tough a lady as any salt-water body anywhere on the globe. An aberrant monster wave caught the bow of the attacking boat. The speedboat flipped and twisted. Then cartwheeled into great balls of fire from an explosion that temporarily broke the sound barrier of the howling wind.

The vibrations from the explosion circled and cycled from the epicenter. Laura turned to see burning and smoking debris raining down on the water. Charred embers and flaming red added to the red of Mitch's dying flare.

The *Folk* began flying south out of control. Laura's hold on the tiller was merely incidental. She was not in command at all. The wind had commandeered her sails. The *Folk* was running on a beam reach, heeled over 40-plus degrees. Laura was trying to reef in the mainsail, afraid she might broach which would snap the mast like a toothpick being used to lever a tire jack.

And then there was the mutiny to contend with. "Hudson!"

she screamed into her own deafened ears as the second mate took flight. Up, up and away, the white bird sailed.

Laura cursed the lake as she fought the waves. She cursed herself as she fought back her tears. She should never have let Mitch go.

Mission accomplished, albeit with unfortunate casualties, Smith's remaining muscle-boat was now coming after her.

❖ ❖ ❖

Ted Moore looked up at the Seal of the Great State of Michigan. He couldn't translate the Latin, *Si quaeris peninsulam amoenam circumspice.* He couldn't translate much of anything that had happened to him in the past six months, except the recommendation about probation for turning State's evidence. And then there was that bizarre call offering to pay off their delinquent land-contract debt. He had held out a long time before they "flipped him," as prosecutors like to say — longer than most men would have, insisting on his innocence and the innocence of the fugitive lawyer. It still didn't seem right. But enough was enough.

Moore looked at his court-appointed lawyer. His lawyer looked at the Judge. The Sheriff standing next to his prisoner looked at his watch. "Let's get this show on the road," thought the Sheriff as he impatiently rubbed two shiny silver coins together, compliments of the Water Cathedral & Casino. They had been presented to every adult of voting and gambling age in the county.

"Mr. Moore. Let me ask you again. How do you plead? The County Prosecutor will not accept a plea of *nolo contendere,*" said the Judge, adding more Latin to Moore's confusion. "You can't say, 'guilty, but I didn't do it.' Either you're guilty or you're not guilty." The Chief Judge of the Circuit Court was growing impatient, too, prompted by his wife who was in the back of the courtroom pointing to her watch with a disapproving look on her face.

Ted Moore turned around and looked at Barbara, who was holding Teddy Jr. in her arms. "Guilty," he said as he hung his head.

The County Prosecutor smiled. The Sheriff smiled. The Judge smiled. The Judge's wife smiled. Even Calley managed a smile.

Mike Kopicubb and the rest of the press corps ran out the door to phone in their stories or do their satellite feeds — before heading to the WC&C for free drinks and all they could eat.

Four hundred years later, what John Donne wrote was still true. But Laura didn't see it that way. She only saw an uninhabited island on the southern horizon, its sandy white shores appearing to float in the rocking and rolling water. If she could only make it to that island, she could beach the *Folk* and run for cover. There were no trees on this end. Perhaps on the other side.

The sole surviving muscle-boat was closing the distance between life and death. But Mitch's sacrifice had bought her precious time. She wasn't going to let him die in vain. She owed him that much. She owed him at least a stanza of "Beyond the Sea." She uncleated the mainsail line and pulled hard, giving back to the wind what she had previously taken to avoid capsizing.

The extra canvas bought her another knot. The *Folk* creaked and crashed through the waves. It was at the outer limits of tolerance, but it continued to fly. The muscle-boat pursued less than five hundred meters behind. But now ahead, she could see something she hadn't seen before: a harbor. The island had a harbor, a harbor that was opening like an intergalactic space station to let in a lost starship fleeing a black hole.

The *Folk* sailed into port. The port cradled around the wooden boat, denying entry to Smith's boat, which swerved at the last minute, leaving only its ugly wake.

A young brave in a Red Wings T-shirt was the first to board the *Folk* and help trim its sails. Laura looked around in awe at the multitude of red and brown faces staring at her from hundreds and hundreds of canoes. From out of the core of this swell of humanity, a giant birchbark canoe glided up to the bow of the *Folk* to greet Laura.

In that canoe knelt a woman with yellow hair. And next to her, doing something that mortals should not do in canoes, stood a man. Tall, brave, and proud, like a Marine. And a great Ottawa Ogema.

❖ ❖ ❖

The vestibule leading to the Grand Hall of the Water Cathedral & Casino was packed. Inside, pews had been reserved for Malone's entourage, dignitaries, politicians and Jonah Wasaquom's faction of the Ottawa Council. Otherwise it was all general admission. People were pushing and shoving to get in, including Smith. Smith looked determined. He was in a hurry. The crew from his speedboat followed close on his heels. They looked wind-blown.

High above them all, Reverend VanderHook was sequestered in the dressing room with his make-up artist and personal assistant. There was a knock at the dressing room door and a voice, "Five minutes to show time."

"I am prepared," responded VanderHook with his trademark authoritarian voice. Early on, that wonderful vocal gift had distinguished him from his fellow Calvinist seminarians, who had been blessed with mere mortal powers of elocution. That wonderful gift of manly, lilting tone and timbre had helped carve the path to this hallowed place where sin and salvation would struggle to a glorious, golden, redeeming end — twenty-four hours a day, seven days a week.

Not taking his eyes off the full-length mirror before him, VanderHook slipped into the long silky robe which his assistant held for him. Just think! All those years in black.

The art director of VanderHook's newly formed company, *Dutch Treat Productions,* had insisted on the color change.

The fellow had learned his craft on the Vegas stage. "Purple Pulpit Passion" was definitely his palette. The robe was quite flattering, VanderHook mused, and for some reason the fringe and the stripes didn't seem nearly as effeminate as he had thought the first time he tried it on.

The blasting bass began to vibrate VanderHook's dressing room. It was the opening act: a young white southern rap group from Forrest City, Arkansas. It was a bow to the Casino's potential youth market, thought VanderHook. Once again, he had to admit that the entertainment professionals from Vegas were way ahead of the creative curve. Sons and daughters of former KKK members doing ebonicly-correct rap was just the right touch. "We be weak, But He be strong. Yo, yo, the Bible told me so. Yo, yo, the Bible told me so ...."

The make-up artist coiffed and sprayed an errant curl. A long errant curl, longer than Custer's last and as yellow as the feed-corn harvested last August in the nearby farmer's field, which had since been paved for the Casino's overflow tour-bus parking.

VanderHook looked buff. As well he should. A lot of people were counting on him. Not just Malone and the Michigan electorate, not just the eternally thirsty patrons of Las Vegas, but sinners everywhere.

The sound of the Forrest City rap group was being piped out on the veranda, when Geltman finally found Rick.

"Where've you been. I've been looking all over for you," said Geltman, concerned at the sight of Rick. The manager of his label's number-one prospect was drinking alone at the vacant veranda bar. "They've already started."

"Yeah, I can hear it from here," Rick snipped.

"Isn't Laura coming on next?" Geltman asked.

"Little white lies are my disguise," Rick announced loudly. "Little lies. Teeny tiny lies. Whoppers aren't the problem in this world. It's the nasty little ones that cause all the problems."

"Is this some kind of psych job to get more money out of me? Or just maybe you don't manage her anymore? Maybe you never did?" Geltman was getting warm.

Rick sneered at Geltman and signaled the bartender for another one.

"That's it, isn't it? You don't manage her anymore. You let her get away. You were too small-time for her. I knew it the first time I laid eyes on her." Geltman was agitated. "You're just a beer-joint band hustler. She was too good for you. Wasn't she?"

Rick grabbed Geltman by the lapels of his expensive designer jacket. He pulled him close enough so that Geltman could see the bloody county roads etched in his eyeballs. "Take yes for an answer," Rick said before shoving the startled record exec against the bar.

Geltman straightened his jacket. "Might as well shoot some craps," Geltman said with disgust. He walked off the empty veranda to join the rest of the throng congregating into the Water Cathedral & Casino.

"Is that just furniture or does that piano play?" Rick questioned the bartender after paying for another Stolys. The bartender shrugged, as if to say, "I don't know. I just work here."

"Rap is crap," Rick blabbered as he walked with an unsteady gait towards the baby grand, which like him had been sitting all alone on the veranda for the entire evening. He threw off the soft chamois cover revealing a virgin keyboard, spilling half his drink in the process.

❖ ❖ ❖

A red light went on in VanderHook's dressing room. It was his final cue from the sound room, which was located equally high on the opposite wall of the Cathedral. His personal assistant and make-up artist bowed slightly as VanderHook walked a few steps to a tiny door that opened into the Cathedral.

It was time to feed their heads. He grabbed the silver door-handle. It was in the shape of an alewife fish, one of the first non-native species introduced to the lakes via the St. Lawrence Seaway. VanderHook turned the handle and squeezed his towering frame through the opening.

He emerged on a balcony. In front of him was a pulpit made of some kind of PVC plastic, shaped like the basket of a utility company's cherry-picker. It was mounted on a pneumatic base.

VanderHook was no fool. He knew that Malone's interest in him might well wane after the water-gambling referendum passed. The cherry-picker was just one more device to enhance his presentation, to maintain top billing above a lion-taming act or magician from Vegas, who VanderHook expected would soon be competing with him for center stage.

Behold his magnificent Water Cathedral & Casino!

Even as he surveyed the enormous space, VanderHook nodded discreetly to his devoted wife seated in one of the pews. She was accompanied by a few of the deacons from his old congregation who had remained loyal. On the other side sat Calley, the odd but brilliant legal mind, who had been there for the Reverend at the time of his personal crisis with poor troubled little Peter.

Next to Calley was seated Jonah Wasaquom, Malone's silent minority partner, always ready to do whatever it took to keep this monumental construction project on schedule. Then there was Malone, the son of a Western pioneer, who had inspired *The Gospel of Wholly Material Salvation and Redemption.*

And last but not least was Malone's lovely wife Tammy, who looked particularly stunning this evening. She waved at the Rev, even as she was rising to her feet to exit the pew. Curiously, that goon Smith, Malone's chief of security, was escorting Tammy and Malone out of the nave.

Perhaps Mr. Malone had political flesh to press. VanderHook did not dwell on it. He was too caught up in the momentous occasion to consider what possible last-minute details could be so important to summon his mentor away from the grand opening ceremony.

VanderHook's eyes feasted on the gigantic edifice. The massive sandstone structure ran parallel to the lake bluff. The walls of the Water Cathedral were intended to be a mere extension of the sand, which had been blown and ground to constantly form and reform this shore for thousands of years.

The organic design of the Cathedral's exterior belied a frantically baroque maze of wires and plumbing inside the walls. On the interior, except for the rows of pews reserved for penitents and those holding tickets to shows, the Cathedral was a pantheon to all games of chance. Cards, dice, slots, OTB, and much, much more.

Dominating all this spectacle, all this Michigosh, was an

amazing open roof. Above them was nothing, only sky. A gull swooped overhead, curious about all the noisy glittering machines and people milling below.

Timing was everything, with his sermon slated to interrupt gambling. It was a tight window of opportunity within which VanderHook had to work to begin the process of salvation. For most of the patrons, it was a process that might well take years, perhaps a lifetime. At least, that was Malone's hope.

Precisely at seven, with the aid of the building's powerful computer system in the sound room, all the action on the floor ceased. Slots stopped chinking. Wheels stopped spinning. Dealers stopped dealing. A thunderous silence came over the floor of the casino. VanderHook stepped into his cherry-picking pulpit. All eyes were on him as he began to rise.

The Right Reverend began by preaching to these charter members of the WC&C about the life-and-death importance of a "yes" vote in the August gambling-water referendum. He explained, as logically as possible, how their salvation depended on its passage. While a few of his newfound flock were restless to get back to their roulette or blackjack (especially those showing aces against dealer face-cards), the crowd remained generally reverent and respectful, placated by the happy-hour prices being offered during the sermon.

VanderHook was eloquent. His enunciation impeccable. His cadence enchanting. "... There are charlatans, hucksters, and heretics who speak of resurrection of that renegade. These are lies! These are unholy lies perpetrated by flag-burning fag environmentalists," raged the Reverend, sounding a theme that he knew would deeply resonate with his right-wing constituency, many of whom were watching at home, thanks to the miracle of cable TV.

"In open and notorious consort with the Devil himself,

these hustlers and heretics perpetrated those lies to thwart your wholly material redemption ...." Vigorous applause interrupted him. As he gathered himself for the strong close to his speech and the "roofing of the cathedral" finale, VanderHook gazed to the west from his lofty cherry-picker. He temporarily paused, as he beheld with wonder and amazement a vision: hundreds of canoes in a vast flotilla, streaming onto Algonquin's golden shore. It is a sign, thought VanderHook.

"Verily, verily, it is a sign!" VanderHook resumed his sermon with Messianic urgency. "Twelve thousand sealed out of the tribe of the Ottawa, twelve thousand sealed out of the tribe of the CR, twelve thousand, praise Jesus ...!" He was working himself into a frenzy. Although his animated gestures had the congregation's rapt attention, none of them had any idea what he was preaching about. His dutiful wife Ruth figured it was Revelations according to her husband.

"Then I saw another angel ascend from the setting sun with the seal of the living God! Do not harm the earth or the sea or the trees till we have sealed ...."

Actually there were only about seven hundred Ottawas and three white people — Sarah, Verbrugge, and Laura — who were swarming ashore and beginning to scale the sandy cliff. But accurate numbers did not matter anymore. Things were taking on biblical proportions.

"Twelve thousand! Twelve thousand!" shouted the Reverend VanderHook, flailing his arms to the heavens.

The raising of his arms was supposed to be VanderHook's cue to the technicians in the sound room, because even state of the art computer systems sometimes rely on hand signals.

❖ ❖ ❖

In his not so semi-inebriated state, Rick had declared total victory of rock over rap. For no sooner had he started to
punctuate the smooth ebony and ivory on that baby grand with
a simple rock 'n' roll rhythm than the incessant mechanical
beat of the Forrest City Rappers ceased.

"Paper, scissors, rock. Rock beats scissors and rap," Rick
gleefully proclaimed to the guy, who he now considered to be
his favorite bartender in the whole world.

The bartender nodded, "Sure pal, whatever you say."

"Yeah, that'll work," Rick said as he grabbed a couple
chords and was off singing,

Rock beats scissors and rap, oh baby,
Rock beats scissors and rap, oh Laura,
Rock beats scissors,
Rock beats scissors,
Rock beats scissors and rap, oh baby ...

And on and on and on and on. In spite of the fact that the
tempo was upbeat and it was as easy to dance to as anything
at the hop, anyone who was still listening could see that it was
all a form of denial. Tears were streaming down Rick's cheeks.
Dripping on the keyboard, running down between the keys,
like diluted honey.

Absorbed in his rock 'n' roll dreams of yesterday, Rick

had not noticed when the bartender and the rest of the WC&C staff fled the veranda. He had not seen the first wave of Ottawas led by David Wasaquom coming over the veranda wall. Nor the brave in the Red Wings T-shirt. Nor the hundreds of Ottawas still beaching their canoes and beginning to follow their risen Chief up to the walls of the new Jericho.

When the blue-eyed angel first spoke the words to him, "Mitch is dead," Rick had not looked up from the piano. He had just kept playing on like a broken record. Wallowing in alcohol-enhanced depression, Rick had assumed it was a voice-over that some technician was laying into his sound track, just like that "Paul is dead" thing on *The Magical Mystery Tour.*

"Rick, Mitch is dead," the angel had spoken again. It was then he had looked up and seen his star standing in front of the piano, surrounded by the burgeoning Ottawa war party. Her skin was brown, too, from being wherever she had been since the day of the great snowdrifts. And there were the blue eyes. There were no tears in those eyes, only steely determination.

"These people killed Mitch," the blue angel had spoken, pointing to the adjacent towering temple of money changers. "You've got to somehow get inside and play this for me. This place must have a control room for light and sound. You know how to make those things work." The angel had shoved the cassette into the palm of his hand, much like it was a baton, much like Cheer Cheer had done earlier that day to Mitch.

If the sight and sound of his long lost Laura was not enough to suddenly sober Rick, there was the risen Chief standing before him. He was giving field orders to his people. "Red Wing. You go with Piano Man here. Find the sound room. Play the tape."

The Chief spoke quickly and decisively to the rest of his people on the crowded veranda. "I want the main war party to encircle the exits. I shall enter this place alone. Bloodshed is only a last resort."

Chief Wasaquom had directed that comment to the angry young braves and maidens, especially his former cadre of environmental lawyers and law clerks. They had exchanged their law books for the weapons of their ancestors, as well as an assortment of the repeating rifles of the long knives. Ever since the Ogema had been restored to life out on the lake waters, which he had so valiantly fought to protect and defend, the young men and women of the re-united Ottawa tribe had been itching for a fight.

Now their chance had come. Popping sounds of gun fire came from the woods in the direction where Smith had hurriedly exited the Cathedral with his charges, Malone and Tammy. This prompted more field orders from the Chief, who deployed the remainder of the tribe as they emerged up out of the freshwater sea.

❖ ❖ ❖

"He's waving at us. I think it's a sign," observed the first assistant in charge of hydro-technics, when VanderHook began flailing his arms skyward. The first assistant squinted out of the glass-encased sound room across the expanse of the Cathedral. He was studying the physical antics of the Reverend, which were causing the cherry-picking pulpit to bounce buoyantly in mid-air. "Is that suppose to be our cue? He's digressing from his prepared text." The technician turned the pages of the script which VanderHook had submitted the week before.

"I am not sure," responded Gil Bates, the software designer, who was standing behind his first assistant in the sound room.

"That's the sixth time he's raised his hands like that. I know that signals a touchdown in football," said the first assistant looking for some direction from Bates, who was looking through binoculars trying to render his own interpretations of the Reverend's frenzied gyrations.

Bates spied through his binoculars what was, according to the first assistant's calculation, the seventh sign. "Go with the flow." Bates handed the assistant a silver-colored key. The engineer took the key and unlocked the second of two plastic covers, revealing several red buttons on the control panel. He pushed the red button labeled "Roofing."

A low rumble rose up from the bowels of the earth, like a

gusher about to blow from a newly-drilled wildcat well. "What is that?" the first assistant questioned with the wide-eyed fear of a child hearing something go bump in the night.

Gil Bates knew exactly what it was. "It's the pump for the main well-head. It's sucking in almost an acre-foot of water per minute." He listened carefully. "I'm not sure they anchored it with enough concrete. Maybe I should have warned them, but hey, I only do the software."

The first assistant ripped off his headset and stood up. "What in hell is that?" he once again asked, but this time with more feeling.

With his binoculars, Bates was scanning the floor of the casino. Idle red and blue chips were jumping on green felt. All the sinners in VanderHook's congregation, which is to say all of the congregation, were fixated in terror on the trembling temple walls. Bates put the binoculars down. He looked at his right-hand man. They were almost eye to eye in the intimate sound room. The first assistant was sweating profusely, anxiously waiting for an order to abandon ship.

At that moment, the door to the sound room blew open. An Ottawa brave in a Red Wings T-shirt rushed through the threshold gripping a hunting bow with a sinewy, formidable forearm. Bates and the first assistant ran for their lives, fleeing out the same door and down the narrow dark stairway, pushing past Rick as he followed Red Wing into the sound room.

Rick quickly surveyed the three computers which dominated the control panel. The trembling of the Cathedral's sandstone walls escalated to shaking. Everywhere, drinking glasses began shattering on the floor. Concomitantly the only window in the casino (because casinos do not have windows) blew out. It was the window which encased the sound room.

Rick and Red Wing peered out the newly exposed opening. Three stories below them, raining fragments of glass sent dozens of worshiping gamblers running and screaming.

The irony of this was not lost on Rick. The last time he had clutched a demo which Laura had begged him to play, there had been a low-level Richter. He had been in the San Fernando Valley studio recording White Lies. Those tremors had barely made the natives restless, but they had reminded Rick that drab gray Michigan winters did have some pluses.

Rick and Red Wing were now visible to the maddening chaos in the casino. "Piano Man. Are you okay here?" asked Red Wing, who had concerns for the safety of his risen Chief.

Rick was without fear, not only because of his elevated blood-alcohol level, but also because he would finally play one of Laura's demos for Geltman, whom he spotted on the floor of the casino, desperately trying to get out of a clogged exit door which was being blocked on the outside by one of the armed Ottawa war parties.

"I got everything under control." Rick was not boasting. He was merely confident.

Red Wing was out the door. Rick slapped the tape into one of the cassette decks on the console, as if he was shoving a clip into his Glock, which unfortunately he had left at home. Either the tape was blank or it had an extra long lead. But it didn't matter. In the instant that Rick inserted the cassette, the shaking stopped.

A solid sheet of water. Suspended in mid-air. One single, shimmering, solid sheet, running from the east wall to the west wall. The velocity of the jets in the sandstone walls was such that not a drop fell onto the scene below.

Eat your heart out, Sistine Chapel! It was a magnificent, surreal, translucent ceiling of pure water. When the water hit the stainless-steal beam on the far wall, it was sucked inside catchment troughs, to be recycled back into basement pumps and piped up again. As the water flew on its high-speed journey across the open expanse of the casino floor several stories below, much of it evaporated. Rainbow-like halos began to float above the Cathedral towards heaven.

As soon as the roofing commenced, the hypnotic screen-saving devices on the three computers automatically downloaded Bates' colorful new program, "Carrara" Ceiling Illustrator. Sensing this might be a last-minute chance to help showcase Laura's American debut, Rick grabbed a mouse and started clicking through the software's files listed in the folder labeled "church, cathedral, etc.," He viewed thumbnail scene after scene of bloody biblical justice. Quite unsatisfactory, thought Rick. Inebriated, Rick started hacking through the rest of the design files, hoping to find something, anything, that would put Laura in the best possible light.

With the dexterity of a Michelangelo and a Pentium chip faster, the Piano Man surfed the program's image bank. It was a virtuoso keyboard performance, for up on the Cathedral ceiling soon appeared a more lyrical host of saints and sinners: Jimi Hendrix playing like a witness from the watchtower; Marvin Gaye no doubt questioning what was going on; Dennis Wilson on drums, a true beach boy to the end.

Rick had barely finished up-loading a likeness of St. John, when the risen Chief and the blue angel appeared to the assembled multitude.

❖ ❖ ❖

Murmurs of, "He has risen. He has risen," and "She's the one. The terrorist's girl," raced through the unholy assembly. Mike Kopicubb jumped up on one of the blackjack tables in one of the alcoves on the perimeter of the Cathedral to get a better view. He was quickly joined by other members of the press.

At the urging of Calley, a couple of rambunctious off-duty deputies moved to arrest the risen Marine and Laura. But the Sheriff in charge restrained them, thinking it might be bad politics. Besides, he wanted to hear what this was all about.

VanderHook, high in his cherry-picker, who had not stopped preaching throughout the quaking, was finally speechless. Like the rest of the masses, he was mystified by the showdown on the floor of the Cathedral. His wife Ruth sat alone praying. Jonah Wasaquom was nowhere in sight.

An aisle began to clear all the way to the altar, like a parting sea. Laura had persuaded the risen Chief to let her enter the temple with him. "I will walk beside you. They cannot hurt me anymore," she had calmly told the Chief on the veranda, after Red Wing and Rick had dashed off in search of the sound room.

Laura and the Chief walked up on the stage where VanderHook had always feared the lion tamers and magicians would someday appear. The room was silent.

But before either Laura or the Chief could speak of the

sins of gambling with water, the celestial sounds of a boy's choir, humming ever so softly and sweetly, filled the chancery. 'Twas a tune that all leprechauns cherish and those of the orange persuasion need to work hard to hate.

Then the singing faded, and as the cassette being broadcast on the sound system hissed along, a voice familiar to a few of those present spoke to the multitude — a voice shaky at first, and then growing with Celtic eloquence.

"Mitch Miller never killed anyone. It was Malone and his henchman. Barstow was murdered with an arrow shot by Jonah Wasaquom. Calley ordered the arrow-wound covered up with a shot-gun blast from Ted Moore's gun."

Cheer Cheer's voice penetrated to every corner of the Cathedral. "As for Judge Alkema, what the resurrected Indian is saying about him is all true. He is as much a disgrace to the legal profession as I am.

"Mitch, the rest of this tape consists of recordings I made of my meetings with Malone and Calley. I think it's admissible. You're a good lawyer. You can figure that out."

There was a brief pause. Then Cheer Cheer continued.

"Mitch, forgive me. You were a great friend — for a Wolverine. And one more thing. Tell Stacey I loved her more than a National Championship."

With the butt of Barstow's deer rifle, the same rifle which had been removed from the crime scene on orders from Calley, Jonah Wasaquom caught Rick on his scapula only inches from snapping his cervical vertebrae. It was enough force to knock Rick headfirst into one of the computer screens, cutting him above his eye.

His head slumped over on the computer keypad. In a dazed

suspended state, Rick watched through a trickle of blood as Jonah Wasaquom shouldered the stock of the 30.06 and sighted someone in his scope.

"Laura!" whispered Rick into the public-address mike, which was switched to "On."

Whether by the grace of the saints, his Nana, or all of the above, Rick summoned the energy to his aching body to lunge across the narrow abyss between himself and the sniper. Rick hit Jonah Wasaquom. The rifle discharged, but not in the vector intended. The projectile ripped through the voice box of Calley, who had just confronted the two special guest stars on stage.

Calley dropped to his knees, clutching his throat as red blossomed between his fingers. Incredibly, the life-threatening wound did not kill Calley. However, it would later require him to testify by computer in Judge Alkema's federal bribery and extortion trial as part of a plea bargain that would send Calley to a kinder, gentler federal correctional facility.

All eyes turned from center stage to the scuffle going on in the exposed sound room, which looked like a bombed-out balcony. Rick's head craned out over the cathedral floor, three stories below. He was on his back in a contorted position, a reluctant participant in a torturous inverse bench-press competition.

Jonah Wasaquom was slowly pinning Rick by the throat using the deer rifle like a cross-checking hockey stick. As his arms began to give out, Rick felt jagged glass from what was left of the exploded sound-room window press into the bruised flesh covering his cracked scapula.

Like a magician and a lion tamer, David Wasaquom seized the hunting bow from Red Wing, who had jumped up on stage to intercept Calley. He pulled an arrow from Red Wings' quiver.

He aimed. He fired. The arrow zipped across the expanse of the Cathedral. William Tell didn't cut it any closer. Its guiding feathers stopped only inches from Rick's nose.

Jonah Wasaquom's body jerked and went limp. The arrow had pierced the bad brother's heart.

Before Rick could extricate himself from the dead weight of Jonah's harpooned body, a thunderous wail filled the temple. Some would later say that it was heard from Isle Royale to Niagara Falls, from a Sudbury saloon to the concrete canyons of Chicago's Loop. While that may rise to myth, there can be no question that it was heard for miles and miles along Michigan's sandy western shore.

The wailing sound was not of man. And although hawk-like, it was not truly of animal. Nor was it exactly mechanical either — although some witnesses would later say that the saxophone tracks on Laura's instant platinum *Blue Album* (released the following year with Geltman's masterful marketing) mirrored that funky wailing sound.

For though it was plaintive as any true wail, it also carried a sweet breath of thanksgiving and a tincture of hope. It could only have been one thing. Actually, five. The sisters were celebrating on the wind. Celebrating their liberation from waste and corruption. Playing themselves in concert like shiny stratospheric guitars, reverberating in mind-blowing feedback.

To the ardent gamblers, the wailing sound brought migrainous head-banging pain. Some writhed on the floor clutching their ears. However, to true believers like Laura, the Chief, and Red Wing, and to new converts like Rick, Geltman, and Kopicubb, the sound brought a temporary reprieve from the death and destruction they were witnessing.

As soon as the sisters began to wail, the three computer screens flashed a red as deep as the fresh blood on the keyboard: "Warning — Intake Valve Malfunction!"

Rick managed to push Jonah's heavy body off of himself. He got back on his feet. He looked at the screens. All three of the screens flashed the same alert. The wailing ceased. For a few seconds, whirlpools of wind played out in the alcoves by the slot machines. Then there was nothing. Only an ominous silence.

Reflexively, Rick looked up at the Cathedral ceiling. Jimi, Marvin, Dennis, and St. John had vanished. Instead, snow had begun gently falling in a scene on the watery ceiling. And there appeared a solitary stranger with long hair, wearing jungle fatigues and a policeman's cap. The stranger had one foot up on a blue milk-crate. A paint-chipped Fender Stratocaster with a worn fretboard rested on his knee. The man was playing some simple chords on the guitar, which he had borrowed from a star. He was smiling and laughing. And he was catching snowflakes on the tip of his tongue.

Two years later in a deposition given on behalf of the risen Chief and his "renegade" tribe in their billion-dollar civil fraud and conspiracy suit against MDDC and Malone's estate, Rick would admit that, at Laura's request, he had hidden the blue milk-crate from the police search.

However, Rick would swear on his Nana's grave that he never up-loaded that final scene on the Cathedral ceiling.

❖ ❖ ❖

The "Intake Valve Malfunction" was all Malone's fault. Smith's plan for a quick escape to the airport by ground transportation had been thwarted. Their limo had gotten stuck in the log jam of cars, trucks, and buses all trying to get into the grand opening of the WC&C.

Malone, Smith, and the rest of his men had abandoned Tammy in her designer dress and high heels with instructions to "find Calley and just take the Fifth." Scattering in the woods, Smith's men had been run down by the renegade Ottawas. For the most part they had surrendered docilely. However, Malone and Smith had managed to elude capture.

Trying to reach Smith's beached speedboat, they had decided to circle deep in the woods and double back. Lost and running scared, they had tripped and rolled down the blind bluff. Finding themselves on a deserted stretch of beach, they had followed it back north until they spotted hundreds of canoes and, just beyond that, the inlet where Smith had beached his muscle-boat. They had crawled on their bellies through the beach grass, waiting and watching as old men, women, and children, the last of the Ottawa armada, had scaled the bluff up to the Cathedral.

"What the hockey puck do you mean you can't swim!" Malone had exclaimed, when they realized that there was a short distance, maybe seventy feet, between them and the speedboat where the bluff jutted out into the lake without any beach. To get to the Riva, they would have to swim out around a grapevine-covered outcropping of sheer cliff which ran straight down into what looked like deep water.

"I grew up in Tonopah, Nevada. I never saw water outside of a horse trough, until I got to the fountains and pools on The Strip," Smith had replied defensively.

"Gosh darn it. I'll throw you a line," Malone had said disgustedly as he waded in.

Looking like a gargantuan mutant penguin in his tattered tux, Malone swam out into the lake. His strokes were not that smooth. But it was amazing to Smith, who remained behind watching from the water's edge, just how fast and effortless "the boss" glided through the water. So fast and effortless, that for a moment Smith thought that Malone's screams, when he was already halfway around the outcropping, were just a way of mocking a land-locked boy from the desolate Nevada desert. Even when the swimming penguin sank out of sight, Smith had thought Malone was just playing with him.

Then Smith realized his boss was being pulled down into a mighty whirlpool. Malone was in deep sucking trouble.

When the roof fell in, VanderHook was its first victim, perhaps because he was closest to the hand of God. The torrent of water jolted him out of his pulpit, which was bobbing about like a yellow rubber duckie under a bathtub faucet. For a few seconds, the Reverend managed to hold onto the rim of the pulpit, like a basketball player making a career-capping slam dunk.

His long legs scissored frantically in mid-air high above the Cathedral floor. He looked more like silent film star Harold Lloyd hanging from the hands of a giant clock than like Gary

Cooper at high noon. Then his grip broke and he plummeted three stories, coincidentally about the same height little Peter had jumped to his death that past Thanksgiving. The Reverend Peter V. VanderHook, Sr. was dead on impact.

When the drowned penguin plugged the intake valve, causing the water pressure to fail and the roof to fall, Laura, the Chief, and Red Wing found themselves in the relative safety of the Cathedral stage. It was like they were standing behind a majestic white waterfall in a tropical rainforest cave. They watched as the enormous weight of the cascading roof of water showered and pounded patrons to the floor.

Across the way, Rick watched from his high and dry perch as the Cathedral filled with water. Marked cards floated. Loaded dice sank. Rick spotted the portly woman, who had hit the slot on the veranda, trying to keep her overflowing cup of coins above her head as the water rose up to her short neck.

People were scurrying up to any higher ground they could find. Geltman appeared to be captain of a floating craps table. Kopicubb was trying to hang onto a roulette wheel like it was an inner tube.

If the Cathedral's ceiling didn't meet code — and a lot of building inspectors had been bribed to sign off on that — at least the exit doors did. Just as the swimmers were being clearly separated from the non-swimmers, the exit doors released. Soaking wet gamblers shot out of the Cathedral on a free water-slide ride, which sent many of them all the way down the bluff to the lake.

❖ ❖ ❖

In the immediate aftermath of the roof cave-in, Verbrugge quite naturally assumed the role as press spokesmen for the pro-Lakers. Out on the veranda he was conducting an informal press conference, as emergency personnel attended to mostly minor injuries.

"... And look at them. You can see through their eyes to their souls," said Verbrugge, gesturing towards hundreds of gamblers who still looked dazed and confused from their non-elective baptism. "They are swing voters now. Everyone of them. They will swing in our favor. We will free Ted Moore and defeat the referendum!" Verbrugge was animated.

"I think your opposition is already dead in the water," Kopicubb said dryly in spite of his soggy appearance. He pointed towards the horizon. A mile from shore, the U.S. Coast Guard was fishing out a body from among the debris of what was left of the splintered speedboat. It was one of Smith's men. It would be a few more days before divers would find Malone's body wedged in the underwater intake valve.

"When do we get an interview with the resurrected Indian?" Kopicubb's colleagues pressed Verbrugge.

Verbrugge glanced beyond the low veranda wall to where dozens of young Ottawa warriors, male and female, had formed an impenetrable circle of humanity around the risen Ogema and Sarah. "I suppose when he's ready," Verbrugge responded curtly to the reporters.

Under a small stand of sugar maples which had avoided the wrath of the MDDC bulldozers, the great Ottawa chief was contemplating his killing act and the future course for his tribe. In the grand oratory of great Ottawa leaders, he pledged that his tribe would fight to preserve and defend the life-giving gift of the Great Lakes from wasteful plunder. No pipeline would siphon off lake water to make the gamblers' desert green. That should never have been in question, David Wasaquom said to the circle around him.

The problem remained that too many of the things his brother had spoken were true. He cautioned his followers about the wholly material world that the red man had grown dependent on. The "New Buffalo" was such a strange creature. Was it a perverse penance for the white man, a payback for centuries of greed and racism? At best it could be used for good, like every bone and tendon that dead buffalo rendered up. But such sacrifices should come with a prayer for the generosity of the earth, our mother, who must be protected from harm.

Sarah was kneeling behind her mother. She was tenderly brushing her wet hair, like her mother used to do for her so many tears ago. "Don't say that. You still have a lot to live for." Sarah was trying to console her. "Grandchildren need grandparents," offered Sarah. Sarah looked to her future husband for confirmation of his forgiveness.

Sarah's loving voice was a welcome intrusion to the Chief's troubled thoughts. He looked Sarah's mother in the eyes. "You are *Ododem*," he spoke gently. "You are of the family."

An ambulance with lights, but no siren, waited to take Rick to the hospital. The vodka and the adrenalin had worn off. Rick felt a throbbing pain in the back of his head where the rifle butt had struck him. He looked up at Laura, who was standing over him. "I'm sorry about Mitch. And I'm sorry about us." Rick paused for a moment as a current of pain flashed through his body. "I've always loved you," he said sweetly.

"You've always loved all the girls," said Laura. She kissed him on the cheek.

Geltman helped the attendant lift the stretcher into the ambulance. "Why don't you come with us?" Geltman pleaded.

"You go with Rick. I'll be along," said Laura.

"Shake on it?" Geltman anxiously asked.

"Shake on it," said Laura, mustering a handshake and a faint sad smile for the record exec.

Geltman hopped up into the back of the ambulance with Rick. "I can already see the video ...." Geltman's words were cut off as an EMT hustled to shut the ambulance door. Nearby police escorted Smith in handcuffs into a squad car. Tammy was arguing with a couple of plainclothes detectives, who were taking her in for questioning.

Laura managed to slip around the other side of the Cathedral, away from Verbrugge's press conference, away from the maddening crowd. She walked on hallowed ground where Hazel Hanker used to sit in her Biedermeier chair and read Norman Vincent Peale by the light of the silvery moon. Where Albert use to steal a few tokes on his corncob pipe after awkward father-daughter conversations.

Even with the outlandish edifice, which had irreparably scarred the land, Laura felt like she knew the place, if not the people. During their enchanted time together on the Georgian Bay, Mitch had set the snow-driven scene at the Hanker cottage in her mind's eye.

As she walked to the edge of the bluff she imagined his gallant deeds. She embellished those deeds more than he ever had, because she had the benefit of knowing that her disenchanted young lawyer had attained the kind of justice he had always hoped to find.

The sun was setting in the west, touching the water. Through tears from those deep blue eyes, she saw a bird fly high above the shoreline and beyond the sea. The Coast Guard vessel was gone. Bits and pieces of debris from the speedboat were beginning to wash up on shore.

And then the bird was back again. It made a swooping dive-bombing maneuver. Her eyes followed the bird as it landed on a sea-wall that jutted out into the water.

Slowly, Laura started to side-step down the steep bluff. The bird began to squawk loudly, obnoxiously, like when he used to beg for food on the *Folk*. Laura knew it was him.

The man emerging was shoulder-deep in the water, centered in the orange path of the setting sun. She hit the beach running. She ran into the water until she was up to her waist.

There was something extremely reverent about the way they embraced in that Great Lake.

Mitch looked at the holes in Albert's wall. He looked at Hudson, who was respectfully silent. He looked at Laura.

"I could hear your voice singing 'Beyond the Sea,'" Mitch said to Laura. And they kissed. Again and again.